The Soul Merchant

Isabella Hush Series, Volume 5

Thea Atkinson

Published by Thea Atkinson, 2020.

THE SOUL MERCHANT

First edition. July 21, 2020.

Written by Thea Atkinson.

CHAPTER ONE

"He wouldn't get circumcised," said the woman sitting next to me at the bar. "So I dumped his sorry ass."

I was perched atop a stool at Fayed's Rot Gut Tavern, a place I frequented, well, frequently, even though I'd recently discovered it was a bar for Kindred and not for humans.

That didn't mean that humans like me didn't come in; it just meant they might not get out again.

I was one of the few and fortunate exceptions; mostly because Fayed, a centuries' old vampire, had taken a shine to me. I didn't take that privilege lightly. I couldn't afford to.

I had reason to be in a vampire bar just a couple hours after the sun set, and I had a burly protector from all things fangish in the form of the vampire owner, Fayed.

The woman sitting next to me, on the other hand, was no doubt already living on borrowed time. She just didn't know it.

While I still wasn't comfortable with the thought of vampires being a reality, let alone having their own bar, I was getting better at dealing with it all. I'd been thrust into the supernatural world whether I liked it or not. I had already managed to get into and out of more trouble than I cared to when it came to all things strange and unseemly, and that included the tavern.

Fayed had alternately tolerated me, welcomed me, barred me, and welcomed me again.

I might be safe here for now, but I didn't take it for granted.

So, I lifted my glass of Rot Gut, a drink named for the tavern, and I waggled the stem of the glass at my companion so the crystal of absinthe at the bottom sparked a brilliant green in the incandescent lights.

Because she wanted a response, I knew. Her tilted her gaze in my direction indicated exactly that. She even leaned back on her stool snuggling into the backrest, confident I would have something to say to her risqué confession.

Trouble was, I was still racking my brains trying to come up with an explanation for why she really should hightail it out of the bar altogether. The dangers of the Rot Gut might be easy enough to miss if you were human, so she couldn't be blamed for hanging out here too long. But the risks were real, even if she was oblivious to them.

I was afraid if she haunted the place for much longer this evening, she might end up haunting it for rest of her afterlife.

So, while I worked out what exactly I should say to get her ass off the stool and out into the dark alley where she'd be much safer, I tilted my glass toward her in a mock toast.

She was nursing a martini of some sort, her fourth in the last hour, even if this one had sat in her grip so long it had to have grown warm by now. She hung over it like a sad vulture. A sad, gorgeous vulture.

She smelled of frankincense. Her long, black hair was ombre-dyed on the ends to a light mauve that had been curled into perfect beach waves, which she touched every now and then with fingernails done in French tips. When she wasn't adjusting her hair, she tapped the stem of the glass as though she hadn't really made her mind up about the man in question, no matter what she said.

I dumped my drink back in one unceremonious swallow, all the better to excuse myself from commenting about her uncircumcised beau. I caught the absinthe crystal between my teeth as I considered just telling her to get the hell out of Dodge without any sophisticated preamble.

She drummed her nails on the bar and watched me.

"You meeting someone?" she said.

"Yes."

I thought about Maddox, who I was indeed, waiting for. He wasn't a vampire, but he was Kindred. If I had to describe him to a casual human acquaintance, I'd call him my new boss and owner of an estate auction house. I wouldn't say he owned a place called the Shadow Bazaar, or that he was the owner of an even shadier business he called Recollections. I would leave out the fact he was the kind of male that women would have fought to bear their children in the days of yore, when he'd been a mere man instead of an immortal.

Hell no. I wouldn't even admit that to myself. That way lay madness.

"My boss," I said. "I'm waiting for my boss."

I'd already been waiting for Maddox for an hour, and was wondering when he'd finally deign to show his sorry ass. I might be relatively safe in Fayed's bar, but it was foolish to assume too much.

"I didn't know ladies like us had bosses," she said. "But there you go. Progress marches on."

She lifted her martini glass high over her head in a mock celebration of time and progress. Booze sloshed out over the edge and onto the floor.

She snickered as though she thought my mention of a boss was a euphemism. I ignored her deep-throated chortle. She could think what she wanted so long as she left whole and alive.

"It's pretty dark out there," I said, priming the conversational pump. "I hope nothing happened to him. Bad neighborhood and all."

"I'm sure he's fine." She waved her long fingers at me.

I placed the glass back onto the counter.

"He's late."

Fayed was busying himself adding a few droplets of blood to a glass of ale on the other side of the bar for a rotund, hairy looking man, who, if he was a vampire, lacked all the legendary charisma so enjoyed in fiction.

"Imagine," she said. "Refusing to have it done when I was at his beck and call."

So we were back to that, it seemed. She huffed as though it was truly the most incongruous and unimaginable thing she could think of.

Fayed must have heard her comment, because he glanced my way ever so subtly and his eyebrow lifted enough to indicate he was interested in my reply. A smirk rode his full lips, revealing the tip of one of his elongated canine teeth.

Fangs, I told myself. Vampires called them fangs.

I was still getting used to the idea that there were vampires and all sorts of other creatures big, small, good, and bad. Kindred, Maddox called them. Kindred was the word for humanoid creatures that were of this world but not human.

My twenty-six years of humanity colored my view of things because most people, according to Maddox, had no idea there was a supernatural world seething beneath their feet. Nine worlds to be exact, and most days, I dearly wished I hadn't either.

There was a certain bliss in ignorance. I wasn't sure who had coined the phrase, but it fit perfectly.

I was unabashedly and painfully human myself, despite some pretty awful events over the last couple of months.

For instance, once upon a time, I'd thought the absinthe crystal in my drink was something they created by distilling the liquid until a hard chunk of chemical was left behind. I didn't even know if that was a possibility, and hadn't cared. But nope, I was wrong.

Now, I knew that the crystal was created from magic. I wasn't sure what kind, and while I hoped it wasn't fae magic, I didn't want to know. Not really. When I'd drank the concoction in the past, I expected to hallucinate, but apparently, the servers only gave the human clientele–of which there were precious few–a placebo unless they were targets.

They saved the real thing for Kindred who knew how to deal with the magic.

The woman beside me downed her drink, a sanguine martini, I think she called it, and told me she'd had a hundred lovers in the last decade, and not one of them refused to be circumcised.

"I'm celibate," I blurted out. "So it's not an issue for me."

I didn't confess my current state of celibacy was involuntary, or that it was also attached to the fact that I'd murdered my ex-fiancé, Scottie, who had brutalized me in ways few women ever managed to escape from with her psyche intact. Made me sort of gun-shy to jump on that pony again.

And yeah. Not even for the gorgeous Maddox. Who as it turns out, *is* actually celibate.

Didn't matter that my ex-fiancé was going to kill me or worse. I'd taken Scottie out, and Maddox had cleaned up the mess after me. Wherever he put Scottie's body, whatever he'd done with it, I didn't want to know.

It was bad enough knowing I was a murderer. Not just a thief and a runaway.

A killer. That's what I was. That kind of truth does things to your psyche.

And he, the man who wasn't a man, who had lived hundreds of years, who had conveniently cleaned up my mess, and who had centuries earlier taken vows of celibacy, had declared how badly he wanted me.

Such is my life.

So, I was broke, working for a man who wouldn't give me a job or a roll in the hay, and confused as hell with how I felt about it all.

And he was late.

The woman beside me waved Fayed over, and I pushed thoughts of Maddox aside for the time being.

"Another," she said perfunctorily when Fayed laid his palms on the bar counter. She then shifted her attention to me.

"Celibacy is for monks and nuns," she said in response to my comment as she inclined her gaze back in my direction. "No self-respecting woman—vampire or otherwise—would rob herself of an orgasm or two each night."

Each night? I might have asked how she managed to keep up that pace, but found I was too insulted by her insinuation that I wasn't a self-respecting woman.

"I didn't say I was sexless," I said, shifting on my barstool awkwardly.

I winced, not entirely due to the way the spring on the outer edge of the stool bit into my thigh.

"My small friend, if you have to do it on your own," she said. "You aren't owning your sexuality. Take what you want when you want."

She pulled at the stem of the fresh martini glass as Fayed laid it down just within reach. "One for the China doll, too," she said. I could almost hear the smirk in her voice.

Fayed avoided my eye altogether as he reached to clear my glass and replace it with another. "Isabella prefers absinthe to blood in her drinks." His smokey voice was full of innuendo.

The woman reeled back on her stool and looked me full in the face.

That's when it hit me like a cool breeze. Her earlier comment had gone right over my head.

She was a vampire.

And she thought I was too.

"She's human," Fayed said, almost unnecessarily, judging by the flash of narrowed gaze and involuntary widening of the woman's nostrils as she studied me afresh. "I thought you understood that."

"Human," she murmured with astonishment as she looked me over. I wasn't sure if the color I saw in her face was from embarrassment or the blood in her drink, but when it rose to her cheeks, I could really make out how pallid her complexion was.

I don't know how I'd missed it before.

It didn't make sense. I couldn't imagine what exactly circumcision entailed for a vampire, and I felt duped that Fayed let me sit here drinking with someone he knew I thought was human, but wasn't.

He must have read the sense of betrayal on my face because he shot me an apologetic look. I stared back, still wrestling with the knowledge that my companion was a vampire and expected her lovers to get a procedure done that obviously wouldn't take or would have to be done repeatedly.

"Circumcision for a vampire," Fayed explained as he drummed his fingers on the bar counter. "Involves the teeth."

He coughed into his hand.

I stared at him, astounded.

"Are you embarrassed?" I said, not sure what it could possibly involve that made him blush too, but I found the idea delightfully funny.

The woman reached across the bar to grip his wrist.

"Oh, Fayed," she said with such a pitying tone that I couldn't help chuckling out loud into my glass. "Don't tell me you're not circumcised. Your poor lover."

Fayed rocked back on his heels and pulled his wrist from his grip. "My lovers don't complain, unlike you, Cleo."

She spun to face me on the stool and for a moment, I thought she might explain the concept, but then I caught something different in her expression. Something that hadn't been there before but that I'd seen plenty in Scottie's face when he was feeling especially amorous.

"So," she said with a predatory note in her voice that wasn't there before. "You're human."

The tiniest tip of her tongue darted out the corner of her mouth. Like she was mulling something over. Something she found incredibly exciting but taboo.

Then the pity and sympathy she'd shown for my state of celibacy all but dissolved from her expression.

In its place was something more feral.

CHAPTER TWO

C leo must have decided she would forgo that extra martini and snack on the real thing, and she made no bones about her desires. It rode her features the way lust does. It's unmistakable. You don't need to hear someone say they want you when they want you that badly.

I felt for the floor with my feet because I had a feeling I'd be needing them on solid footing in a moment or two.

Fayed must have seen it too, because in a heartbeat, he leaned over the bar to put his body between us. His back was to me and his shoulders made a mountain of rust-colored gabardine that undulated over the muscles in his back.

"She's protected here." he said to Cleo. "You've been drinking with her for an hour. I thought you'd guessed she wasn't vampire."

He reached for my arm and settled his fingers around my elbow. Urgency made his grip rough. He yanked at me, hard enough that I almost fell off the stool. It clunked as it wobbled against the wood. I had to brace myself against the bar to keep my ribs from jamming into the edge.

Cleo stood when she noted his obvious unease, but it wasn't because she felt she'd done anything wrong. Quite the contrary. A sense of indignity coiled about her demeanor. She was shorter than I'd thought. Her figure was full but petite. Even so, she had a regal bearing, one that indicated she wasn't used to being denied.

I fully expected Fayed to defer to her under that direct and commanding gaze. It certainly seemed as though his every fiber wanted to. I laid a hand on his shoulder, doing my best to tug my arm away from his iron grip as I did so. I needed to be free if I had to bolt.

He was a friend, but the way his shoulders trembled beneath my palms told me he might not be friend enough to resist her.

"I should have guessed," Cleo said, scanning him with that unblinking and penetrating gaze. "The way you've been watching us from the side of your eye."

She directed her stunning gaze at me over his back. I felt my legs start to sag beneath it.

"You want her," she said to him.

"She's already mine," he intoned. "When she's here, she's mine. I thought you guessed that."

Despite the tension in the air, I wasn't sure I liked that statement of proprietorship.

"Hello?" I said, jamming my index finger into the meat of his shoulder. "I'm not some meat sandwich wrapped in jeans and Spandex. I'm probably the only thing in this bar that isn't yours. I'm nobody's possession."

Maybe it was stupid to argue the point right then, but after Scottie, I'd decided I wouldn't be anyone's possession ever again.

Fayed didn't look at me, but I felt his body tighten at my words. It had affected him all right.

"You don't know how it works, Isabella," he said without looking at me and shrugging off my probing fingers. "But I can assure you, when you are in my bar, you are under my protection. So, yes. Mine."

That last word was said with a ferocious bite, then he moved so quickly I didn't realize what he was doing, until I felt his grip beneath my arms and I was plucked from the stool so easily I might have been a flower in a vase. He retreated to his side of the bar, pulling me with him as he went.

My torso didn't even fetch up against the lip of the bar. I felt weightless in his grip, until my boot caught up on the edge and lodged there.

I was stuck for a few breathless seconds until it wormed itself free of my foot. My boot fell to the floor with a thunk as Cleo pushed her sanguine martini aside almost too calmly. The sound it made as it slid down the surface of the bar would be one I knew I'd hear in my nightmares for weeks.

"If you've claimed her, why isn't your scent of possession on her?" she demanded of Fayed. "She has no brand either."

She swept my throat with a piercing eye, no doubt looking for pinprick scars that would indicate I'd been fed from. Seeing none, she inhaled deeply. "She doesn't even smell human."

"Fae magic," he said. "She walks in the door, she's cloaked. No Kindred might know she's human unless she's revealed."

Revealed. I guessed that meant Kindred were able to suss me out by talking to me or if I admitted it. I hadn't needed to; he'd done that just fine with his explanation. Even if he hadn't meant to out me, he'd done it. There was no turning back now.

I felt safer behind the bar with Fayed, certainly, but his words made my heart squeeze painfully even so.

If I'd been cloaked by fae magic, it was news to me. And it wasn't welcome.

"Cloaked?" I said, with a knot in my voice.

I knew fae magic. No good ever came from it. Not in my experience. I wiggled my toes against the bar and felt my socks stick to something gooey. There hadn't been anything there before. I tried to swallow down my unease that the fae magic might be turning on me from the heels up.

"You're sure it's fae magic?" I said.

He didn't look at me when he answered but kept his attention on the vampire on the other side of the bar, who had begun to look decidedly less gorgeous and much more frightening.

"After the last time," he said without taking his gaze from Cleo's face. "After my kin tried to...well, I couldn't risk you getting hurt again. I pay a guy for a subscription of sorts now."

He was talking about the time his progeny, Isme, and a swarm of other vampires had attacked me in his bar. She had tricked him into making her. A sorceress turned vampire, who to be honest, was one nasty piece of work. Bad enough that The Morrigan had sent the bitch to Hell for me, swapping her life for mine in a Devil's bargain I didn't ever want to see reneged upon.

I still didn't know if Fayed was aware I was the reason his progeny was true-dead, but I intended to keep that secret.

But if he was forking out for my protection because he felt guilty, then I at least owed him the chance to retract it in light of the dangers he was taking on in doing so.

"Oh Fayed," I said. "You shouldn't do that. Fae magic is never free."

"I hired a rogue," he said. "A fae with a taste for a certain kind of drink he can only get here. He renews the magic once a month and I water him. You look, smell, and sound like Kindred, to other Kindred."

"Except now I know," Cleo said with a side glance at me. Her voice fell to a whisper of awe and longing. "And the magic has fallen from you, human."

She poked me over the bar with a finger as though I was a piece of meat on a grill. I told myself if she stuck her finger in her mouth and made an *mmm* sound, I was going to holler.

Loudly.

Fayed tugged me close, turning so that he faced the door with me pinioned between his two meaty arms. He had to look over his shoulder at Cleo, indicating she would have to go through him to get me. I, however, was facing her, and I could see that she very well might, and very well could.

I braced myself for a good kicking and screaming bout. Then I tried to work out how far I could run with only one boot on.

"I told you," Fayed said, interrupting my mental prep. "She's already taken."

He held his finger against my mouth when I thought to protest. "You might not think you are, Isabella, but trust me. You are mine when you're here. Otherwise, how do you think you'd come and go with such ease?"

"Fae magic?" I said in a choked voice beneath his finger. "Cloaking?"

He made a sound beneath his breath that indicated his patience was waning.

"Just trust me. Running away won't always work. There are some things you just can't run from."

I didn't relish the thought of being spoken of as a thing a vampire might enjoy over a sanguine martini, but I wasn't stupid. I shut up.

Cleo narrowed her gaze to little slits of burnished and copper-shadowed eyelids and didn't look the least bit convinced. Or impressed.

"I could make you give her to me," she said to Fayed

That thought terrified me.

"You have age on me," Fayed said. "But where would you go to moan about your lovers if not here, Cleo. No one bothers you here." His tone might as well be warm oil being massaged into a warm body. I could almost hear the perfume in it.

"I want her," Cleo said.

"Is she worth not coming here ever again?" he said. "I can't resist your order to give her to you, but I don't have to allow you back."

"Look," I cut in as I twisted around Fayed's shoulder to catch her eye. I tried to inject a bit of casualness to my tone but fell woefully short. "We were friends just ten seconds ago."

"Friendly," she said, staring at Fayed pointedly. "Not friends. And that was before I knew you were human."

I tried to invoke the camaraderie of the last half hour. "Oh, come on," I said. "We were having fun talking about lovers. I'll tell you about a man I know whose circumcision as an adult went horribly but hilariously awry."

Her tone when she spoke was flat and emotionless. She might have been reciting some lesson from a classroom.

"Humans who know about us are dangerous. You can't be trusted to be anything except a lovely feed on a rabid stomach."

Her use of the word rabid instead of empty made me quail. I looked from Fayed's face to Cleo's. He trusted me. Did he think it foolish and misplaced? He'd ordered me to stay away from his bar for my own safety but let me back in when I needed him. He protected me from the other patrons. He'd kept Kelliope at bay when she'd attacked on the day my involuntary initiation into all things supernatural started.

Trust, however, didn't seem the most relevant word, though.

I was about as dangerous as a cricket on a hearth. Totally at the mercy of those within. That any vampire would feel threatened by my humanity was laughable. That this vampire could claim fear as a motivating factor for claiming me from Fayed, when she was so utterly and obviously the one with the most power despite her stature, was astounding.

And yet, that's exactly what she did.

"She's a threat," Cleo said to Fayed's stubborn back. I noted he refused to turn around to face her now that she had made her intentions known. "You know it as well as I. We don't harbor humans. We use them. We feed from them. Occasionally, we stable them."

I squeaked at the word stable and she swung her gaze to mine even as she kept addressing Fayed.

"If you're going to spout arcane rules and morals at me, like I'm an insipid pupil at my lessons, then let's take it all the way to the test."

She spread her arms out, palms on the bar as she leaned into it. Her face was so close to his shoulder, he must have felt the heat of her breath.

"Look at me, Fayed," she said, and those black eyes lost all semblance of empathy as the pupils swallowed the irises.

He shifted, ever so subtly, but enough that he wouldn't have to look over his shoulder at her. If he wanted to, he could catch her eye with a side-glance. It seemed to be all Cleo needed.

"Give her to me," she said.

I made a sound like a mouse might make when frightened and took an involuntary step back. The bottles on the shelf beside me clanked together.

I felt something shift in Fayed's posture.

"Oh my God," I said, realizing he was indeed about to hand me over. "Seriously? You're going to just pass me over like a bit of prosciutto?"

"He has to," Cleo said with a lazy smile. "I'm an Ancient One, and the rules demand it."

Fayed looked down at me, his face filled with regret and angst. "I'm not *just* handing you over," he said.

"Damn straight," said a voice from the doorway that was loud enough, harsh enough, and commanding enough that even Cleo balked and took a step backward.

Fayed's grip trembled on my arms at the sound of it, but I had the feeling it was relief and restraint rather than fear that made it quake.

I didn't need to turn around to see him to know Maddox's voice. I might have peed myself with relief if everything hadn't shrunk inside to tiny bits of dried tissue.

"You aren't just handing her over," Maddox said to Fayed. "They're vampire rules, not mine. I don't have to obey."

His boots scuffed across the floor toward us at a pace that indicated he had all the time in the world to do so. Meanwhile, Fayed's grip had gotten even more painful.

"Let her go, Fayed."

I craned my neck so I could see over my shoulder.

Maddox had extended his arm toward me without a flicker of recognition of who I was or that he wanted with me. His expression was a death mask of calm and command. There could be no disobeying. Didn't matter how old Cleo was.

There was a moment. Just one, where I thought Fayed would fling me toward Cleo. But then, just like that, I felt Fayed's grip go slack.

"Sweet baby Jesus," I said with a relief I didn't bother hiding.

I stepped out of Fayed's arms and started backing my way toward Maddox without checking to see if I was on track to meet him. I had eyes only for the gorgeous vampire in front of me.

Cleo stood like a pillar of salt. Her diminutive stature might have been a glamour for the way she commanded the space she stood in. I thought she was ready to pounce like a leopard might, and I wasn't taking my eyes off that female vamp until I was safely in the alley and could pound my feet as fast as I could against the pave.

Except I didn't get any further than three steps before Cleo launched herself with a shriek that pierced my eardrums.

I cringed involuntarily and dropped to a crouch, thinking she might sail over top of me and give me time to elude her.

And she did. She leapt right over my head.

Then ran straight for Maddox.

CHAPTER THREE

It all happened so fast I felt the breeze of her movement catching my hair. At the same time, Fayed grabbed my wrist and yanked me to my feet with an apologetic look on his face that did nothing to make me feel inclined to forgive him. He passed me my boot and I crammed it on, hopscotching in place until I had it secure.

I noted he kept his mouth set in a tight line and that he avoided looking at Cleo at all.

I pulled my hand free of his and hitched up my collar where it had fallen down over my shoulder. I shot a glance toward the doorway, toward Maddox.

"Well fuck me," I said as I noted that Cleo had already wrapped her legs around his waist and was climbing him as though he was a tree.

I hadn't noticed up to that point that she wore a black split hem turtle neck sweater dress with above-the-knee leather boots. The amount of leg that showed, and the way she used them to hook around Maddox, was enough to convince me she worked a pole to keep fit.

And Maddox didn't seem to mind one bit. He held her with a soft grip, one that fell a little too close to her hips to be useful at keeping her from doing anything but clinging to him tighter. Maybe that was the point.

"I need a drink," I said, cringing as one of her muscled legs wrapped around the backs of Maddox's thighs.

"You and me both," Fayed said.

With an adroit movement, he leapt over the bar and disappeared behind it. He came up with a bottle of whiskey and a vial that held a tarry looking substance. He clunked the bottle down and then ran the vial under the hot water tap, all the while with his jaw set in a tight clench. Steam rose to cover his face and dissipated quickly when the tap squeaked off.

I kept wanting to look back at Cleo and Maddox despite my own determination not to, and it was only the sound of a screw cap spinning off its glass threading that freed me from the inclination.

"Canadian whiskey," he said as he held my gaze. "Good for what ails you."

He spun the bottle on its rim to show me the label then palmed it with a toss in the air. Whiskey poured from the spout into a Rot Gut Tavern shot glass in a fluid motion that put me in mind of the show bartenders across the city who entertained more than they watered their clients.

In a quick one-two motion, he upended the shot first and then the vial into his mouth.

He swallowed with a moan of pleasure.

I didn't need to be told the vial was blood but at that point, I didn't care.

Behind me, Cleo was cooing and Maddox was murmuring something unintelligible beneath his breath. Or he was whispering it.

Fayed flicked his gaze in their direction then pushed the whiskey bottle along the bar toward me without a word. I contemplated it for a long moment. I'd already drank my share already. I couldn't risk being too drunk in this neighborhood.

"You cut your beautiful hair," Cleo said to Maddox.

I grumbled non-words to the bar top at the sultry sound to her voice, but it didn't stop me from stealing a look at them again.

What she'd said was true. The auburn man-bun Maddox always wore was gone, and in its place was a buzzed cut with a stylish bit of flipped bang.

"Bit woosey if you ask me," I mumbled.

"Me too," Fayed agreed.

I directed my stare back at the whiskey. With a resigned sigh, I palmed the bottle and tilted it toward Fayed in salute. He grinned. I grinned. Things felt back to normal. I guess he could be forgiven for almost passing me over to a strange vampire, considering he had no choice and that he kept such liquid heaven in his bar.

Before I could pour a shot, I heard Maddox chuckling beneath his breath. It was enough to make me steal another glance their way. Cleo whispered in his ear as though she had a secret she wanted only him to hear. Sweet nothings, they would have been called in ancient times, and maybe she'd had first-hand experience with it. Maddox certainly didn't seem to mind.

When he glanced my way, one corner of his mouth tugged upward.

He had the gall to waggle his eyebrows at me.

I flipped him the bird.

"Virgins," I said out of the corner of my mouth. "They'll do anything to look like they get some."

Fayed canted his head at me.

"Virgin?" he said with a note of surprise that made me pretty damn happy in the moment.

Maddox must have heard it because he extricated himself from Cleo's arms and stepped out of the python grip her legs had of his.

"Bourbon, Fayed," he said, distracting the vampire from any commentary on his sexual status by giving him a reason to turn away and do what he was bid.

With Cleo in tow, Maddox approached the bar, telling her with each step, and in that husky, charming voice he had, that it had been a long time since he'd seen her last.

"Too long," she said, trailing along behind him with her eyes on his ass.

"He's not circumcised," I said beneath my breath, and Maddox obviously caught just enough of it that as he escorted her in the direction of the barstool she'd just vacated, that his brow lined up into questioning furrows.

"I was just saying that I've been here an hour," I told him.

Cleo stabbed me with a long, hard look as Maddox helped her—quite needlessly—onto the stool all the while giving me long, pointed looks.

Pointed. As though I was somehow being bad company.

"You know this human, Maddox?" she said then ran her gaze up and down the length of my body.

When her gaze lingered a little too long on my neck, I told myself that at least the predatory look had disappeared. Not that what I got now was much better. The look she gave me when her eyes returned to my face told me I was inconsequential.

Invisible.

Nothing.

Maddox didn't seem to notice.

"Ah, you've met Isabella," he said as though he'd just come upon a stranger meeting his filthy kid playing in a puddle.

"Fayed said she is his," Cleo said with a hint of accent I'd not heard during our earlier friendly chat. I wondered if it was European, and tried to place it as she swiveled on the stool to present her best profile to Maddox. "His, Maddox," she said "And yet you were able to make him give her up."

Her last sentence was said like a statement, but I read the accusation in the lilting voice. Not that Maddox caught it through all his rapt attention of her ample side boob peeking out through the gap in her sleeve.

"You know how it works," Fayed interjected, placing a glass of something that did not look like bourbon down onto the bar in front of Maddox. The ice cubes chinked together as they ricocheted off the sides of the glass.

"I do." Maddox waggled his fingers at me and when I glared at him, he shrugged. "If Fayed believes she is his when she's here, then it's as true as it can be."

"But," he said and I waited with fists clenched for him to retract the statement, because he had to. He knew how I felt about being owned.

"Isabella is her own woman," he said to Cleo. "No one owns her."

My fingernails eased out of my palm as I shot Cleo a victorious glare. Not that it mattered. She wasn't looking at me at all. Her eyes were for Maddox.

"Mind you," he went on as he picked up the glass and sniffed it. "Sometimes it would be easier if someone did show her who was boss."

He sent me a long look over the rim of his glass that traveled from my face to my feet, and then rose again to land on my mouth. He pulled in the drink slowly and noiselessly and he swallowed just as languidly, never taking his eyes from mine until he was at the bottom of the drink.

Damn, he had that smoldering look down.

I felt hot and beneath that gaze and thought I could forgive Cleo at least her swooning over the man. He was, indeed, a fleshed over Michael Angelo's David, even if he was a virgin.

I caught sight of Cleo watching him too. Her eyes narrowed as she watched Maddox's face and there was hunger in it as well as suspicion. Too much of both for my tastes, to be honest. I didn't think Maddox should be left alone with her. She would eat him alive and the poor virgin wouldn't know what hit him until he'd cast his vows to the wind.

I poured a shot and downed it, then dragged the bottle along the bar top with me as I made my way to the stool I'd been sitting on when we'd drank so companionably together earlier. Cleo's eyes followed my every movement as I climbed onto the stool next to her, claiming it with a territorial lean onto the bar that I figured looked far more confident and casual than I felt. Fayed smirked and busied himself with his point of sale table.

"And who is this human that she would command two Kindred so easily?" Cleo said Kindred like it had an extra E in it...like, *Kindered.*

It was obvious she had given in, but she was far from done with the subject.

"If you knew Isabella," Maddox said. "You wouldn't have to ask."

I plopped the bottle down on its bottom with a noisy clunk then stuck my free hand out to shake hers.

Cleo glanced down at it and then back at Maddox. Dismissing me.

"You asked me here," she said to him. "To meet a human?"

The pause in between her phrases turned that last sentence ripe with condescension. I decided I'd like her as much as I liked Isme.

Maddox rocked back on his heels and stuffed his hands into his pockets as he addressed her.

"I asked you here because I have a lead on your item."

She actually startled me when she bolted off her seat. I found myself grabbing for the edge of the bar in reflex.

"My potions chest," she said without actually squealing and yet, her tone rose an octave, enough that I got the sense that this potions chest was pretty valuable. "Have you really found it?"

"I have a lead," he said, lifting one finger in the air to hold her off. "That's where Isabella comes in."

She spun on her heel and managed to make it look like a ballet move. No. That wasn't it. It was more of an Arabian dance move. I had visions of her in a belly dancer's belt, coins clinking musically.

I decided to tack on a greasy looking, ugly master to the image for good measure.

"She?" Cleo said. "What can she do that a man like yourself cannot?"

"She can tell you to go fuck yourself," I said with a pleasant smile.

Cleo's fangs slipped behind her full lips as she frowned at me. "I don't like her, Maddox."

Fayed had taken a few steps back after Maddox had inched near, making a show of reaching for my bottle but not picking it up.

"Careful, Isabella," he said to me under his breath. He didn't pull his hand back but let it rest on the bar close to me. I caught his eye and he held mine. *Don't mess with her* his look said.

I swung my gaze back to the petite figure perched on the stool next to me.

"I don't like you either," I said. "And I don't care what Maddox thinks we need to know each other for. I don't have to please anyone anymore."

I pushed the whiskey bottle back toward Fayed. "Can you call me a cab, Fayed? I don't fancy walking home in this neighborhood."

Maddox pressed himself between Cleo and I, with his arm outstretched over my chest. Although, I was impressed with how he managed to fit himself into such a small space, I looked down at it and then up at him until he retracted it.

He cleared his throat.

"Isabella, Cleo hired me two hundred years ago."

I laughed out loud. "She didn't get what she paid for then."

"Recollections doesn't run like that," he said. "We get requests that we keep in a ledger. Then if items come up, we reclaim them, notify the owner, and they pay us the full and remaining remittance."

I quirked an eyebrow. "By reclaim, I take it you mean steal."

He smiled and tapped his nose before easing back out from the space and touching Cleo on the arm. I thought I saw him run his palm down the back of her shoulder.

"If we have to, we do. If we can buy it, we buy it. Many objects are found in the strangest of places. I once spied the book of Thoth in a second hand book shop—"

"I still have it," Cleo interjected. "It's been useful over the years, I admit, but it's a pale replacement for my chest."

"And I found the *Draupnir* in an old jewelry box out of Errol's pawn shop. That cost me dearly, of course. Errol knows his merchandise and he knows their value. It's hard to pull the wool over his eyes."

I had no idea what either of those things were, and it didn't matter. I heard the things he wasn't saying. I wanted to be clear that he understood that I did.

"So, most of the time, you steal the artifacts."

"Reclaim," he corrected. "Since those who often have possession of the relic are not the true owners. The Draupnir, for example, went to Odin's son, Thor, and he paid me handsomely to hand it over to him."

I was beginning to realize why he wanted to meet both Cleo and I at Fayed's.

I drummed my fingers on the bar counter, punctuating certain words with a hard tap.

"So, you want me to steal something for the vampire," I said and was pretty sure I heard Cleo growl beneath her breath.

Maddox sighed. "Cleo collected poisons."

"Potions," she corrected.

"Of course," he said with a subtle bow. "But the chest went missing soon after..." he let the sentence trail off as though he'd said too much.

Cleo looked at me directly, almost defiantly. "Soon after I died," she finished for him.

"So how long ago are we talking?" I said. "Long enough that you've found it in a museum and I need to deal with alarms and police and late-night curators, or just some bloke's pawn shop?"

Cleo barked out a laugh. "I doubt you'll be able to carry the thing. It's inlaid with gold and precious stones, but it's not the whole chest I really care about. It's just one small vial."

Her eyelids closed and her nostrils rounded as she inhaled deeply. She tilted her head slightly back, more, I guessed, to retreat into memory than out of nostalgia. I doubted this creature had any empathy left in her to feel such emotion.

"It's the palest blue at the top, colored by copper and fading beautifully to clear white glass," she said. "It's encrusted in diamonds to make it sparkle like sun on water when you hold it to the light."

She opened her eyes and leveled them to mine. "Anyone with any intelligence will know it by the stopper. Not made of gold, but of silver and stamped with my seal. The vial is shaped like a tear bleeding down a lover's face."

I blinked stupidly at her expression, one that made me doubt my belief she couldn't feel. She was enraptured, that much was clear.

"You can do what you will with the chest, Maddox," she said, turning her gaze to him. "If it has survived these centuries, I don't care. I only want that bottle and what's inside."

"And what is that?" I said.

"Were you not listening, human?" she snapped. "The bottle holds my lover's tears," she said. "They speak of his pain and his grief and his agony to leave me at the moment of his death."

She squared her shoulders, all semblance of nostalgia gone as quickly as it had come. She turned with an all business-like demeanor toward Maddox.

"I will reward you handsomely," she said to him. "But you will not use this disgusting human to reclaim it for me. I don't care how much it costs to procure a collector worthy of the task. I won't have her filthy hands pawing at the last of my Antony."

CHAPTER FOUR

Antony. This woman turned vampire, with the regal bearing and the slightly exotic accent, that called herself Cleo. I stared at her dumbstruck for a moment as I tried to process my revulsion for her and the awe of knowing, I was standing in front of Cleo-fucking-patra. The woman who had seduced Caesar.

In the end, it was something else entirely that won out.

I had put up with a lot of things in my lifetime. I'd proved it time and time again when I'd let Scottie degrade me in public, hit me in private, and promise me in front of his cronies never to do any of it again. No one in Scottie's posse had ever made the slightest act of contrition for what they allowed their boss to do to me. No one stood up for me. Hell, I'd not stood up for myself, and I suppose the blame for all that lay on my shoulders.

But Cleo's words struck a nerve. It felt so ludicrously familiar that at first, I couldn't find the words to defend myself. Without thinking about it, I let it slide over me like a bit of breeze to a body accustomed to hurricane force winds. I even felt myself grow smaller out of habitual posturing and it felt normal.

"Isabella?" Maddox said as he eyed me. His face held a peculiar expression, one I couldn't quite make out. "Did you hear what she said?"

I shrugged my answer. "She wants a different agent."

I mean, if Cleopatra wanted someone else to do her bidding, she was entitled. Who was I to such a pedigree?

I was aware that Fayed had taken to looking from Cleo to Maddox and was seesawing his jaw back and forth.

I leaned toward her, not sure why, just feeling as though I suddenly had an insight into history that no one would ever truly get, and I forgot for a moment she was a vampire.

I couldn't take my eyes off her. I wanted to memorize each feature. Was her beauty a glamor cast over her facade by vampirism, or was it sheer charisma that made the hooked nose just a fetching bit of wabi sabi? If I looked her up on the Internet would I find a face like the one that was in front of me now?

"Isabella?"

Maddox again. I blinked and swung my gaze to his.

"Yes?"

"You heard her, right?"

I nodded. "Do I look deaf?"

He canted his head to the side. I watched him scan me head to heel and then swing his gaze from Fayed—who stood looking strangely tense—to Cleo, who refused to look at me at all.

"Say you're sorry," he said.

I sagged against the bar as I remembered telling the Queen of Egypt and the Nile to go fuck herself. The familiar haunting sense of shame cloaked my spine.

"I'm sorry," I said.

Maddox breathed out an exasperated sigh and when he spoke, his voice was flinty and brittle.

"Not you, Isabella. You have nothing to be sorry for. I was talking to Cleo."

"Me?" Cleo's hand went to her hip as though she was indignant, but I noted she didn't so much as step backward in surprise or shame.

I assumed she'd never felt indignant or ashamed in her entire few hundred years. In fact, she looked so regal, it was all I could do not to fall into a sort of curtsy.

Maddox held his ground and all vestiges of charm disappeared. He was demon warrior in that moment and I saw in him what demons must have seen in his days as a Guardian of the Stone. I would have quailed at the way he set his jaw, at the tension in his shoulders.

Cleopatra merely looked furious.

"You forget who you're speaking to, Maddox," she said.

"I know exactly who I'm speaking to. A woman who dearly wants her lover's last tear. A vampire who, no matter how old she is, can still be slain by just the right warrior. A client who has paid an already handsome fee to a procurer of the most delicate treasures."

I noted he saved the last to remind her why we were all here in the first place, and didn't end on a threat.

But she heard the threat anyway. I had the feeling her psyche was finely tuned to the smallest hint of insult.

She all but scalded me with a hateful look over Maddox's shoulder.

"Get her out of here," she said to Fayed in a tight voice. "If you don't remove her at once, I will use her blood to flavor your keg of craft beer."

I sent a little wave to Fayed. Things were getting out of hand, and I couldn't see any way to smooth it over. Time to hotfoot it.

"Thanks for the drinks."

I started to head for the door, not entirely sure I wanted to hide tail and run now that I was doing so. It felt wrong. Shades of Scottie tried to wring out a note of warning in my head and I remembered I had killed him. I was no better than the vampires and demons of the world. I didn't deserve to be apologized to. I was guilty. Guilty as sin.

"Isabella," Maddox said from behind me.

I waved at him over my shoulder without turning around. I couldn't turn around. I felt a sting in my eyes that was as unexpected as it was sudden.

"Let me know when you have work for me," I said over my shoulder.

Before I made it three steps, he was in front of me. His palm swept over my arm and down to my elbow where it cupped the joint and sent warm pulses through me.

"Don't go," he said. "She has no right to say those things to you."

A flash of memory swept through me; of him touching me when Scottie's henchman had beaten the living snot out of me and left me a ball of blood and tissue on my kitchen floor. Maddox had taken the pain from me with his touch. I don't know what magic had allowed him to do it, but it had been the first time I'd felt kindness in years.

It was too kind. I hadn't been worthy of it then. I wasn't worthy of it now.

"It's OK," I said, shrugging him off as gently as I could. "I'm sure her work will bring in a tidy sum for you. I'll just wait for something else. I've got a few irons in the fire."

I didn't. I'd lost so much when I killed Scottie and entered the world of the supernatural. I didn't dare use any of my human contacts for fear they'd end up endangered by my proximity to all things Kindred. I mean, look how long I'd gone on ignorant and it hadn't protected me when the magical elements crossed my path.

It was inevitable that I put my small network at risk. Many of them were vagabonds and kids with eyes and ears all over the city. They were invisible enough to hear and see without being heard or seen.

But they were still human. I'd let go the pretense that I could continue to use them after I'd returned from Hell.

Maddox's offer of work had been the only thing I could cling to. But I couldn't—wouldn't—confess that.

His lips pressed together and he huffed through his nose with a definite sense of finality.

He spun to face the interior of the bar.

"Fuck you, Cleo," he said. "Find your own potions chest."

He extracted his hand from my elbow and ran it over the small of my back as he guided me to the door.

Cleo slammed something down on the counter behind me. It made a distinct shattering sound that told me it was one of Fayed's martini glasses.

"You're dead, human," she said.

CHAPTER FIVE

I fled the bar with that voice and all of its sultry accented sylla-bles filling my ears. I knew any threat made by a Kindred should be taken seriously, and all I could think of was to high tail out of the district before she decided to come looking for me in dark alleys on the way home.

And that's exactly what I did. I was halfway down the alley before I heard Maddox behind me.

"Wait up," he said.

"No time to wait," I said over my shoulder. "You heard the Queen of Egypt. I'm dead."

I was so busy craning to see over my shoulder at him in the barely lit alley, that my boot rammed into something hard in the dark, and while it didn't hurt, it put me off balance. I hop-scotched a couple of feet before I could get good footing again.

Something clattered out of sight into the shadows.

I peered into the darkness after it. I hoped it was an empty can and not my cell phone. I felt down my jacket, testing for its telltale bulge. I only relaxed when I felt it in the back pocket of my jeans. But then I thought; what else might it have been if not my phone or a tin can, and I shuddered inside my jacket.

"Isabella?"

I swung around, mindful of the debris scattered over the al-ley floor so I didn't stub my foot on something else or step in something disgusting. It was odd, all the litter. Fayed normally kept his back alley neat and clear.

"Isabella?"

I dragged my gaze from a pile of fabric clotted on the ground next to the dumpster.

"What?" I said. I had to mince around a logger-jam of pizza boxes and what, in the darkness, looked like a medical cooler in order advance any farther toward the street.

"I don't have time to chit chat, Maddox. I need to get a cab and get the hell out of here. Like yesterday."

His sigh behind me was filled with resignation.

"You don't need to go alone," he said. "I'll come with you."

I shuffled through a pile of filthy tissue paper like it was fallen leaves and balked when a blast of air from a grate blew scraps of them up toward my face.

Swatting them away was more a panic-filled exercise than a strategic one. There was no telling what was on the litter in this part of the city, and I didn't want to imagine what the worst might be.

A piece of paper covered in goo stuck to my sleeve when I failed to bat it completely away. It glowed purple and I followed the direction of the light to a black-light lamp post.

"Oh fuck me," I said as I tried to pluck the paper from my sleeve without actually touching it.

Maddox by then had come up next to me. He stripped it from my arm with two fingers and wadded it up before throwing it into the dumpster a few feet away.

"Here, he said with a move to take me by the elbow.

I shrank away from him.

"Don't touch me with that hand," I said. "God knows what you've got on your fingers now."

"It's ketchup," he said, jerking his chin in the direction of the dumpster. "From a bag of fries."

I backed away. "Sure," I said. "We're in the alley behind a vampire bar and you think it's ketchup."

His lips twitched, and I was so sure he was going to stick his fingers into his mouth to tease me with a fake taste test, that I put up my hand in protest.

"Don't," I said. "If you do that, I swear I'll puke on your shoes."

"Fear not, dear maiden," he said with a sweeping bow. "Your gorge is safe with me."

I watched somewhat impatiently as he started scouting the alley, peering into the shadows, kicking aside bits of debris. A can skittered across the asphalt and fetched up into the dumpster with a clank.

The sound of it indicated that whatever had rolled away earlier most definitely was not a can.

I hugged my arms around my waist as I tried to decide whether to bolt or wait for him. The hairs on the back of my neck were standing up and I had the terrible feeling Cleo was creeping up on me from the shadows along the building.

"To hell with this," I said. "I can't stand here while you look for a snack."

I started to head back toward the mouth of the alley when an awful shriek froze me in my tracks. It was awful. The kind of sound something makes when it's either terrified or enraged.

Neither sounded particularly encouraging, and I might have leapt for Maddox and the boxiness of his arms if he wasn't already halfway across the alley from me, hunched over and staring down into a plastic milk crate.

Another awful shriek rent the air.

Evidently, it was coming from the milk crate.

"Hey," Maddox murmured down into it.

From the indulgent tone in his voice I could tell there wasn't some otherworldly miniature vampire or worse clamoring for blood from inside the box.

Curiosity overrode my thoughts that Cleo was lurking about and waiting to pounce on me. I paused to watch Maddox kneel on one knee and reach for the box.

Without thinking, I edged closer.

A hiss leaked from the box at about the same time as Maddox yanked his hand back to his chest. He cradled it with his other hand.

That's when I knew what was happening.

"Oh fuck me," I said with a chuckle. "You found a stray cat."

The six-foot-four man fell to a crouch as he leaned toward the box, scanning the inside with a wary sweep of his gaze from left to right. The light from Fayed's back door lamps made the buzz cut of his auburn hair look a weird shade of magenta. I felt the most insane urge to run my hand over the top.

Instead, I went on tip toe to crane toward the box over his shoulder, making sure it was indeed a cat and not a rat. I'd been fooled before and it was how I'd acquired my own stray cat, who by now had shredded every pair of socks she'd found in my laundry basket.

I felt him lean against my legs for a moment before he pushed back onto his feet. He surveyed the contents with arms folded over his chest.

"How old do you think it is?" he said of the tiny ball of fur inside.

I dropped to a crouch beside the crate, deciding that if Cleo did find her way out into the alley, Maddox would be able to charm her off my neck. At least I hoped so.

"Few weeks," I said of the kitten. "Maybe a month."

It really was tiny. But its size didn't stop it from hissing furiously when Maddox bent over as if he meant to pull it out of the crate.

He yanked his arm back again, then straightened up and squared his shoulders, frustrated.

I nudged him in the ribs.

"Slow learner, huh?" I said.

"It's so tiny," he murmured. "Poor thing."

His jaw seesawed back and forth as he looked down at the kitten. Yet again, as if the moment before had not happened, he dropped to one knee again and made to scoop the kitten into his hand, this time by pulling his sleeve over his palm. The cat swiped at his arm.

He recoiled in time to avoid another nasty scratch.

I had to choke on a laugh.

"I guess it goes to show you... pussies don't like virgins."

He planted his arms on his knees as he regarded the box and spoke to me at the same time.

"Real funny, Isabella."

"No, seriously," I said. "For a virgin, you sure do have a way with pussies."

I didn't look at him, but I was sure his mouth was pressed into a tight line. It was enough to encourage me further.

"Most pussies prefer a confident touch," I went on, enjoying his discomfort.

He huffed an annoyed sigh.

"Pussies like it when you stroke them,"

"Enough," he said and pushed himself to his feet.

"That's what she said," I intoned with a snicker even though that last was a bit too cliché even for a teen to enjoy.

"We can't leave it here," he said with a sigh.

"Well," I intoned. "A pussy needs an experienced..."

"What makes you think I'm inexperienced?"

He swung his gaze to mine and even the black light of Fayed's lamps couldn't mask the bald desire I saw in his face. He might be a virgin, but he wanted me. And I didn't just know it because he had said so over the holidays. I knew it because the air was electric with lust. It was enough to make my throat ache.

"Virginity is what makes me think you're inexperienced," I choked out, knowing that despite his celibacy, that if he did touch me, I'd melt. "You're a monk."

"Was," he said without taking his eyes from my mouth. "And I wasn't exactly a monk. I have lived a long time, Isabella. You don't really believe I've never touched a woman."

I didn't really believe it, no. I wanted to. Some awful part of my mind whispered things to the inner Isabella that she wanted a man who was dirty and rough and knew how to make a woman feel as though the only soft edges were his thumbs as they whispered over her skin.

And that was the most awful thing. I always fell for the wrong guy.

I took a step sideways, more to move out of the line of his stare than anything else. I cast about for a memory that could support my argument that he had no idea what to do with a woman and found one.

Just one.

"There's a very well-known god named Pan who knows all about your past," I said.

"Not all of it," he said with a smirk and then peered back down into the box while I enjoyed the memory of meeting Pan, and discovering that the man who acted like a player was indeed a celibate virgin who all but blushed at the preponderance of nudity that had surrounded the god.

He shoved his hands into his jeans pockets as he considered the box.

"Should we take this little one home with us?" he said, neatly changing the topic.

I shook my head and strode toward the street, leaving him standing over the box.

"I already have a cat," I said.

"We can't leave it."

He sounded aghast, as though I was some callous beast or something. I wasn't. There were two very good reasons why I was not volunteering to home that kitty. One was that I knew he couldn't just leave it there. He was drawn to cats for some reason, no matter how much they hated him. The second was more obvious to both of us.

"You've seen my cat," I said.

"Demon," he corrected. "Your cat is a demon."

He leaned over the box. "This one is too little to be so evil."

"Mine was little once too," I said. "They all start out that way."

He bent, this time to pick up the box instead of the cat, so he had obviously learned from his earlier, thwarted attempts. With it clutched against his chest, he swiveled toward me as the tiny thing inside growled with a deep-throated rattle.

"So you think this one will grow into a demon too?"

He looked so damn earnest standing there, I couldn't stand it.

I sighed and waved him closer, then I rubbed his arm encouragingly when he brushed against me. He jostled the box accidentally and the little thing leapt from the bottom to grab the edge with one claw. It hung there, caught by its tiny nail on the plastic washed in the black light of the alley.

"I'd say it's well on its way to making scratching your eyes out its favorite past time."

I scraped the kitten's claw off the edge of the crate with my pinky nail. It fell back down with a yowl and then balled itself up in the corner, where it started to shiver.

"Oh," I said and reached in to stroke its little head with the back of my fingers. It was soft despite the grime in its fur and the face was broad and flat like a rag doll breed. I thought maybe the fur would be a creamy beige after some grooming.

I lifted my eyes to Maddox's face. He wasn't glowering at me, though he did look put-out that the kitten responded to me but not him. His russet eyebrows had scuttled downward in an upside-down V.

He pushed the box at me, a little too gruffly.

"Maybe you should to keep it."

I laughed out loud. "Oh, no. I have a cat, remember? She's all I can manage."

I lifted the tiny ball against my chest, though, and it began purring. "It's perfectly loving," I said. "Maybe you just need a little practice with..."

"Don't say it," he said, but I noted he leaned in closer toward the ball of fur, encouraged at the sound coming from the puff of grimy softness.

He smelled of woodsmoke, the way he often did, and what I imagined aged whiskey would smell like if its color had a fragrance. I had clear sight of the bristles of his buzz cut and the tops of his ears as he leaned in. I had to close my eyes to pretend he wasn't right there in front of me, head down the way he would if he were to nuzzle his way down from my neck to my breasts.

"Just leave it in the box and feed it until it gets used to you," I said, and buoyed by the sound of a level voice, continued. "It will love you like its own mother."

I eased the kitten back into its corner. It shivered harder and tried to ball up into a tight knot to hold in its warmth.

Maddox shoved the box against my chest and took a step backward.

"Hey," I protested but then he unzipped his jacket and yanked it from his shoulders, and I realized what he was doing.

When he flung it over my shoulder, I could still feel the heat inside the lining.

I hadn't realized how chilly it was until I felt all the warmth draping over my shoulder to my back, blocking off the cold.

I might have been content to pull it over my shoulders, and call it a good image for a long night of boredom, but the man was digging into the waist of his T-shirt and peeling it upward. Right there in front of me. As if stripping down was the most casual and normal thing in the world. The shirt stripped over his shoulders and head, and he stood there for one insanely cliché moment before he tucked the material around the kitten, ignoring the hissing and swipes it made at his wrist.

"There," he said, looking at me with a heart-stopping sense of victory that gobbed up my throat and kept it being able to elicit one note of intelligible response.

He had to coax the box from my grip, and I might not have noticed the nasty scratch that went from his wrist to his forearm, except he snapped his fingers in front of my face.

"Still think I need more practice, Kitten," he said with a chuckle, and then hugged the box close to his chest as he strode toward the mouth of the alley.

CHAPTER SIX

There was no way I was going to get left behind in that alley, knowing Cleo could come out of the bar any minute. She might have seen me leave with Maddox but that was no guarantee she wouldn't decide to hunt me the whole way home. You couldn't trust a vampire. Evidenced by the fact that one I'd thought was my friend nearly turned me over to his elder on a simple order from her.

So it didn't take me long to realize that Maddox either expected me to follow him or was leaving me there, and I most definitely was not going back inside the bar. I could call my own cab, but I reasoned that it might be far safer to do that walking alongside him than to peck at numbers on a screen in the dark alley behind Fayed's tavern.

That meant I'd have to run to catch up to Maddox as he was already rounding the mouth of the alley. I could hear him talking to the box and even though it slowed him down a bit, in a heartbeat he'd be onto the main drag. I had to hotfoot it if I wanted to catch up.

Maddox was six foot four and made of sinew and muscle from his toe to the top of his scalp. My short legs and weeks of languid living made the exercise a frustrating one. Each of his strides was like three of mine.

Even so, I was an above average runner, and I pelted it down the alleyway like the devil was behind me.

Maybe she was.

I exited the alley to a street that was empty of vehicles and casual pedestrians. The moon was out and hovering over the top of the buildings like a clipped toenail flung skyward. The air was even chillier now that we were out of the lee of the alley. Smoke billowed up from manholes.

"What's with leaving me behind back there?" I demanded as I drew close enough for him to hear without me shouting.

"I wasn't worried about you," he said without taking his eye from the box. "You're a fighter, Isabella. And if all else fails, you run."

For that last word, he laughed.

I grabbed for his bare arm and hooked it to hold him back so I could keep pace. Of course, it was me who fetched up, not him. His jacket fell from my shoulders and I made an instinctive but hasty grab for it. I noticed one of the hookers down the street had caught sight of his bare chest and was swaggering toward us.

"Good grief," I said. "Put some clothes on before your delicate chastity is impeached."

He halted finally as he caught sight of the hooker.

"Good gravy; she looks hungry," he muttered beneath his breath, but I caught it and smothered a laugh. I wasn't sure if his comment was hopeful or worried.

"Put this on," I said and tossed his jacket over his shoulder. I took the box from him so he could pull the sleeves over his arms.

The kitten inside saw me and tried to climb out.

Maddox huffed as the small ball of fur made it as far as getting its two front paws dangled over the top. He pulled his arms back out of the jacket and plopped it over the top of the box, effectively cutting the kitten's vision off. Then he gripped the edges of the crate.

"Don't want it getting out," he explained with a cast look over his shoulder.

The hooker paused directly beneath a street lamp so she was bathed in yellow light. She struck a pose with one foot lifted and her knee crossed beneath the other. With a long smile at us, she ran her palm down her hips.

"Fuck, that's hot," I said with a tilt of my chin toward her. "Don't you think that's hot, Maddox?"

"You're the devil, Isabella," he said.

"I've met the devil," I said, not totally joking. "He's hornier than a hooker."

"Hookers aren't horny," he said. "And I know all about Lucifer."

There was a pensiveness to his voice that made me cant my head at him, curious. Was he remembering that the devil had had trapped me and made me wear gimp leather for his pleasure before I'd managed to escape, or was there something else seething beneath the surface of his admission? I had the feeling that Maddox's whole past was an iceberg: poking a mere tip to the surface but leaving a dangerous swell of jagged blades beneath.

"Do tell," I said.

"Long story," he said. "For another time."

He started backtracking, in the opposite direction from the hooker, and guided me along with him by his shoulder. "We need to get you home before the rest of the nasties make their way onto the streets."

He scanned the drag up and down the way a soldier pans a battleground, and I was content to have him at my side. His survey of the area was a good reminder of how bad this area could be for those who didn't know about the supernatural element. Heck, it was dangerous for those of us who did.

In my naive days, I'd lingered in the area for specific reasons and none of them that took me too far past midnight. It had to be pure luck that I'd not chanced on danger before, and now that I knew how bad the place could be, I only ever came here for new specific reasons. Case in point...Maddox's request to meet me.

But I'd stayed too long in the borough waiting for him, and if it was late and dangerous, it was his fault, not mine.

The fact of it reminded me of why I had taken the risk in the first place.

"You had a job for me?" I said. "That was why you wanted to meet."

"Had," he said. "You sort of botched that one."

I bristled at the thought that he'd consider it my fault that Cleo was racist. Or was it specieist?

"I could easily have slipped into wherever it is that you found her chest hiding," I said, deciding it didn't matter. "We can sell the chest somewhere. Keep the vial just because. Her loss."

We walked together down the street, and I had to do double time to keep up with him. There was an even better reason why I was willing to meet with him in an area lousy with Kindred. I needed the money. The last few weeks recovering from doing nothing work-wise except running from supernatural baddies had sorely depleted even my bug-out bag of resources.

"I've been waiting weeks to get started. I have bills. Rent. Put me on the case anyway. She doesn't need to know."

"I'll find you something else," he mused aloud and held me back from crossing into the intersection by holding the box out in front of me.

"I need something now," I said. "Tomorrow is the first of the month."

He gave me an odd look.

"Rent," I said. "Humans pay rent."

I waited for him to comprehend the basics of humanity. They needed shelter. Food. Warmth.

"Well?" I said when he said nothing, and as I watched him and the way his face remained carefully composed despite my pressing on, I realized the truth.

"You don't know where her potions chest is."

"I wouldn't say I don't know exactly."

"Then why bother at all? Why get my hopes up that I'd have a job? Why get that vile vampire involved and have her put yet another damn target on my back?"

He inhaled deeply, I thought to construct a lie, and I was cast back to the times when Scottie kept things from me, expecting me to just do his bidding by trust only.

Well, I didn't trust blindly anymore. But I'd never be free, it seemed, from Scottie. It was enough to make me antsy and angry all at the same time.

I pushed the crate back toward him and made to cross the street on a red light. There were no cars coming, after all. There were precious few vehicles in this district, strangely enough. I guessed either Kindred didn't drive much or the human element made up for far more motor cars than I'd realized.

He made short work of my intention by stepping in front of me.

"Isabella, it's not what you think."

I side-stepped him and he blocked me again.

"I know where it is. I'm just having trouble acquiring it. I need you. She'll come around."

"Maybe you can arrange for us to work together without her knowing."

"I wish it was that easy."

He shifted the crate as the light changed, indicating we could walk, and we started to cross over to the other side.

"Forget it then," I said. I hugged myself and looked longingly at the jacket keeping the cat warm inside her box.

"You're not cold?" I pointed an elbow at his bare chest and wondering what sort of blood he had running through his veins. "Or worried about getting arrested for indecency?"

He laughed. "You think if human police ever decided to beat this area, they'd live long enough to arrest anyone?"

I mulled that over. I'd never given thought to how devoid of police presence the borough was. The thief instinct just sent me reflexively where their law presence was low, and I gave it no more thought.

He skimmed me with an assessing gaze.

"You're cold, though," he said and brushed against me so he could wrap his free arm around my waist.

"Maybe you should give some thought to my offer," he said.

"You mean the one where you move in with me and watch me like a hawk so that someone doesn't decide to use me as a conduit to Lilith's power? That offer?"

"Something like that," he said.

"No." I shrank into a smaller ball beneath his arm to harbor all that glorious heat. "I can't have someone watching my every move. I lived that life. I won't live it again."

"You mean you don't want anyone knowing what you're do-ing. That's a remnant of your old life, Isabella. You don't have to worry about human jail or your boss trying to take what's yours. You work for me. I will look out for you."

"I don't want to answer to anyone, Maddox. I need to be my own boss. We agreed on that. You could contract me. I call my own shots."

He didn't laugh, even if I'd just been begging him for work a moment earlier. It was a complex thing, this freedom. Even I couldn't work out all the things Scottie had done to my psyche. Only time would let that happen for me.

The thought made me halt on the sidewalk, though.

"You want me to fail," I said. "That would put me right where you want me. You wouldn't have to sniff around from afar to make sure Absalom doesn't come for me."

He lifted one shoulder. "I can't say I'd be disappointed for you to end up having to come under my protection. It would make my task protecting the stone's energy a lot easier. But no. I don't want you to fail, Kitten."

"I'll find you something," he said. "Can't see you go hungry or homeless because of your spiteful nature."

He stared off up the street as he spoke and I followed his gaze to see a yellow vehicle, the only car on the street, strangely enough, approaching.

"Cab," he said, jerking his chin at the car and easing the crate onto the ground between his feet. He lifted his hand and just like that the cab pulled over.

"Your magic," I said. I wasn't averse to walking but I couldn't shake the feeling of doom that dogged me since finding out Cleopatra was a vampire who considered human kind a pest to be rid of or food for her larder.

"That wasn't magic, actually," he said. "At least not the kind I have."

I yanked open the door of the cab and pushed into the bench seat, scooting over to the middle to make room for Maddox and the box.

He passed the cabbie something that didn't look the least bit like money. In fact, it looked more like a ticket of sorts. He mumbled what sounded like my address except for a few words that might have been in a different language, then he flashed me a smile and closed the door.

"Hold up," I said to the cabbie who had put the car into drive at Maddox's nod. I scooted back across the seat and struck the window button so I could lean out.

Maddox stood there, still shirtless, with the kitten's box hitched up to his hip. I could see the jacket undulating upward as the tiny thing tried to climb out.

"Aren't you coming?" I said out the window.

I had been on my own for years. I'd braved the worst of men, and the devil himself, and yet I couldn't shake the feeling of dread prickling my spine. It wasn't just Cleo. Something was off. A girl on her own got used to listening to her intuition.

He leaned in and tugged my jacket collar up around the muff of my neck.

"I'd love to go home with you, Isabella," he murmured. "But I have my hands full already with a sassy female."

He shifted the box to his left hip and ran a thumb over my chin with his free hand. It was dry, rough, and delicious feeling.

"Lock your door tight," he said. "And don't let anyone in."

CHAPTER SEVEN

D_on't let anyone in_ was something you told a person when you were worried they would accidentally invite in a vampire. Maddox had said it with a grin on his face, so he obviously thought my anxiety over Cleo was overwrought. But how could he be sure?

"You're not helping," I said.

"Just testing."

He chuckled, but it sounded off, not like him at all. He was calm. Collected. Not the kind of guy to get weirded out by a threat from a vampire who obviously wanted to make him hers.

Nervous Maddox was an anomaly.

"Testing for what," I said, suspicious of the man who had only ever displayed anxiety when he'd been surrounded by a bevy of sexed up, naked nymphs, sicced on him by the god Pan.

The cabbie complained that we were taking too long, but he didn't turn around or even look at us in the rear-view mirror. That was strange enough, but when Maddox shot him a glare that drew his glance to the same mirror, he shook out his shoulders as though he wanted to argue but didn't.

Right. Definitely odd.

Maddox turned his attention back to me.

"I'm worried about you," he said.

I sucked the back of my teeth to indicate what I thought of that comment.

"Right," I said. "You sure sounded worried when you laughed about Cleo worming her way into my apartment and draining me dry."

"I did not laugh."

"But you did ask to meet me and a woman you knew was a vampire, in the darkest dregs of the supernatural district?"

He sighed. "This isn't the darkest dregs," he said. "I just wanted to check in on you, make sure that you were fine."

"Why wouldn't I be?"

He ran his hand over his new buzz cut and shifted the box to his other hip. The kitten inside complained with a loud yowl.

"You know why," he said.

Did I now? I couldn't imagine the reason I'd suddenly be cause for concern. All I saw now was that he'd put me in the cross hairs of a vampire threatening to visit my house in the dark of the hour before dawn.

"If you were so worried, you shouldn't have asked me to meet you and a bigoted vampire at the Rot Gut," I told him, and meant it.

"That's not it," he said. "Cleo is all bark and no bite."

I could just make out the sound of something scraping along the asphalt, as though he was worrying his boot back and forth across the pavement.

"Are you doing alright, Isabella?" he said as he put his hand on the bottom of the window. "Mentally, emotionally?"

I had a moment of blazing understanding. I leaned toward the window so I could punch down on his hand.

"Oh my God," I said when he didn't so much as wince. "That's why you offered me this job that you knew would come to nothing."

He flipped his hand over just as I pulled mine back, and caught me at the wrist. I yanked away.

"It's about Scottie," I said. "All of this is about Scottie. You knew Cleo wouldn't want me involved in your recollection of that god-forsaken chest of hers, but you couldn't think of another way to get me out of the house. You thought a job might tempt me."

He leaned his forearm onto the window as I retreated into the back of the cab.

"You weren't answering my texts," he said, and flicked his gaze to the cabbie's in the mirror. I caught some kind of communication pass between the two of them and that infuriated me even more.

"There wasn't a single question to answer," I said. "There wasn't even a dick pic. Just little shots of your dinner. Punchlines from jokes. I mean...what did you think?"

"I thought you'd answer one of the damn things." He pushed his head through the window. "I'm not good at technology."

"Well, a dick pic at the least might have got a response."

The cabbie turned on the overhead light and I could see that Maddox had pressed his lips together and was struggling with something I thought he didn't want to say.

"Shut the damn light off," I said to the cabbie. I didn't want to look at Maddox right then. I didn't want to see the look of worry that rode his expression, because it said more about me than it did him, and I wasn't going to go there.

"You weren't leaving the house," he said. "You haven't come out of that hovel in weeks."

"That's not true," I said, crossing my arms over my chest. "I came out at Christmas."

I felt a flush of warmth prickle up my throat to my cheeks as I thought about the party he'd convinced me to attend. He had faked a job then too, and for the same reason.

I fell for it again.

"You're a one-trick pony, Maddox," I said. "You need to be a bit more inventive if you want me to leave my hovel."

My words sounded sour and I kicked the back of the seat in the hopes of urging the cabbie to finally pull out. I pushed at Maddox's arm to release it from the window, but he kept it anchored there as though his strength alone was keeping the cab grounded.

"If you were fine," he said, "you'd go get groceries. Pizza. Put the cat out."

"She has a litter box."

"You know what I mean."

This time it was my turn to lean onto the window. He'd taken a step backward, evidently having some trouble with the kitten trying to claw her way out of the box.

"Have you been watching me?" I said.

He toed the pavement and peeked under the jacket to the interior of the box instead of meeting my eyes. He didn't answer.

"You said you wouldn't do that," I went on.

Maddox dropped the jacket back down over a tiny claw that jabbed out from the edge.

"Maddox?"

He looked at me finally, and his face in the dim light of street lamps said everything he wouldn't. I felt my chest burn.

"You said if I worked for you, I wouldn't need someone staking out my apartment twenty-four seven."

He lifted one shoulder. "You think I can leave you to Absalom and his greys? They know where you are, Isabella. They know what you can do."

I'd spent three years on the run from Scottie, watching over my shoulder for the day when one of his henchmen would find me. I didn't want to live my life knowing someone was watching me. I didn't care what the reason was. Absalom and his greys were a distant threat, if any, right now. I needed space to find out what my life could be as a truly liberated woman.

"I would have left you be," he argued, and I thought he hated having to explain himself. "I took vows," he said. "You know I'm a guardian, Isabella. I can't risk Absalom finding you and using your energy."

"Oh, so it's not me you're worried about after all. It's the damn Lilith stone."

"For Pete's sake, of course I'm worried about you." He pinched the bridge of his nose. "Sweet Pagan Piety, it's times like this I'm glad of my celibacy. You women are just not rational creatures."

"You Kindred are the complex creatures," I said. "Can't my behavior just be because I need to find myself?"

He leveled his gaze at me again.

"Look. You weren't yourself, alright. Not even after Scourge." There was a pause, however brief before he spoke again. "Especially after Scourge."

He flicked his gaze to the interior carpet of the cab, and I knew he was thinking about how he'd declared his want for me on Kindred's most savage eve, how he'd chased me with the intent of showing me that need because he couldn't help himself.

"Scottie," he said, finally, tearing my mind away from the things that had happened that night and back to the present. "Or rather, your mental state now that he's gone. You seem normal again, act normal. But..."

"But what?" I demanded, my voice a little too sharp. "I'm up off the sofa. I'm getting dressed. Going out to meet people, who evidently don't think my time is valuable."

It was as I was speaking that I understood exactly what he'd been worried about after all. Me, a fragile, vulnerable human being, with all the rampant emotions he and his kind didn't understand but exploited.

"You thought I wanted to kill myself," I said with a harsh laugh. "After all the things I've been through? After I fought like mad to live? After I, after I..."

I couldn't say the words, *after I killed Scottie*. I couldn't. Instead I found a round-about way to answer to the concern.

"Listen, I'm not sure how I feel about being a murderer but I didn't go through all that just to swallow a bottle of pills. I need work, Maddox. I need to earn so I can live. Do what you promised and find me a real job please."

He rocked back on his heels as though my words were striking him in the chest.

"Okay, okay. I believe you."

He didn't look like he believed me. I didn't care in the least. I leaned toward the door to press the window button.

"Take me home," I said to the cabbie.

He didn't move to take the car out of park.

"Now," I said and then added, "please."

The cabbie ignored me but hunched down so he could look through the back window at Maddox, who finally knocked on the door of the cab and yelled to the cabbie to take me straight home.

I leaned back with a sigh and laid my head on the back of the seat. At least the cab was warm and clean. I watched the city blur by as I pondered the situation I was in.

I'd taken out the kingpin of a criminal group, but there were always brutes willing to take on the mantle. Whoever took Scottie's place might decide on vengeance.

But that wasn't my big fear or the thing Maddox was worried about the most. The Lilith Stone Maddox had given his vow to was a powerful one. It kept Lilith's energy trapped and needed guardians. Maddox was one. His father, who now possessed the stone and was skipping his way through the nine worlds to keep it safe, was another. The last two guardians of the stone.

And there was the big issue. The stone had sent me to Hell. I'd escaped with help from the Morrigan, but it now made me a conduit for the power. I had no idea what it meant, but it was sufficiently threatening to make Maddox decide I needed to be surveilled.

The cabbie took a route I was unfamiliar with. The buildings looked empty. No one walked the streets. Even the hooker had disappeared and in her place was a tall pillar of glistening rock.

I was tired. Adrenaline had a way of doing that to a gal. And I knew better by now than to question what I might be seeing in the borough where Fayed's bar was found. As a new-comer to the city three years earlier, I'd found it by wandering about and making contacts as I scouted potential places to loot. I'd been a thief for Scottie for years. It was all I really knew or had known since I was in my late teens.

But Scottie was gone, and now I was tainted with some sort of Hell aura. I'd barely escaped the dark sorcerer Absalom and his minions, and while he needed to regroup, it won me time to learn about the things that went bump in the night.

How much time was anyone's guess, but Maddox was sure he'd return. That he'd strike when the time was right.

But I couldn't live with that sort of piano hanging over my head. I'd decided to just live.

Except, apparently, I wasn't doing such a good job of it.

Or maybe Maddox was being too much of a Nancy boy.

What I was really worried about was Cleo and her threat. That one was a clear and present danger. Much more than an absent shapeshifter and his minions.

Maddox might have been joking about me not letting anyone in, but the fact that he'd hired me a cab who obviously had some connection to Kindred and perhaps even a direct connection to him, spoke volumes.

He was worried about it too. He'd used the premise of taking care of the cat to put me off, but I imagined he'd be staking out my apartment soon enough, or would have this cabbie do it for him.

And I'd been a bit too hasty in declaring perfect security of my apartment. In truth, things had been going downhill with my landlord lately. I'd not noticed it at first, because I had been doing exactly what Maddox said I'd been doing. Namely, lying on the sofa and moping around.

All while my landlord waged his subtle and not-so-subtle war with his neighbors. It was an affluent enough neighborhood, but it hadn't always been. McMansions had grown up around his brownstone for the last decade, according to him, and the zoning committee wanted him to sell and vacate his buildings.

Like my cat, my landlord was ornery. He refused to sell, and even past that, found new and innovative ways to irritate and taunt his neighbors.

The most recent was breeding rats and letting them go on garbage pick-up day. I only realized it when he carted my garbage can back from the curb and onto the back of his pickup truck. He drove away at dusk as I watched through the window at rats scampering over the neighbors' trash bins and into flowerbeds around basement windows.

I shivered as I thought about it and made a note to turn on my cellphone light when the cabbie let me out. The last thing I wanted was to run into a nest as I walked up my steps.

"Take a left here," I said and the cabbie grunted.

"I know," he said.

Of course he would. Whatever silent communication that had occurred between Maddox and him, I wondered if it hadn't been set up in advance.

Upon arrival, I pushed out of the cab wearier than I'd felt in days. Despite Maddox's assurances he'd find me jobs so I could parlay my skills into something that would pay my bills, so far, nothing had materialized.

Instead, he was playing me with kid gloves, seeming to think that my funk would somehow infect my ability to reclaim objects he knew his clients wanted.

I shut the cab door when the cabbie informed me it was all paid for and I shuffled up the sidewalk to my front door. It wasn't until I tried to shove the key into the lock that I realized something was wrong.

The lock didn't disengage. When I twisted the knob, the door pushed open far too easily.

That's when I knew.

Someone had broken in.

CHAPTER EIGHT

I was no stranger to break-ins. I'd done a few myself in the early days for Scottie when he was a small-time boss and had his minions do small-scale grab and steals. Because I was petite, I was often the one slipping into houses through windows and crawl spaces. And because I was quick, I was the one responsible for taking off with the lightest, but most valuable stuff if trouble presented itself. I knew what a break-in looked like. This had all the hallmarks of it.

I felt the sure prickle of adrenaline as I flattened myself against the outside of the door. I wasn't sure if whoever might be inside had seen the cab pull up, and I certainly didn't want to just walk in as though I didn't realize someone was inside.

The last time someone had broken into my own apartment, it wasn't so they could steal my television or laptop.

It had been on Scottie's orders, and the brute had beaten the daylights out of me.

Even if Scottie couldn't possibly have ordered something similar, I was cautious. Calling the police was out of the question. A gal like me did not do that for any number of reasons. It was prudent to go in, but it would be slow and deliberate, with my wits about me.

I had placed a bat by the door after the last break-in. I knew where it was, and I could grab it pretty much without entering the foyer. So I twisted the knob and eased the door open a crack, just enough that I could slip my arm around the door jamb and felt for the handle. It was rough and solid in my palm. I pulled it out through the doorway and palmed it the way a pitch hitter might.

Then I slunk through the door, nice and quiet, pushing it aside with my shoulder.

I'd left a light on over the kitchen sink, and I could see the glow of it from the hallway. The steps up to the third floor were filled with the boxes and books I'd put there because I didn't use the third floor. Nothing looked disturbed.

If someone was here, they were not up the stairs.

I listened for the telltale signs of an intruder, prepared to wait perfectly still for almost five minutes. I knew from experience that a professional intruder would freeze for at least that long if there was any inkling they'd been heard. I didn't think I'd made much noise to alert my presence, but I wasn't taking a chance.

Even knowing all that, my heart was hammering against my ribs, and my breath was short and sharp. I waited with the bat clenched in my fists. I barely breathed because I wouldn't be able to hear with my rasping breath in my ears. My lungs protested even as tension tightened the muscles in my legs.

A minute passed.

Two.

I swallowed, certain that the sound of it was far too loud.

My nostrils whistled as I exhaled.

Still, no sound inside the apartment. The breeze from the door clawed at the back of my neck but I was too amped up to care.

When I was sure at least five minutes had passed and there was no sound within the apartment, I took a long slow, noiseless breath and inched forward, craning my neck to peer around the doorway to the living room.

Nothing.

Well. Next to nothing. The cat was stretched out on a pile of socks in the middle of my sofa with her belly exposed. The most recent purchase of a pair of Harry Potter character socks lay in a ball on the floor, threads cast out in every direction.

I dropped the bat onto the floor with a thunk and closed the door. There was no way that feline would be so relaxed if someone was still in the house. Her fur had just grown back from the scorching it got from the dark sorcerer who'd found my digs.

I stared at the knob and replayed that information in my head. Sorcerers, fae, Scottie and his thugs. All had gotten in to my humble abode.

And now, apparently, someone else had decided to let themselves in. Or had they?

I scanned the knob and the lock. It hadn't been forced. Only one other person had a key. My landlord. He'd obviously let himself in and not bothered to lock back up after he'd left.

That explained the cat's exhausted respite on the sofa. She loved my landlord. But what he was doing in my apartment at all was the real question, and why he couldn't be bothered to secure it afterwards was enough to make me decide that I didn't care what time of late night hour it was, Mr. Smith was going to get a call from a very upset tenant.

I yanked out my cell and stabbed at the contact list until his number showed on the screen. The speaker rang in my ear several times and still he didn't answer.

"Bastard," I said and the cat perked up her head.

"I know," I told her. "I love him, but he can't just come in here when I'm not home."

She flipped onto her belly and arched her back in a huge stretch before jumping down and strolling toward me. She rubbed against my legs and purred up at me, but it did very little to assuage my annoyance.

"Did he feed you at least?" I said. "I'm guessing not." I picked her up and carried her to the kitchen where her bowl was empty.

"I think his neglect puts him in deserves-to-get-woke-up status, don't you?"

She purred and climbed up onto my shoulder, all the better to leap onto the counter. I opened the cupboard and let her pick the can of food. Tuna. The good stuff.

"You're one expensive pussy," I said, then recalled Maddox and his new kitten and got riled up all over again, because his demand to meet me meant I wasn't home to growl at Mr. Smith for taking such liberties during a decent hour.

I had already decided to visit the landlord by the time I dumped a can of albacore solid white into her bowl. Before I could rethink it, I was out onto my stoop and closing my door purposefully. I rattled the knob to make sure it was locked.

He lived two doors down from me. The air felt crisper now that I'd been inside, and I had to hug my arms to stay warm as I bustled along the sidewalk to his door.

His porch light was on and he had piled half a dozen garbage cans along his sidewalk. A trash heap of broken furniture and electronics held up the fence on the edge of his property. I caught a whiff of feces and urine, and spied a small opened bag of diapers. My landlord was in his sixties but I knew he wasn't incontinent. He'd somehow collected a bag of baby diapers and deposited them on the side of his property that bordered that of a year-old McMansion.

The war had gone too far as far as I was concerned. I was pretty sure he would have all of it conveniently removed by the time the city came to investigate, but it made me wary as I inched my way up the paving stones. The last thing I needed was to have a rat scuttle across my feet or a raccoon leap out at me.

The state of his yard, however small, was indicative of how badly he wanted to piss off the zoning committee. I knew they had a quarrel, but I had no idea it was this bad.

I made my way onto his porch, only narrowly escaping the wide swath of spider web that stretched from rafters to pillar because the hallway light shone out onto it through the doorway window.

I stood before the sidelight with my finger hovering over the doorbell as I considered exactly what it was I was about to do.

It was nearly two A.M. What seemed like a good idea in the warmth and light of my home showed itself to be a ridiculous decision now that I was standing there.

I peered in through the slat of lead glass. There was more illumination inside than I expected for this time of night. As far as I knew, he wasn't a nighthawk and the lights in the hall foyer weren't the only things on in the house. If I peered through the window just right, I could make out a light in the living room, and beyond that, the kitchen. The television cast images of the news into the room.

His brownstone was laid out similar to mine. I knew he used his third floor as an office. Light streamed down the stairs from there as well.

I didn't feel the least bit guilty pressing the bell then. It rang inside the house with all the old-fashioned charm I'd hoped mine would have had if it worked. All I got was an annoying buzz and I'd made him disconnect it the first month I moved in.

I waited, stomping my feet on the porch to warm up and hugged myself tighter. I was beginning to regret my hasty storm to his property. A smart woman would have grabbed a sweater.

A few moments went by without a sound coming from within. I rang again, thinking he was up on the third floor. Just in case, I held the buzzer longer.

I expected the rudeness of the bell would bring him running, cursing, to the door. When it didn't, I tried one more time, this time getting up on my tiptoes and peering more judiciously through the window. I hadn't come out without a sweater for nothing. I wasn't going to waste the stupidity by running back home without speaking to him.

It was in craning to look downward that I noticed his slippered foot lying at an odd angle at the bottom of the stairs.

My heart pummeled my chest as the connection of all the dots came together. He'd fallen. Maybe broken his neck or his back. Terror clutched at my throat as I grabbed the handle and twisted. It should be locked, but I had to try.

Yet it swung all the way to the left as easily as my own doorknob. I pushed at the door and it bumped into something. A body. His body.

"Mr. Smith?" I yelled. "Are you alright?"

I hoped he'd answer. I wasn't surprised when he didn't. I pushed at the door, shouldering it with all my weight to get it to make enough room for me to slip through.

"Wake up," I said when I made just enough space between the door jamb and the door that I could wiggle my way in sideways. "Are you alright? Mr. Smith?"

I pulled in my breath and lifted onto my toes, lengthening every fiber of tissue that I could.

"Mr. Smith," I said again, this time louder. When I realized he was lying on the floor sideways, I finally understood he couldn't have fallen. The angle wasn't right.

He must have fainted or something. I hoped it wasn't a heart attack.

I managed to free myself from the gap in the doorway and fell to my knees at his side. He looked pale and gray. Greying hair with a nice salt and pepper beard were the most color he had from the V-neck of his yellowed, white t-shirt to his hairline.

His arms were flung out sideways. His mouth was slack and open.

"Oh fuck me," I whispered as I leaned over his mouth.

I listened, trying to smother the sound of my own heartbeat in my ears for the telltale sound of his breathing.

Nothing. Not one breath. If he was breathing at all, it was infrequent and shallow.

I suffered a searing moment of panic. Should I breath into his mouth, start CPR, phone 911?

Phone 911. That should come first. God knew how long he'd been lying there already. I laid my palm on his chest as I did a quick visual scan of the hallway. Maybe his phone was handy.

Thankfully, I felt a faint heartbeat.

"Sweet Jesus," I said to his chest. "You are one lucky old man."

I pushed myself to my feet as I scoured the area. Umbrella stand. Box on the floor. Coat tree. Table.

No freaking phone.

Unless it was on the wall. My foster parents had an old-fashioned phone on the wall. I pivoted on my heels, swinging in a circle.

There. Right by the stairs.

"Thank you, God," I said and ran for it. It had a long, winding, twisted cord, one that I could bring right over to him as I spoke to the operator. I laughed out loud at the good fortune.

At least it was push buttons and not a rotary phone. I jabbed at the numbers and in seconds, an operator barked out at me, requesting my emergency.

"I need an ambulance," I said and gave the address and a description of the scene. "Should I do something?"

CPR apparently. I left the phone on the floor next to me so I could talk and hear them at the same time.

I sweated as I pumped at his chest. It was taking forever. The operator said the ambulance was dispatched. Moments if anything. I'd be relieved soon.

"Do you know what happened to him?" she asked. "Is there a bottle of pills nearby? A knife, a gun?"

Laughter burbled up as my anxiety increased.

"No," I said. "Nothing."

I scanned the area as I spoke. The floor was neat and swept. There wasn't a lick of dust on any of the surfaces, a stark contrast to the outside of the building.

"I don't see anything out of the ordinary," I said loud enough for her to hear.

My gaze landed on a box lying on the floor next to the table. It looked like a boutique box of some sort tied with string.

String that was lying on the floor too.

"There might be something," I said. "A box of some sort."

"Give it to the paramedics when they come," she said. "Don't stop compressions."

I was getting tired but the box kept nagging at me by virtue of its position. It didn't lie straight up. It had been tipped over, as though it had fallen. I eased up on my haunches, trying to read the label or see inside as I worked at my compressions.

That was when I saw the side of the box had a weird rusty spot on it as though something had dripped and bled down the side. The more I looked, the more I realized I knew exactly what it was.

Blood.

I hesitated on the next compression. My gaze went involuntarily to Mr. Smith's face before I began again. He looked dead. He just did. There was no two ways about it. He'd gone too far with his taunts, and someone had sent him something dangerous inside a beautiful boutique box.

Someone had just tried to kill him.

I believed it right until I noticed the label. It too, looked boutique. Big and square, it had lovely script written out in curly letters as though it was a formal invitation to a highbrow party.

His address was clearly readable.

The trouble was... the name on the label was clearly mine.

CHAPTER NINE

My first thought wasn't one of panic. I was already soaked in adrenaline, and it took a while for the paranoia to creep in past it all. With each compression onto Mr. Smith's chest, I grew more certain someone had sent the man a death package.

But they hadn't meant to. That was the kicker. That package was for me. You can mistake an address, but you can't mistake a name.

Sirens wailed up the street, making the nervous ringing in my ears a bit less obnoxious. I flicked my gaze from my landlord's face to the box again as I considered what to do with it. I was supposed to pass it over to the paramedics in case it had some sort of clue inside.

I knew it was a clue all by it's lonesome. I couldn't give it over to the paramedics. Not until I knew what was in it.

I ran through the possible culprits pretty quickly; Cleo, the new kingpin of Scottie's vast criminal enterprise, the shapeshifting Absalom—who wanted whatever power was tethered to my soul by the Lilith Stone. I even threw in the incubus Errol for good measure. He hated me plenty. With good reason.

But Absalom was the one that won the round of Who's Your Villain and I was already sorry I'd ragged on Maddox for being so careful. Stupid, Isabella. Just plain dumb.

The wail of the alarm grew louder as the flashing lights filled the entrance sidelight. The ambulance had arrived, and I was more sure than anything that I'd have to at least look inside before I even thought of passing it over.

There were three short raps on the door that nearly scared the bejesus out of me but I managed to holler out that the door was unlocked.

The paramedics had the same problem I had getting in. The door butted up against Mr. Smith's shoulder for a moment, but while I'd been just one small woman pushing her way in, there were two paramedics. Big burly gorgeous men who pushed both me and my landlord aside as easily as if we were scraps of cardboard sliding along a waxed floor.

I was never so happy to see an official.

"Move aside," the first one said as he yanked out a mask and strapped it onto Mr. Smith's face. "How long have you been doing the compressions?"

"What is his medical history?" the other fired at me. "Is he diabetic, cancer, heart issues?"

"I don't know," I said. "I just found him like this."

"How long ago?"

I backed away, giving them room as I stammered out that I couldn't be sure. A few moments at least. Maybe ten. I couldn't tear my gaze from the activity. They seemed to have five hands a piece, and each of them roamed over the unmoving body at the same time as they shot questions at me and scanned his face, mouth, and eyes.

"He's in his sixties," I said. That one I knew. "I'll go look in his cabinets for prescriptions."

I clung to the banister railing as I waited to see if that was a good idea. At least, I thought that was what I was doing, waiting. I realized I hadn't budged to go looking for meds, and that I was wringing my hands. I liked the old codger. Despite the idiosyncrasies, he was a good man. Odd, but good.

"Is he going to be OK?" I said.

One of the paramedics shot a look at me over his shoulder. He had kind eyes. Liquid brown with molten bits of gold in them.

"I hope so," he said. "He's still breathing. But knowing his meds would help. Are you his daughter?"

I shook my head and felt the need to swipe at my cheeks. My fingers came away wet.

"I'm his tenant," I said.

"Do you know where he keeps his meds?"

I nodded although I really shouldn't have. I had no idea if he was even on meds or where they'd be. A moment's thought assured me that if the house was like mine, he'd have a second-floor bathroom as well as the company one on the first floor. No doubt his meds would be upstairs. If he needed some.

"I'll go look," I said.

The box caught on my toe as I strode for the stairwell. It scuffed across the floor and butted up against the wall. Right. The box. I'd almost forgotten it.

I stooped to pick it up and held it against my chest. A strange smell wafted up from it. My nose wrinkled involuntarily as the stink perfumed my nostrils, coating them in an oily fragrance not unlike that of fish.

"That's it," said one of the paramedics. They weren't talking about me or the box, but to each other. "Right there."

"Get him on the gurney," said the other. "Call it in."

I swiveled to look at them. They were already hoisting him onto a gurney they had hauled into the hallway when I'd stepped away. They'd found something. I could tell.

"What is it?" I said. "What's wrong?"

They were all business. Strapping him in.

"Get a list of his meds," the first one said to me. "And bring it to St. Anne's. It will be helpful for them to know what he needs if he recovers."

"If," I said. "What do you mean if?"

They were hustling out the door and I had to follow them onto the step.

"The box," I said. "Don't you want the box?"

It was empty. The stain was blood, I could see that now. But it wasn't exactly useful to me. It would be more useful for the doctors. Might help the old guy.

"Did you find anything?" I said.

"Some kind of bite," the first one said, swinging those compassionate eyes onto me again. "Snake maybe."

He jerked his chin toward Mr. Smith's arm where for the first time, I noticed two bloody dots surrounded by a black and blue bullseye rash on his crêpey skin.

"Looks like it might be poison."

Poison. His voice didn't change as he said it, just delivered the news as if it was something he said every day. Maybe he did.

Maybe they were trained to show no emotion or let emotion rule them. It would be useful, wouldn't it, that skill?

Even so, I couldn't shake the dread that made my shoulders pinch together as he and his partner rolled the gurney along the sidewalk toward the back of the ambulance.

I was left alone in the doorway, watching them hoist the gurney into the back of the vehicle. Lights swept across the yard, illuminating the garbage and the rats and diaper mountain near the fence, and then it flared over my face, making me squint.

When I opened my eyes again, the first paramedic had disappeared into the back with the patient. The second slammed the door and rounded the vehicle to the driver's side.

I blinked as the breeze burned my eyes.

I realized I was still holding the box. I felt as empty as the contents as I stepped back inside and closed the door.

I couldn't just go home and pretend none of it had happened. I'd make myself useful like I'd said I would. I'd gather the meds list if there was one. I'd put the box in a bag to keep it untainted and make sure it got to the hospital.

I stooped to pick up the string and laid it inside the box, then ascended the stairs in my shoes, feeling the familiar haunt of the thieving Isabella lurking in my psyche. I told myself this time I was using my skills for good instead of evil, and then I tittered aloud to myself when I realized I'd never truly been evil. Not compared to the things I'd seen since moving here.

The meds in his medicine chest held vitamins and a prescription for Viagra. I tried not to judge what a man his age, with no apparent partners, might be doing with a scrip for 60 of the things dated a month earlier and was half empty.

I tried not to judge as I noticed his bathroom was filled with lotion bottles and lube and one single latex glove.

None of that was any of my business and I decided if he got out of this safely, that I'd hire a high class escort to make up for the lonely taint of need I witnessed in his lavatory, because in the end, I couldn't shake the sense that I was responsible somehow.

If it was a snake, if it was poisonous, it was meant for me. That was the truth of it.

And that was when it struck me. The snake.

It wasn't in the box.

So where the heck was it?

The Viagra bottle fell from my grip to the tiled floor with a smack as I realized it had to be still slithering around the house somewhere.

The back of my neck went cold.

I glanced down at my feet with more than a bit of trepidation. Everything took on a different hue. Every space could be a hiding spot. Could the damn thing have found its way up the stairs? How long had it been anyway? Did one of those things die if they discharged their venom? Were they less or more angry if they had to use up their stores of poison?

I decided to scout the damn house like a cop on a murder scene. If I could find the thing, I'd drop the box over it and answer that question later. Or not. Depending on whether I could put my hands to a hammer or not.

The upstairs was a clean sweep that took me about ten minutes to go through. There was one bedroom, a closet, and the bathroom on that level. I could see the third-floor door was closed so I doubted the snake would have gone that way.

That left downstairs, and I tread down the stairs slowly, panning my gaze left and right, barely blinking. I could see the box on the hallway table and the string draped over its edge. From my vantage, it was obvious there was nothing in the foyer. It was sparsely furnished and perfectly clean except for the mess the paramedics had made.

I edged around the box, staying as close to the open areas as I could. I had to admit, my experience being quiet and careful came in handy. My ears were primed to hear the slightest noise as I shut down the sound of my heart hammering inside my head.

I made for the kitchen first so I could grab a broom. Suitably armed, I backtracked to the living room. It was filled with furniture and bric-a-brac and the drapes were heavy things that made for perfect camouflage.

I swept along the bottom with the handle of the broom, pulling the drapes out horizontally into the open space. I stayed far back, out of reach of what I assumed would be striking range.

"Come out, come out you dirty bastard," I said, singing it to the tune of Hide N Seek.

I had a short moment of panic when I caught sight of a long brown coiled up thing close to my foot, until I realized it was the lamp cord.

"Jesus, Isabella," I said. "Get a grip."

I continued on that way, intermittently scaring myself and chiding myself until I'd gone through every inch I could think of. All that was left was the wall shelf that took up the southern part of the apartment.

I had no idea my landlord had such eclectic tastes. While his sofa, chair, and furniture were a mix of Shaker style and Arts and Crafts, his kitchen furniture was more modern. Mixed steel and grey appliances complimented everything in a way that would beg a decorator to cry out for joy.

He decorated with a good eye, I had to admit. There wasn't a single sock on the floor, either. So. No cat, obviously. But the shelf was another matter. It was a hoard of material, like a cache of mismatched treasure.

The thief in me was drawn to it.

I laid my hand on what looked like a medieval crown, the kind you'd expect to see in movies. Beside that was a velvet-lined display box of ancient coins. My mouth twitched at that. I had no problem stealing from someone I knew, but he'd miss those and he'd certainly know who took them if he had a rational brain at all.

But the insignificant, even dusty looking book lying on its side underneath a heap of other books took my attention. It looked like the grimoire I'd seen in Lucifer's display room, except it was smaller than the arm sized one and held vellum pages written on in red ink, in a language that was all symbols. I doubted Mr. Smith knew what he had or, judging by its placement and the dust on its page edge, that he paid it much mind.

I knew a grimoire had to have an original owner.

Maybe one who was still alive and looking for it.

In one second, I reached for it. I had to push past a few other larger items to get to it. But when I wrapped my fingers around its binding, I knew I'd done the right thing. I had something to offer Maddox. Something to earn a few rubles to keep me floating a bit longer. He could keep me off Cleo's case and I could earn some coin.

I had my fingers on it, my forearm resting against the wood of the shelf as I used the leverage to heft it from its spot. And in that moment between lifting the book and pulling back, a flash of black shot out from the depths of the shelf to strike at me.

I dropped the book onto the floor and yelped in pain. Heat streamed up my arm as though I was running a line of boiled water over my skin.

My one thought as I clamped down on the bite with my free hand was that Cleopatra had been looking for her poison's chest.

And she'd been killed by a snake.

CHAPTER TEN

I flicked my arm sharply to the right out of instinct. The thing that had bit me remained attached.

"Fuck," was the most intelligible thing that came out of my mouth. Not just because of the pain that was already coursing up my arm, but because I knew what dangled from it, refusing to unlatch.

The snake.

I felt dizzy seeing it hanging there. I wasn't sure if it was because of terror or adrenaline or a blast of poison moving through me that was making me feel that way, but I definitely was losing my cool.

My feet spun. I whirled in circles. I shook my arm like I thought I was about to lift off on my own steam.

All I knew was I wanted the thing off me. I didn't even care if it tore a hole in my skin.

It. Had. To. Come. Off.

The snake was stubborn. The more I shrieked and shook, the harder it clamped down. The more the strike site hurt. The dizzier I got.

It was pure terror that sent me back to the bookcase. Books and knickknacks got swept aside in my haste to lay my arm against the shelf. I braced. Inhaled. The snake hung from the edge with its tail curling and uncurling in time with the waves of nausea cramping my belly.

My own breathing was so loud in my ears I knew some part of myself had separated and stood aside my body. That part of me was cool and collected. It measured exactly how bad the situation was, eyed the length of the snake, and then added it all up to pretty freaking bad.

I grabbed the nearest item to me with my free hand. Something solid and heavy. I swung.

It connected to the snake's body with a dull thudding sound that told me it had done nothing to injure the serpent at all.

I struck again.

And again.

Whatever I was holding collided against the edge of the shelf through the snake's body and bounced off.

Bile rose up into my mouth, but I hammered at it once more.

I let go a little sob as I felt it unlatch and dropped clean off my skin. It fell to the carpet near my feet.

I hopscotched out of the way with a yelp, then blustered at it with the object—a See No Evil monkey statue as it turned out—and dropped the weight down onto the serpent's head three more times.

Only when a small smear of black ooze seeped into the carpet did I stop.

I fell onto my ass and stretched my legs out in front of me but kept the snake within view.

Even after all the blows, even after it bled black fluid, it still didn't look dead. Just stunned. The glassy crimson eyes rolled back in a very human way. Long, thin, and shining in a way that made you think of wet tar on the streets in summertime. The head made a popping sound and with a squelching sound reformed as though someone was blowing air into its cheeks.

A shudder wracked my shoulders.

"Fucker," I said, and went at it again.

This time I left the weighted statue on top of its head for good measure and when the popping sound returned, the monkey careened sidewise an inch before it settled, a drunken looking statue slightly off keel.

I needed to put it into something. A box maybe. Or a plastic container with a tight-seal lid.

Smother the mother, I figured.

But I didn't dare leave it. What if the thing got away? It survived the pretty brutal beating I gave it and even now, its tail was curling up and out at the very tip.

I don't know how she did it so quickly, or how she had found me, but I knew the vampire Cleopatra was responsible.

And Maddox was responsible for that.

I rolled onto my palm and pushed myself to my feet. With my eye on the snake, I backed into the kitchen and rummaged through the cupboards until I found a bag. Plastic for some reason, which eluded me. Maybe the man was an old hippie who didn't believe in saving the Earth.

I somehow found the courage to grab the snake by its tail and dropped it into the bag. Then I rolled the bag down over the bulge inside. Only then did I feel as though I could breathe easier. I shook it for good measure.

No responsive movement from within gave me the courage to carry the bag into the foyer and drop it into the box. I plucked the string from the table and tied it up nice and tight.

There was no way I could bring the box to the hospital. Whatever the heck that was, it wasn't normal and I had no doubt it hadn't come from any place that a human would be able to re-search.

And there was no way I was going to try to explain it or be responsible when someone poked around inside and got themselves bit.

There was only one man I could trust to leave it with.

I swaggered on my feet as I looked at it. I felt pretty certain Mr. Smith was not going to be OK.

I twisted my arm and looked at my skin. Two tiny dots sat in the middle of a purple bruise much like two eyes in a blushing face. But there wasn't a bullseye rash like on my landlord's skin. That had to be good, right?

A small red speck adorned one edge of the bruise. It looked like a freckle. A tiny, innocuous, friendly freckle that took the sting out of the fear. Whatever poison the snake had, no doubt it had discharged all of it into my landlord. Surely, it had to be so. Otherwise, I'd be lying on the floor wheezing out my last conscious breath.

I laughed out of relief and nerves. That was close. I was still standing metaphorically speaking. Dizzy maybe, and a little swoony from all the adrenaline. My knees were weak from the exhaustion of the rush of it all.

But I was alive.

I blew out a breath and kicked the box toward the door. I was loathe to touch it, but I needed to bring it to Maddox. To hell with the hospital. They wouldn't find what they needed from it. But Maddox needed to know what his client was capable of.

And she needed to be held responsible. At the very least, she should be made to provide the antidote for Mr. Smith.

I looked at my arm again and decided I might need a swig of one too. For good measure.

I decided to go back into the living room and pluck the grimoire from the shelf too. If the old man lived, he'd owe me at least that much. If he didn't, someone would just come in and clear out all his stuff anyway.

I might as well have the things that could help finance all the damage to my brownstone that he'd let creep in over the weeks.

I pulled my cellphone from my back pocket and swiped the screen to bring up the text app. I didn't have many people on my contacts list. I scrolled past Kassie's entry, one I had continually updated and changed each time I gave her a new burner phone. I stared at it a long time, feeling a longing for the teenager I'd thought was a runaway. I still didn't have the heart to delete her, even knowing she was actually the Morrigan.

I sighed and scrolled past to Maddox's number. The last text he'd sent had been a bad joke about vampires and colds and coughing when you sleep. I'd not responded to that one and he'd called me instead, asking me to meet him at the Rot Gut Tavern. That was just a few hours ago.

I touched the screen over the phone icon. It rang once.

"That was fast," I said.

"You sound tired," he said. "What's wrong?"

I kicked at the box, making certain the snake didn't make noise inside and just hadn't alerted me it had come to. No movement. So far, so good.

"Isabella?"

I realized I'd been glaring at the box and that Maddox was waiting for a response. I shook my head to clear it.

"I've got something," I said.

"I'll be right there."

"You don't even know what it is."

"Unless it's the mumps," he said. "I don't care. Where are you?"

I nudged the box with my toe and hefted the grimoire to my hip. It was getting awful heavy for a little thing.

The sound of his voice rose sharply through the phone speaker.

"Isabella?"

"At my landlords," I said.

"I'll be there in five minutes."

I stared at the phone as though he could see my disbelief and pique.

"Five minutes?" I said. "Are you staking out my apartment?"

Silence on the other end.

I hustled back into the living room to pull the curtain away from the window so I could look outside. I craned to see around the pane toward my brownstone. I couldn't see a thing, but I had the feeling Maddox had already stormed my door and was rampaging through my apartment. I listened hard for the sound of a cat's complaining yowl. There was the sound of a door closing and I knew he was inside my house.

I sank onto the sofa and let the curtain drop as my butt met the cushions.

"You know," I mused aloud as I eyeballed the living room. "I always expected his house to look all messy and dirty, but it's immaculate. His sofa is soft. Really soft."

I ran my palm over the supple leather. Calf or kid. Whatever it was it was as good as velvet.

"Kitten?" Maddox said. "You sound weird."

"Shock," I said, spreading my knees wide and leaning forward so I could lay the cell phone on the floor face up. "I think it's shock."

I hung over my knees as I spoke, telling myself the sudden shadows on the edge of my vision were quite normal for a gal who'd just got a pretty bad scare. That the sound of wind coming through the cell phone speaker was a vortex I was slipping into as I passed out.

"Where are you?" he said and added a shocked, "Ouch!"

The cat no doubt. She'd probably swiped at his ankles from beneath the sofa. I giggled.

"You do remember what I said about pussies," I said.

"Where. The. Fuck. Are you?"

There was absolutely no humor in his tone. In fact, it sounded pretty angry.

I inhaled slowly, fueling my lungs. "I told you."

"I don't know where that is, Kitten."

I could imagine him pinching the bridge of his nose. I glanced toward the hallway and spied the package.

"Well, if you saw the box you'd know," I said in a clipped tone as I thought of the neatly lettered address label, and then rattled off the address, which if I thought about it, was not quite next door but two doors away from my front porch.

It wasn't but three minutes before the door swung open in the hallway and I heard the box slide across the floor. I lifted my head just enough to see Maddox filling the space in the foyer, and the box butted up against the table again.

"Careful," I said. "The box is loaded."

My head felt heavy, and it was all I could do to watch him without succumbing to dropping it back onto my neck or completely over my knees.

He had put a fresh shirt and jacket on, I noticed before I couldn't hold my head up anymore.

Next I knew, he was crouched on one knee in front of me. The smell of woodsmoke whirled around me.

"You look awful," he said.

"You do have a way with..."

"Don't say it, Isabella," he murmured. "This isn't funny. What happened?"

He didn't wait for me to answer, but instead hoisted me more firmly onto the sofa, grabbing a lacey throw pillow as he moved. He tossed it against the back of the sofa to fill in the space at the small of my back as he guided me in place. With a swift movement, he lifted my legs to stretch out along the cushions and sat beneath them. He leaned over my legs and torso toward me. The backs of his fingers fleeted along my throat until he reached my pulse. There, he spread his fingers over my skin and breathed deeply, making my heart tick up.

I imagined my pulse was hammering along quite nicely. My heart was certainly stuttering. He always did that to me and yet...

His fingers moved to poke at my eyelids and while I expected the annoyance to shift the swoony feeling off, it did nothing of the sort, and that pissed me off more than anything.

"Bugger off," I said and tried to swat his hand away.

"Your eyes are different," he said with a narrowed gaze.

I jerked my chin toward the grimoire I'd dropped onto the floor.

"I told you already. Shock," I said. "It's a physiological thing." I wasn't dismissing it, but I wanted him to pay more attention to the book. "I found that on his shelf. What will you give me for it?"

He tilted his head toward the hall, giving the box his renewed attention before he regarded me again with a narrowed gaze. The molten flecks of his eyes sparked like flames dancing within. I felt his weight against my chest.

"What was in the box?" he said

I lifted a finger to correct him. "What *is* in the box, you mean."

His gaze darted again to the foyer as he realized the difference in verb tense.

"Yeah," I said. "About that. It's got a snake in it."

I saw him swallow.

"Nice big black one with bright red eyes," I said nodding at him as his expression went ever so carefully blank. I knew from experience that he didn't want me to guess what he was thinking.

"I wish you wouldn't do that," I said.

His russet eyebrows scuttled down. "Black, you said."

"Yup. Black as Cleo's heart. It bit my landlord. Poisoned him. Paramedics took him to Emerg."

He reached for my eyelid again, and I whacked his arm with the back of my wrist, blocking his touch.

"I came over to complain to my landlord because my door was open and the lock broken. I found him on the floor. I found the box on the table, and I found the snake on the bookshelf."

I tried to hoist myself onto my elbows but a gentle pressure from his palm on my chest held me down.

"Speaking of our Queen of the Nile, I want Cleopatra's head on a platter," I said. "A silver one. And then I want you to buy back the platter so I can melt it down."

"Explain," he said and so I did, filling in the best I could.

"It won't do any good to bring you her head," he said. "Vampires don't die that way. But if she did send the snake, she would have had to do it at least week ago. She hadn't even heard from me then."

My stomach gurgled and I felt the awful wracking's of bowel complaints. I clutched my belly and tried to roll off the sofa. Even though he sat beneath my legs, his weight from the waist up as he leaned over me was too much. I fought off a wave of sweat and held my breath till it went away and I could talk again.

"I don't understand."

He scooped beneath my knees and shoulders and in one movement stood with me in his arms. I felt even dizzier with the movement.

"I know the box style," he said. "It's from a shop in my bazaar. They have a long waiting list."

I sucked the back of my teeth as I tried to look up at him and failed. I ended up letting my head fall backward. It felt much better that way.

"I should have known your dastardly bazaar would be involved," I said as he strode for the door with me hanging like a doll in his arms.

I didn't mind him carrying me home. To be honest, I didn't think I had it in me to walk alone so I wasn't going to protest. But I wasn't so out of it that I would forget the next most important thing.

"Don't forget the book."

"We have more pressing things to worry about than an alleged grimoire," he said with that same clipped tone.

"Like what?" I said, trying and failing to stretch out toward the book in the hopes of snagging it on my way by.

"Like keeping you alive."

CHAPTER ELEVEN

I didn't doubt his worry for me, but really; it was unfounded. I knew the snake had released all of its poison into my landlord. That was why the poor man had been taken out on a stretcher and I was still—sort of—standing.

I wasn't quite as concerned about my imminent death as Maddox seemed to be. There were other things that needed to be addressed. Like Cleopatra getting her just desserts for such a heinous thing as to send a rattlesnake via cake box delivery. But I played along, and enjoyed the feeling of being in his arms as he headed from the living room.

"The book," I insisted. "It's my pay. I'm not letting you take me out of here without it."

He grunted in the back of his throat, but at least he looped the box's string around his index finger, freeing up his other hand to hook the book. He carried both as he strode to the hall, opened the door, and carried me out onto the stoop where a breeze washed over my face and made my eyes water. I was just glad it didn't carry a wave of diaper stink to my nose.

Maddox pulled the door closed behind him with an audible click.

"Don't lock it," I said with a yawn. "I don't know if he has his key with him."

"Don't worry," he said. "I'm not interested in keeping his apartment safe from thieves."

He didn't so much as look at me, but I could make out the movement of a half grin on his mouth. I imagined he thought his little jibe about my vocation would make me laugh. It didn't.

We were standing on the stoop and while I could feel a fresh breeze against my cheek, it wasn't cool like the first one. In fact, everything was starting to feel as though things were brushing against skin that was numb from cold. There was pressure where I rested in his arms but no real sensation.

I must be really exhausted. I all but stretched in his grip like a cat in the sun until he looked down at me and broke the spell.

"You look funny," he said.

"You see in the dark now?" I said.

His jaw clenched for a moment as he shifted me higher against his chest as he went down the stairs to the sidewalk. I thought he would say something sharp and stern because I was changing the subject and he was detail oriented at best. But he didn't.

He gave me a tidbit of information I didn't expect to hear instead.

"I've always been able to see in the dark," he said. "Part of what I am. What I was. The demon fighter in me, I guess."

"I thought all you did was guard that damn stone," I said, sincerely surprised, even as I loathed the thought of the stone that had taken me to Hell.

I didn't want to think about the stone itself or where it was, off in his father's clutches, safe as far as we knew, and protected from evil men like Absalom who would use the power within for God only knew what.

I was just glad it was gone. The tether I had to it, that was created when I traveled to hell and back had nearly made me immortal like Maddox. I'd come within stink's distance of living forever.

Instead, the magic just clung to me like a bad smell.

I looked up at the chin that had set itself into a position that made me think he would have a headache later.

"So," I said, trying to tease out even more of his past because up to that point, the most interesting thing I'd learned about him—and quite by accident—was that he was a virgin. "You were some sort of warrior before you were a cheesy bazaar owner?"

"I wasn't always a guardian," he said tightly. "I did have a life before that, Isabella. Many lives, in fact."

"Sheesh," I said. "Snappy much?"

He obviously wasn't interested in talking about himself. Not that it surprised me, but it did disappoint me. I shifted in his arms, trying to find a way out but he clutched me tighter.

"You can put me down now."

"I told you, you don't look right," he said.

"No doubt it's the narrow escape from a nasty vampire and a poisonous snake," I said. "Fear can do that to a gal."

He made a small grunting sound in the back of his throat that indicated he was not of the same mind as I was.

"I'm feeling better," I said, mentally running down my body parts and testing out how each one felt. I was surprised to feel as though I was telling the truth. My legs were heavy, I was still dizzy, but the spot where the snake had bit me on the arm didn't sting quite so bad anymore. I could even feel an almost pleasant warmth stealing its way from my solar plexus, which had to mean my heart was beating oxygen through my tissues just fine.

"Put me down," I said as he strode down the steps and aimed himself in the direction of my apartment. "I'll just go sleep it off in my bed."

I tried to stifle another yawn but he caught me and snapped at me.

"Don't you dare go to sleep. We have to get you to the bazaar."

"What?" I said, perking up at the mention of his bazaar enough to lift my head off the cushion of his arm. "You didn't say you were taking me there." I struggled in earnest then, but he tightened his grip enough that I protested again.

"I'm not going to the Shadow Bazaar."

He didn't argue but neither did he stop walking with a determined stride that indicated he had already made up his mind.

"It's almost morning," I said, pleading now. "You've got a lovely grimoire to sell thanks to me, I saved my landlord's life, and I, unlike you, am a human in need of rest."

He stepped up his pace and was rounding the short fence where Mr. Smith had added several extra garbage cans to border the property. The stink indicated he'd filled at least one of them with fish.

He was muttering words I couldn't make out, and I got the feeling he was talking more to himself than to me. I needed to remind him he wasn't carrying a sack of flour.

"I want to go to bed."

"Kerri has a shop in the bazaar," Maddox said. "She might have something that can help."

"Kerri?" I said, intrigued, despite myself. I hadn't seen her since we had stolen an ancient coin from the museum that Maddox said belonged to her. That had been months ago. I would be happy to see her. But it wouldn't be in the bazaar. Not if I could help it.

"You're baiting me," I said.

"No, I'm not. She really might be able to help. It's why I need to take you to the bazaar."

He rubbed at his nose with his finger, squeezing me close enough that I could feel his heartbeat against my cheek. The corner of the box knocked into my nose and made my eyes water. I could sense the snake inside recoiling.

I batted it away. At least, I tried to. I ended up swatting at it like a quadriplegic trying to grab a spoon.

"And why is that again?" I said, absently trying to wiggle my fingers and grapple with information at the same time. For some reason, doing both seemed impossible.

"She has a potion shop there."

"And let me guess. I need a potion," I said, wriggling in earnest now that I realized my fingers weren't truly obeying me, and realized that the harder I struggled, the less I seemed to move.

"Oh great," I said. "You're not playing fair."

Whatever he was doing to me, it was making me pretty damn tired. "You and your magic can just leave off. I'm not going through that Blood Gate again. Not ever."

My arms and legs felt logy. They didn't obey me so easily. I slumped in frustration. I couldn't remember being this tired.

"Maddox," I said, giving it another try before giving up. "I'm really tired. Can't you squeeze me through some less evil portal tomorrow?"

I watched the way his throat tensed into bands of muscle.

"Maddox?" I said again.

"You won't have to go through the Blood Gate or the Fire Gate," he said. "Don't worry."

I noted he was heading toward my basement window instead of my stoop and while I thought about questioning him on it, his tone shifted to something akin to apology.

"I made a gate for you so you wouldn't have to travel the worst of them," he said. "Now that you're my employee, the gate will recognize you. Only two beings can go through it. You. And me. At least, theoretically."

He said this last part with a bit of a musing tone and I gathered that while he was feeling a sense of urgency, he wasn't so sure that his magic would work on me.

"Oh fuck me," I said. "You don't even know if I can go through the damn thing."

I gave a good go at struggling but discovered I couldn't move, a fact that he seemed to notice at the same time I did.

"Good Gods, Isabella. You're like dead weight," he complained.

"Then put me down," I said. "No one asked you to manhandle me in the first place."

He grunted as he hitched me up higher. "I'm not sure why I was so worried about you. You certainly haven't been wasting away on that sofa."

"Chips and vanilla ice cream," I said, feeling a bit ashamed as I envisioned myself dipping rippled chip after rippled chip into a big bowl of French vanilla ice cream.

"Feels more like a few dozen plates of Canadian Poutine."

I had no idea what poutine was. I didn't care.

"OK. That's it," I said. "Put me down."

He looked down at me as we neared the basement window. His head canted to the side for a moment and then he released me.

Just like that.

Pulled his arms away and I landed on my butt on the grass before I noticed he'd done it.

I lay there, looking up at him, feeling queerly outside myself. The dew from the grass sopped through my jeans, but I didn't feel cold. The fall should have hurt. I should be angry. Terrified. Something. I should scold him for being so nasty.

"You have a portal in my basement," is what I said.

The box hung from his finger and he dangled it over my face. He tossed the book on my lap.

"How long has it been there?"

He swung the box back and forth. "A while," he said with an exhale.

I did the math on a while. It came out to about the time Absalom had escaped with the threat he'd be back, and when I'd refused to let Maddox move in with me to protect the magic that clung to me.

"So what you're saying is the portal is how you've been watching me. And how you got here so damn fast."

He tapped his temple with his finger and the box swung back and forth in the air. I could hear the snake sliding back and forth and I had the feeling I should wince or something. Instead, I was mesmerized by the motion until he tucked it beneath his arm.

"And what did you call this one?" I asked.

The Blood Gate had required my blood in order to transport me, the Fire Gate had literally been made of flames, that I only managed to pass through because I was tucked in his arms and cloaked by his power.

He grinned as he crouched in front of me. I could just make out the way his eyes flashed in the light from the basement window which I knew, just knew, wasn't really turned on inside my house. I never left lights on without curtains hiding me from outside eyes.

"What do you think?" he asked, and crossed his elbows over his knees.

I had the feeling he'd watched every single bit of junk food I'd crammed into my gob while lying on the sofa in my sweats. The snacks flickered through my mind like a movie.

"Please tell me it's the vanilla ice cream and chips gate," I said.

He chuckled but his expression didn't move into one of humor. He still looked worried and I thought his laughter was for my benefit and not his.

"What else would I call it?" he said. "I had to name it the Pussy Gate."

CHAPTER TWELVE

The Pussy Gate. Since he'd created the portal weeks earlier, I knew the name had nothing to do with the taunting I'd given him through the evening. That could only mean it was an expression of what he thought of me. I was a pussy.

"I'm not scared of the gates," I said, trying and failing to whack him on the arm. "They just fucking hurt."

He caught my arm in the middle of its awkward swing and held it aloft in between us. In one deft movement, he slipped his index finger beneath my elbow and balanced it there like a fulcrum.

"Are you having trouble moving, Isabella?"

He stared at my arm for a long moment and then pulled his finger away. My arm felt like it wasn't attached to me at all. I dropped like a stone.

"I'm tired," I said, waspish. "It's been a hell of a long day."

His face went about the same shade as a piece of old gum as he leaned toward me and into the yellow light that bled out from my basement window. He pursed his lips, but only for a moment, as though he was trying to keep from saying something he'd regret. In the end, he couldn't stop himself.

He scooped me up again by grabbing me by the waist and tossing me over his shoulder.

"You are one stubborn wench," he said.

He adjusted my hips so that the fleshier part rested against his collarbone, more for his comfort than mine, I guessed. I couldn't feel a thing. "And mouthy," he said. "Good Gods, you're mouthy."

I might have kept my mouth shut, out of Scottie-ingrained habit, had I not heard a subtle tinge of admiration in his tone.

"I'm not mouthy," I said. "I have opinions."

He ignored that, choosing instead to sigh deep in his throat in a way that made his breath rattle. He stooped to retrieve the grimoire from my lap.

"And you have literally zero qualms about stealing from someone you know."

"Hey," I said, this time feeling stung.

"Hey nothing."

He was striding toward the basement door much faster, and I was bobbing along behind his back as though I was a doll with too big a head. He hitched me up again when I started to slide.

"It's all true. All that and more of it. I've spent centuries avoiding the wiles of the most demure, most sensual, most manipulative women ever and it's one small, mouthy little human who gets to me."

His hand slid up the back of my thigh as he spoke, but I heard the movement of his dry palms sloughing the surface of my jeans more than I felt the warmth of his touch.

"Well, I tell you," he went on. "I'm not going to let you, let me, let you pretend nothing is wrong because you don't want to see it."

"You're not making any sense," I complained even as I tried to turn my head so that my nose wasn't smashing into his spine every step. He'd said something interesting, hadn't he? Something I'd let slip by? His grumbling was making it impossible to focus on one thing.

I gathered that we had made it to the basement when he kicked at the door with a little more force than I thought was necessary. I smelled the deep musk of non-use and told myself that was a good thing.

"If you die, it's not because I didn't do my damnedest to keep you alive," he said.

"I don't want to die," I told him. "I just want to sleep."

He halted long enough to take a breath that I felt against my ribcage. I had the distinct impression he had patted me on the backside playfully, and I wondered why I didn't care.

"Hold on," he said.

Hold on. I guessed we were about to portal through to the dreaded Shadow Bazaar. I would have gripped him by the waist if I could move my arms. Instead, they just dangled against the backs of his thighs in a most frustrating way.

There was a moment when I thought the gate would engage its magic and I'd either lose my consciousness or feel a scorching prickliness against my skin. The last gates I'd traveled so far hadn't been pleasant, and I didn't expect this one to be either. I held my breath after sucking in a big draft of oxygen.

I waited. Braced myself.

A strong vibration ran through my entire body, and that was how I knew we'd entered the portal. It felt much like the sensation of putting a vibrator to a sensitive spot, except it erupted from my solar plexus and swept over my entire frame, shooting out to my fingertips and toes.

"Oh," I breathed, surprised and delighted at the pleasant sensation. I could feel. Something. I wasn't dead yet by God.

It went on for several seconds, building and letting go, building and letting go. If it kept up, I thought I knew what the result would be. I hoped for it. Cleopatra came to mind—or rather her words about having an orgasm or two a night and I held my breath in anticipation.

But before that climax of sensation could crest, it abruptly cut off. The vibration that had been washing over me from the inside out shot straight back into my solar plexus and went cold.

"What a rip off," I complained. After feeling nothing for the last half hour, that sensation was even more intense. The absence even more acute.

"What?" Maddox said in a distracted voice.

Things swam into focus. I could make out a wooden floor scuffed in places by years, maybe decades or centuries, worth of boots scuffing across the grain. I smelled leather and books and pipe tobacco.

So we had arrived. I recognized the fragrance of his office even if I couldn't see it.

"It sucks," I said, trying to lift my head. "The gate. Ripped me off."

He spun in place and I managed to lift my head enough to see familiar bookshelves and a broad, open-hearth fireplace. It leapt to life even as I caught sight of it. I couldn't be sure he hadn't snapped his fingers to light it. I never knew what sort of magic he owned. It just always came to my aid when I needed it. This time, the warmth of the fire couldn't reach me.

"What did you expect?" he said.

"Like *the Stones* sing about," I said. "Can't get no satisfaction, apparently."

He strode across the floor and the sound of his boots against the wooden boards made me relax as though the sound itself was a lullaby. Man, I was really sleepy now. Maybe the heat was getting to me after all. That or the long-ass night I'd had. Maybe I'd even had that orgasm and didn't realize it.

I heard him drop the box and book onto a table before he spun toward one of the big chairs. Everything was backwards for me but I saw its partner beside the fireplace and assumed as he moved, he was heading toward the other one.

He cupped the back of my head and swept forward, using the momentum to dump me into a wing-backed chair next to the fire.

He knelt in front of me then, adjusting the pillow behind my back and pulling my knees up to my backside. The chair was much bigger than I'd thought. Nice. It was as good as a sofa.

"No satisfaction?" he said as he looked at me. "I don't understand."

One look at his furrowed brow explained that he really didn't. I cleared my throat and looked him directly in the eye, feeling braver than normal.

"Usually when a woman is treated to that sort of vibration she gets to. Well, she gets to. Um..."

I found I couldn't finish the sentence with him looking all naive like that, but I tried.

"Well, it's just that..."

"That what?" he said.

His hands landed on mine and although I couldn't really feel them lying against my skin, I felt the pressure. It was insistent and it was demanding.

"Oh my God," I said. "You have no idea what the gate just did to me."

He canted his head to the side with an innocent, childlike smile that tugged at my heart.

"It purred," he said with pride. "I thought you'd like it."

He was so obviously pleased that I laughed. I laughed and I didn't care if it hurt his feelings.

"Is that what you call it?" I said. "Purring?"

"Why else would I call it The Pussy Gate?"

"Sweet Jesus," I said. "Virgins. Oh my God."

I tried and failed to swing my legs off the chair and onto the floor. He saw me struggling and swept them aside for me, moving to sit beside me on the chair. It seemed to grow to accommodate him, but the fit was snug. I could smell his scent, but that tingle that always ran along my skin when he touched me was gone.

I guess I was spent. Really spent.

"What did you think I named it that way for?" he said.

"I thought it was a commentary on my courage."

He chuckled. "I wouldn't exactly call you a pussy, Kitten. You've faced some pretty nasty business."

"Well, I have issues, OK." I didn't want to say that I always assumed the worst because that was what Scottie trained in me. "Let's just say I believed it right up until the time it treated me to a full body vibration."

"That's what purring is, Kitten," he said. "It's your gate. I thought you'd like it."

"Oh, I liked it."

I tried to wiggle my toes and realized they tingled. Just a little. I caught him watching me and I saw the firelight reveal his slowly dawning understanding. He jerked his chin in the direction of the doorway.

"You mean the gate just... "

I nodded.

He turned around to look at the place we'd just come from although there was nothing there but the wooden slats of his floor and the wall behind us that led to the street.

"You mean it..."

Again, I nodded.

He swallowed and I swore he blushed, but then he straightened his shoulders and heaved himself to his feet. He tugged at the bottom of his leather jacket and went all business.

"Lucky you," he said, very prissily. "Had I known what I was doing, I would have built in an equal experience for me."

"If it's any consolation, it didn't finish the job."

He harrumphed but didn't say anything. Instead, he headed for the bookcase, stopping momentarily to retrieve the grimoire from the table. He slipped it onto a shelf that had nothing on it.

He shifted two steps sideways and pulled out an old-fashioned rolodex from another shelf. I watched him spin it, thumb through, and poke his finger down into it.

"Doesn't the Shadow Bazaar have cell phones?"

He looked up at me.

"Why do I need a cell phone?" he asked. "I'm not calling anyone."

"Then why the rolodex?"

"I need the ley-lines to Kerri's shop."

"The ley-lines?"

He eyed me like a man who wasn't sure he should or could trust the person he was talking to, then he shrugged.

"Her shop isn't exactly one you can find by strolling along the boulevard. This system tracks all the clients who have shops or businesses that can only be reached through certain means."

I groaned. "Don't tell me I have to go through another one of your gates. Or maybe we could go through mine again."

"Yours only goes from your home to my library," he said. "And you won't be going anywhere. She'll come here."

He busied himself rolling through the stack and I couldn't help thinking how thick it was. If these were businesses that weren't accessible strolling through the bazaar, I wondered how big the bazaar was.

"You know you could use a laptop to keep all that stuff. Might be a bit safer."

He flicked his gaze over me. "Safer? Than my own handwriting in a library no one can enter without express permission?" He snorted. "You humans put so much value on technology."

I tried to roll over on the chair to see him better. "Someone could break in," I said. "A thief with no morals."

His eyebrow lifted as he regarded me. His finger was on one rolodex card that started to smoke.

"Are you that kind of thief, Kitten?" he said. "Because I welcome you trying to work out my little system."

I saw the challenge in his eyes. "I might be."

He snorted again as the smoke rose and curled into shapes in the air much like steam. "This is infallible and unbreakable. I'd tell you what the codex is but as you say, I can't be too careful about thieves."

I watched the smoke change color as they transformed into definite shapes. He stood back and panned his gaze from top to bottom, not left to right, and he hummed a little as he tapped his index finger to his lips.

As fascinating as it was, I started to lose interest and laid my head back. I really did feel pretty exhausted. I wondered how many hours it had been since I slept.

"Isabella," he said and I bucked upwards in surprise.

He was standing over me with his arms crossed. The room smelled of a fragrance I couldn't name and didn't recognize. It made me sneeze.

"Did I drift off?" I said with a yawn.

"You tried to," he said and knelt in front of me. I expected when he ran the back of his fingers over my forehead that I'd feel the same tingle of longing I did every time he touched me.

Happily, I felt nothing.

"I can't tell if you have a fever," he said as he leaned closer, enough that I could see a fleck of gold in his eye that seemed to spark with the firelight.

He pulled his hand away and tucked it between himself and the chair cushion. I watched his mouth twitch thoughtfully and before I could assess what he planned to do, he leaned toward me and planted a lingering kiss on my forehead.

I felt the pressure of his skin but not the warmth.

He drew back so sharply I lost focus of him for a full second. He pushed himself to his feet and ran for one of his bookshelves. I watched absently as he ran his finger along a variety of spines.

"Need a recipe?" I said.

"She's not going to get here fast enough," he muttered, though I didn't think he was speaking to me. "I need to find something to buy time."

"Buy me time? What for?"

He spun on his heel with a flat expression that did nothing to quell the panic in his voice.

"For your life, Isabella."

CHAPTER THIRTEEN

K erri came like a thief in the night.

One moment I was watching dispassionately as Maddox pulled book after book from the shelf and tossed it behind him on the floor after no more than a cursory study. The next, I considered it an uneventful and fruitless use of my energy. I didn't even care that something niggled at me, telling me I should have been alarmed at his reaction, but even that seemed to leak from my mind like so much air from a punctured bicycle tire.

So when a flash of crimson slipped through the shadows on the other end of the bookcase, where Maddox was busy spending an inordinate amount of energy, I shifted my attention to watch it.

At first, I thought I was seeing things, and the curiosity seemed to enliven some deadened synapses in my mind. I waited, enjoying almost too much the dichotomy of Maddox on one end flinging books to the floor while on the other side, that flash of crimson started to reveal a long and curvaceous calf, and delicate foot shod in a silver sandal as it too emerged from the shadows.

Kerri. Wearing a Grecian style gown that flowed over her lithe frame as though it was made of living blood. One second it shone in the firelight with a wet sort of glint, the next, crimson satin caught that light and smothered in it, plush folds.

She didn't see me curled up in the armchair by the fire. Instead, as she emerged fully from the shadows, she sought out Maddox, obviously realizing she'd poked that elegant leg into his shop and knowing he'd be nearby. She smiled broadly when she saw him; her full lips enhanced, I thought, by a hint of gloss that might have been saturated with diamond dust.

I should have felt the tight pang of jealousy. Instead I found myself admiring her. She was more beautiful than the last time we'd met. That evening had been the same night I'd decided to steal an artifact from a new museum exhibit and she'd been Maddox's date. Despite her obvious sensuality, and my fledgling crush on a man I'd barely met, I'd liked her right away.

Tonight, her long silver hair was plaited to the side and swept over a shoulder bared by the style of dress she wore. She watched Maddox for a full moment, amused it seemed, by his outright tossing things from his bookshelf. When she decided to call to him by name, it was on the heels of a rather large tome being tossed over his shoulder and landing with a dusty thud onto a pile of discarded books.

It held power, that voice. It was nothing like the very human timbre I'd heard when we'd met at the museum. Tonight, it brought gooseflesh to my skin, and despite the strange sense of disconnectedness I was experiencing, I felt it so acutely I shivered.

Maddox pivoted on his heel at the sound of her voice, with a book still in his hand, spine cupped in his fist.

"Kerridwen," he said.

"You summoned me." She strode toward him with a grace that made me doubt she was even touching the floor. One hand reached out, as she glided across the floor, and ran it along the bookcase as she approached him. Her fingers spider-walked along the edge.

He stood still at her approach like a hare under a hawk's gaze.

"Thank the gods," he said. "I need you," he said.

His voice was calm and measured, a stark contrast to the sound of the weight of the book striking the wooden floor when he dropped it.

Kerri propped a hand on her hip, cocking it with a haughty thrust that indicated she had heard something similar from him before.

"Had I known you wanted me, I'd have worn something more suitable."

I didn't know what could be more suitable for her than the dress that drenched her skin, but I kept my tongue. The dress slid open and closed against her creamy thigh with each movement. I thought of a barber's pole turning endlessly on a rotation meant to tempt customers.

"It's not me," he said, turning toward me. "It's Isabella."

Her gaze landed on me with surprise at first, and then concern. Sometime during the steps it took her to get from the corner to the side of my chair, the dress fell away and was replaced with a simple white collared shirt and black leggings. The scuff of her boot soles sounded too loud as she fell to a squat beside me.

"I'm not averse to women," she murmured playfully. "But I don't take advantage of friends." She inclined her head toward me. "Certainly not ailing ones. Isabella?" she said. "What are you doing here?"

He raked his hand across his buzz cut and then cupped both hands behind his head as he regarded us both.

"She's not well," Maddox said, rather unnecessarily.

"I can see that," she said without taking her eyes from my face. Her eyes glowed like rubies for one moment and then she shook her head.

"You should have called me right away," she said with a sharp tone. "She's losing it."

I heard myself cackle. "Losing it? Lady, if I ever had it, it was on loan."

I decided to try moving in the chair as though I were looking for something beneath the cushions, but I couldn't manage to make my hands or hips work right. I had to settle for grinning at them stupidly.

She and Maddox both pursed their lips at the same moment. It looked rehearsed, the way they both crossed their arms over their chests and scanned me head to heel. While she looked stunning as she did so, Maddox looked like he could use the friction of his lips to light a fire.

"Careful," I said to him. "You might ignite."

Kerri backed up a step and stood next to Maddox. She put a finger to her lips in thought, propping the elbow on her forearm.

"You know what it is," she said.

Maddox looked miserable. He kicked at one of the books on the floor.

"I thought she was just dying at first," he said.

"Just dying?" I barked. "*Just*? What could be worse than that?"

I shifted on the chair, delighted to discover I could move again. I even felt strong enough to sit properly, which I did.

Kerri nodded as she watched me.

"That's not good," she murmured.

"She couldn't move a few moments ago. She was cold and clammy."

Kerri nodded like she understood.

"So will you help?" he said.

She laid a hand on his arm, compassion, I thought, or something else. I thought of the dress she'd worn to come a visiting and realized some part of her loved him. Strangely enough, it didn't bother me. But I liked her enough to alert her to one incredibly useful tidbit that make save her a lot of agony.

"He's a virgin, you know," I said and sat up fully, my back nice and properly straight.

With my feet on the floor, I felt much better. I shook out my shoulders and took in a deep breath all while they watched me as though I was about to collapse.

I eyed Maddox.

"Does she know you're celibate? You shouldn't keep it secret from her, you know. Wouldn't be fair."

He blinked at me but it was Kerri who stepped forward.

"Isabella," she said. "You need to listen to me closely."

I gave her my attention as she pushed next to me on the chair. I was surprised that it seemed to fit us both. I felt her hand rest on mine. It was warm but not moist, firm but not demanding. I lifted my gaze to hers and waited, happy to know that I could feel something.

In seconds that happiness sort of fizzled out, leaving me as full as an alcoholic's last bottle.

She took both of our hands and laid them, my palm first, against my solar plexus. I might have thought it was too intimate a touch, but it didn't feel that way. I felt a subtle jolt of something through her hand to mine, one that spread into my chest. I recognized the feeling of compassion as though it were my own, and it crested over me before settling somewhere at my feet, leaving me feel like a template of sorts. Ready to be used, but useless on its own.

"You are leaking," she said. "It's not critical yet, but there is a definite leak. One you should look into right away."

"Leaking what?" I said, feeling the impulse to check my pants.

She inhaled deeply while Maddox stood in front of us both, his nostrils flaring as she inhaled as though he were scenting me like a dog or a wolf.

I tittered nervously.

Her grip tightened on my hand the way someone might if they thought you were going to bolt.

"Your soul is draining away."

"That's impossible," I said with a snort. Souls were part and parcel of humanity. They didn't just leak out of a body unless...

"Am I dying?"

Maddox jammed his hands in his pockets and spun away from me. Kerri was the one to answer.

"No."

Relief was a short-lived blast of warmth at best. It didn't last.

"I'm just tired," I said. "I haven't slept in god knows how many hours."

She adjusted the open slit of her dress so it covered her knee.

"I understand your Kindred needs to invoke the god you know best," she said. "But I would prefer you not invoke him in my presence."

"Sorry," I said demurely.

"She got attacked," Maddox interjected, and as though he'd conjured it, the box dropped onto the floor in front of us. I suppose while he had been busy avoiding my eye, he'd grabbed the loathsome thing in order to show us. "Take a look," he said. "I bet you'll find it interesting."

Kerri glanced at the box. "A ferryman," she said with a grimace, that indicated she knew what was inside without needing to look, and found it repulsive.

"Pfft," I said thoughtfully. "I didn't even fix a price or see a hooded old man at the rudder." I chuckled softly as I sang the verse in my head.

Kerri frowned at me, her full lips pulling down at the corners but still managing to look entirely sensual.

"It was a snake, Kerri," I said flatly. "Not a hunched up old man."

Kerri sighed and stretched her leg out. Her foot arched, letting the bare toes point delicately toward the box.

"Let me describe to you the thing that attacked you, Isabella," she said and swept her arm in the direction of the box, in case I didn't notice the way she'd pointed at it already.

"A snake denotes a harmless, earth-bound creature. They eat bugs. The occasional rodent. Some of them eat water buffalo in the right parts of your ninth world. Yours was a serpent. Its eyes were like the center of an inferno. Its scales were like living oil, black and glistening and so wet you'd swear you could plunge beneath the depths if it were a river."

She stared at the box as though it was made of clear plastic and she could see through it to the serpent inside.

"Your ninth-world myths call it a psychopomp: an entity meant to guide a soul to its afterlife. You have many other names for them. Angels. Spirits. But they're shape-shifters," she said. "And they are not myth. They are very, very real."

I stole a glance at the box and imagined again the way the thing had leapt at me. I remembered its teeth in my skin. I shook my arm reflexively. I thought I felt the wound tingle.

I hugged my arm to my chest. "But I'm not dead," I said.

Maddox turned away from us to face the litter of books he'd thrown on the floor.

"Maddox?" I pressed, but he refused to turn back around. Instead, he kicked at another book. It sailed toward the shelf and knocked off a rather fragile looking vase.

I felt Kerri's hand on my arm again. Soft. Comforting. As though I was dying. A veil of tears filmed my eyes. It stung. But it also felt like an autonomic function. My chest didn't ache the way it should. I had the horrible sense that she might be right.

"I already told you your soul is leaking," she said. "Someone was out to take it. Someone may actually be getting it."

I started to protest but she held up her hand, anticipating my argument.

"I don't need to open the box to feel its magic. And I don't need to have conjured the spell to scent the magic that remains."

That made Maddox pivot on his heel to regard us both.

"You meant there's a carrier spell?" he said. "Can you trace it? Can you reverse it?"

Kerri ran her palm over my solar plexus in a movement I barely felt but sensed as keenly as the pressure of Maddox's arms when he'd carried me.

"There's more than just carrier magic left over," she said. "There's an attempt to warp the energy, as though the space the soul leaves when it goes needs to become a different shape."

"Fuck," Maddox said and I could swear it sounded like my own voice.

"That can't be good," I said, guessing. "It's why I feel so strange."

Except strange wasn't the right word. It certainly didn't feel like I was dying. In fact, I felt liberated.

"Whoever wanted your soul and used the ferryman for transport, didn't have enough power to actually take it."

"Your landlord," Maddox said.

Kerri glanced up at him, her graceful features confused, and Maddox explained.

"The box was delivered to the wrong address. Her landlord got the brunt of the magic as far as I can guess. He's in a coma in the hospital. Probably got the near full effect of it."

"Lucky for me," I said, and for a second paused as I considered how the words sounded. After a moment, I decided they sounded perfectly fine even though Maddox and Kerri both gave me a queer look.

"No doubt he somehow managed to disengage the ferryman before he totally lost himself to the magic. Isabella probably got the last of it, all that was left. The carrier spell."

He actually looked relieved and hopeful, and this time when he toed the box, whatever was inside rustled around unsettlingly. I made a face at it.

"Whoever visited this shop in my bazaar did not buy the ferryman there," he said. "Of that, I'm certain. They don't deal in that sort of thing. Simple spells are what they do. A few innocuous potions. Mostly for the witches of the ninth world who frequent the shops of the first quarter."

I knew I should have been disquieted by the thought that the part of the Shadow Bazaar I'd been able to see was tamer than most and that there were other quarters if he called it the first one, but I felt nothing but interest.

Kerri nodded her agreement. "No doubt purchased ages ago for some other purpose and used as a convenience and that's all. But you should check to be sure."

I could see death for the unknown buyer written in Maddox's eyes, but his voice was calm when he asked Kerri if she could reverse the spell.

At that, Kerri stood. Her collared shirt rippled and shifted and she wore the blood red velvet again.

"If she dies, perhaps I could be sure she's reborn in a similar human vessel. I can inspire you to find her. I can transform the shape trying to warp her insides into something Isabella shaped, but I cannot restore her soul."

"Fuck," I said, not entirely sure it was an expletive of grief.

"Yes," Kerri said as she looked down at me. "But I didn't say her soul cannot be reclaimed."

"Sweet Jesus," Maddox said. "Not that."

"Not what?" I asked.

"A soul merchant," he said.

CHAPTER FOURTEEN

I listened while Kerri and Maddox discussed whether a soul merchant might be the best option or the worst. They did so without including me in their planning, and to be honest, I didn't care if they silently agreed I didn't need to be included. It was fine by me. I was too tired anyway. I started to drift off as I sat listening to the ebb and flow of their discussion. The flat-out urgency was gone from their tones, but had been replaced by something edgier; dread, I thought. As though what I had was a sickness worse than death.

It didn't feel that way to me. I felt mentally lighter than I had in weeks. The dread and guilt and nagging sense of self-loathing that Maddox had tried to lift by giving me Scourge's gift at Christmas was gone.

As my eyelids started to close, I could sense something sniffing at the back of my head. Mildly interested, I twisted around to see the tiny kitten Maddox had saved from Fayed's back alley. It sat on the backrest of the chair, with one tiny paw lifted as it craned forward to smell me.

It had been cleaned up and fed. I expected a bloated worm-belly, but it was chubby in a healthy way. Its whiskers had beads of milk clinging to the tips. I glanced at Maddox, wondering if he had used his magics on the little thing to take away her pain. I didn't see any evidence in his skin or pallor, and I imagined that small amount of pain on a kitten wouldn't be so much for a grown man to bear. I decided I would believe he'd done that for her.

I reached out to touch the silky looking fur and drew back my hand with a sharp hiss when it scratched me. Her back arched upward for a moment as she decided whether she should bolt or stand her ground.

I made the decision for her with a shove. She fell to the floor with a solid thud and scuttled off into the shadows.

"Isabella?" Maddox said, turning his eye to me.

"The bitch scratched me," I said, clutching my hand.

He cocked his head at me then at Kerri.

"Are you sure you can't do something?" he said to her.

She gave me a pitying look before turning back to him but I could make out the same pity in her tone as was in her expression when she spoke to him.

"Your best bet is the Soul Merchant."

"Blast it," he said.

I gave Kerri the finger even if she couldn't see it because I didn't enjoy being the object of anyone's pity. I didn't need it. I felt better than I had in weeks.

Beyond her, on Maddox's desk, I caught sight of the grimoire we'd brought with us. I ran my gaze over its spine. The writing was in a language I didn't understand, and it had a metallic glint to it even though the color was a deep enough crimson that it looked black. I'd certainly thought it was black leather when I'd first spied it.

But I'd not had a truly good look at it back at Mr. Smith's apartment. Now that I had time, I could see it was smaller than I remembered. It even had a scent that I caught all these feet away from it. Like leather and cotton candy all at once. It might as well have been calling out to me.

I chewed the inside of my cheek as I considered doing what I really shouldn't with the two of them working so diligently to save me from a soulless life. I mean, it would be pretty shitty, wouldn't it?

And yet. Here I was in the Shadow Bazaar. A place where, as I knew from a previous visit, Kindred of all sorts bartered and sold all types of things. What would a grimoire be worth here, I wondered? Would it even have value or could I barter it for something more useful if I found the right client?

And why should I let Maddox have it and reap the benefits, anyway? I was the one who had suffered the bite. I was the one whose soul was leaking.

I swiveled my gaze to the two non-humans arguing now over whether or not it was more dangerous to visit the soul merchant.

"You guys mind going into another room to discuss my misfortune," I said to him and Kerri as their voices rose over some detail or other. "I'm tired and you're keeping me up."

Maddox shot me a look that said he'd already told me not to fall asleep, but Kerri put her hand down on his arm. "It won't matter one way or the other," she said. "Let the poor girl rest."

He sighed and nodded and the two of them shuffled off somewhere I couldn't see them. I listened hard, straining my ears to assess how far away they were. When I was satisfied I was alone, I eased up off the chair and trod toward the desk as quietly as I could. The kitten jumped up on the desktop and spit at me.

I tried to distract it with a piece of string from the ferryman's box, but it wanted nothing to do with it. Instead, it leapt from the desk and bolted out of sight.

I hefted the book in one hand. It felt comfortable in my grip. The leather was soft and pliable. It bent sideways with the ease of a manuscript that had been opened many times over the centuries.

I didn't have a pocket big enough to fit it in, but I hitched it beneath my armpit and tested its weight. I swung back and forth as I held it there, and decided it was easy to carry. Not so big as to be cumbersome, and not so small it would fall out if I moved too fast.

"Perfect," I said, then squared my shoulders as I panned the room. It had been late night or early morning when all this had gone down. I wasn't sure what time it was now.

I tried to fathom how much time had passed and figured that it would be just as easy to find out by opening the door and seeing for myself.

And that was how I came to be standing in the alleyway of Maddox's first quarter of the Shadow Bazaar. And that was how I discovered that here in the bazaar, it was still nighttime.

I'd not visited the bazaar at night before. The old Isabella would have been frightened. But this Isabella had killed her abusive lover. This Isabella had survived a ferryman's bite.

This Isabella knew she could score in this place with this relic better than any other target.

So I headed to the mouth of the alley, each step lit by an eerie purple light from streetlamps that didn't look like they housed regular incandescent bulbs.

The stalls themselves were closed. At least, I presumed they were. No one stood around barking out deals or offers. Each one seemed shuttered by a blurry petition that might have been a foggy shower door filled with soap scum. I guessed they were barred by magic as well. Not the same kind that lit the streetlights, but magic all the same.

It even seemed to have a smell. I inhaled as I passed through the courtyard, figuring if I could memorize the scent, it would be something to add to my arsenal of skills. Everything could be useful if brought out at the right time. I'd used small details before to my benefit when I stole for Scottie.

Mustard, I thought, as the acrid aroma pierced my senses. I wrinkled my nose. Sour and aged like balsamic vinegar.

I hated balsamic vinegar.

I moved as quickly as I could, sticking to the shadows that didn't cling to the stalls. No use taking the chance that something wicked waited within. There were plenty of places where darkness hunkered. I very nearly hopscotched my way across the courtyard on cobblestones that muffled my steps instead of amplifying them. It took only a few minutes to cross. All I had to do was decide which alley might have the best opportunity.

I was still deciding when I recognized a figure several dozen paces ahead of me, heading into another alley. I knew the tilt of her head and the posture well. She was diminutive, the way I was, but I knew her appearance of frailty was all an illusion.

Kelly, the fae assassin, was nothing anywhere near what anyone would call vulnerable.

But the small figure at her side was most definitely vulnerable, and she was what caught my attention the most. A girl. A human girl. Maybe four or so. She was holding tight to a jacket that was bunched around her shoulders and hung to her knees as she tripped and stumbled along to keep up with the assassin.

The girl didn't cry out or complain. Instead, she was strangely silent as she gripped the assassin's hand, but the bow of her head and the tiny steps indicated she was terrified.

I hated the thought that a small child should be here at all, let alone terrified.

I slipped into the alley and hung by the wall of a building to watch them. I followed them out of curiosity because what was the fae doing with a human child? Kelly was the dark fae's greatest assassin. She had dogged me months earlier and nearly killed me when I'd accidentally stolen a fae relic.

If she was here in the Shadow Bazaar, she had come through the Blood Gate, and I knew from experience that if she had entered through that portal, she'd used the girl's blood to do so.

Maddox had been a fool not to change the locks.

There was nothing else in the alley for them to be following. No doors or windows. Just one long bank of stone and grout and the occasional blackened window. Garbage littered the area around a very human looking garbage can, and the alley smelled of all sorts of things I couldn't identify.

I couldn't help slipping closer to watch as Kelly bit down on her wrist and used it to trace a line across the lintel of a doorway, then stooped to sweep it across the transom.

Streaks of fluorescence blazed into the gloom of the alley even as bits of something that smelled of wet dog flung out in all directions. By some miracle, I was spared the fleshy shrapnel from the door's opening. It stunk of rancid meat and old wool, and I made up my mind in an instant.

The first step I made behind Kelly came just as a light shot up in front of her, bathing her and the child in such white light I knew they wouldn't see me in their peripheral.

I sent a silent word of thanks to who or whatever had thoughtfully provided that blast of light, because it disguised me much better than a shadow could.

At the same time, however, it also washed out Kelly's shape. She and the girl were gone from my sight within seconds.

I spun around in the wash of pulsing red lights inside the building, trying to get my bearings.

I saw a dozen or more women, all of them late teens and early twenties, milling through the space naked save for some streaks of paint covering their skin. They carried trays of drinks and passed them out to patrons who spilled over the floor like an empty bag of beans.

All of the female servers were large-breasted, that I could see, long-legged, and long-haired. The male servers were similar specimens of perfection. Each of them were gorgeous and each came in all colors from mulatto to black and brown and white.

Right about the same time I noted this, I also realized they were human. Many of them caught my eye with a spark of recognition then one of fear and despair and then finally, their faces went blank. Gazes traveled elsewhere.

I hitched up the grimoire to remind myself why I was here. I knew instinctively, that I might be a target, that the patrons were Kindred and not human, and that meant I might be vulnerable. Likely, the grimoire might be the only thing to keep me intriguing instead of tasty looking, so I needed to find a way to use that tout suite.

I caught sight of a black-haired girl wearing what looked like a boxer's fighting pants. Her hands were taped up and she was trailed by a ghostly sort of black panther that seemed to have no solid shape as it moved through other clientele without so much as making them shiver.

"Excuse me," I said, flagging her down with a raised hand.

She caught my eye and cocked her head.

"Human?" she said.

I wasn't sure an admission was the right choice. Instead, I pulled the grimoire from beneath my arm and showed it to her.

"I'm looking for someone," I said. "Someone this might belong to."

I didn't say I wanted to sell it. I didn't want to squeeze out any possibilities before I had a chance to mine them and see what kind of gems lurked in the depths.

She drew back as I brandished the book and the panther slipped next to her legs. Its long tail flicked up and around her chest but she seemed not to feel it. At least, she didn't mention it or indicate it by touch or look.

Someone called out *Witchborn*, and she shot a glance over her shoulder in a harried way.

"You smell strange for a human," she said, turning back to me, her eyes narrowing. "There's a whiff of brimstone on you."

"Witchborn," I said, seizing on the word that seemed to get her attention. I hoped it was as good a segue as I could find. "Is that you? Maybe you're in need of a grimoire or know someone who might have lost theirs..." I let the sentence trail, hoping she'd pick up the thread.

Someone else hollered the word again. This time louder. Another echoed it. The sound of gears engaging cranked along the air, and chains rattled somewhere in the shadows.

"I have to go," she said. "They're calling for me."

"Maybe you can..."

She shook her head. "I have to go. But you want my advice? Get rid of that grimoire. And get the hell out of here."

I watched as she fled from me, pushing through a throng of patrons that had suddenly swept in like a tsunami to fill the space. No one paid me any mind. They were intent on something in the middle of the room that was descending from the ceiling.

It looked like a cage. Lights flashed inside of it, streaking the walls with different colors. The pulse of their movement assaulted my chest the way sound does. The room fractured into different planes as though I stood in the middle of a kaleidoscope.

But one thing was perfectly clear, despite the shifting colors and lights. The cage in the middle had halted a few feet from the floor and the black-haired girl and her panther leapt inside and bounced on her toes the way a boxer does.

"Who is my challenger?" she shouted as she squared her shoulders and spun to face everyone.

She glared out as the light spilled over her. The panther paced inside, a spectral beast that snarled and showed its teeth as it prowled.

"Who is my challenger tonight?" she yelled. "Come to me. Prove your worth and see if you leave alive."

The crowd cheered. What I took to be bursts of magic exploded in the air like fireworks.

It was then that I realized what this was.

"Thunderdome," I said and pulled to mind that 90s movie Scottie was so enamored with that he watched the series a dozen times. It was the perfect description for what I saw happening in the middle of the crowd-filled room. One large cage. One opponent already bouncing around inside, waiting to fight to the death.

"The human," someone yelled.

I watched every server freeze in their tracks at the words. One of them closest to me dropped her tray of drinks. She caught my eye and her face spoke of terror beyond words before settling back into that mindless expression she'd held a moment before as she directed her gaze at me.

The throngs of Kindred clustered into small fists of bodies. All of them too, looked at me.

I took an involuntary step backwards. Something in my instinct told me to turn tail and run. That reflex was one I'd relied on for dozens of years in my service to Scottie. It hadn't quite abandoned me now, but apparently it was slow to rise with my soul leaking out the way it was.

I felt a hand on my elbow, yanking me roughly off balance. My foot rolled and I stumbled into whoever had put their hands on me.

"What the..." I started to complain until I saw who had grabbed me.

"Errol," I said.

I knew the incubus well. We'd dealt in stolen items together now and then before I knew he was an incubus. The familiar revulsion for him curled my lip, and I was glad I wasn't too far drained of my soul to recognize something vile when I saw it.

"Ms. Hush," he said with a smirk curving his full lips. He wasn't the greasy porn-star looking Errol anymore. His skin had a sheen to it that looked more like a glow than oil. "What a pleasure to see you again."

He started pulling me along with him as he headed to the cage. "We had other plans for the Witchborn tonight, but someone in the crowd wanted human flesh."

"Someone," I said, attempting to pull my arm away and failing. I managed to buck backwards for one moment, but he got control of me before I was able to wrest my arm from his grip.

He snickered. "Well, I admit that someone was me. *Is* me."

He paused long enough to sweep his free arm toward the cage where the black-haired girl and panther had begun to pace like they were starving.

"Ms. Hush," he said with a flourish in his voice. "Meet Witch-born. You'll be fighting her tonight in the Kennel. A fight, I might add, that is to the death."

CHAPTER FIFTEEN

To the death. It was a phrase right out of a dystopian movie. I thought of those poor kids in Priam and wished I was trained in archery or cake decorating, anything that could give me a leg up on the girl whose face had turned from beautiful to determined. All I had was my instinct to run and my skill at lifting things from pockets.

"Sweet Jesus," I said and tried, without success, to pull away once again. I wished dearly that I felt some sort of primal terror at the words that could lend me the adrenaline I needed to fight against Errol. All I had was my disgust.

"Jesus has no place here," Errol said and tugged me along. We had to press through a throng of petite winged beings at first, but then the clusters of patrons cleared a path for us when they recognized Errol dragging the lamb to the slaughter.

The crowds whistled and hooted the nearer we got to the Kennel. The panther inside roared as it saw me. I was close enough to the steel bars of the door to see its nostrils flare. The girl, the Witchborn, I realized had pulled a mask of apathy over her face to cover over the one of recognition. I could smell blood on the bars around the cage.

Once glance indicated that the bars inside sported razors and barbs. And that was when, finally, my panic bloomed. My survival instinct kicked in with a ferocity that would put the panther to shame.

I kicked at Errol's shins.

"Let me go," I said. I wrenched my arm this way and that, but each movement only brought more hoots and whistles from the crowd. They enjoyed the struggle. They wanted more.

I wasn't about to disappoint.

I bucked backwards, found an inch of floor to grab with my feet, and bucked again. I was too small to wrestle the man, too weak to fight him, but there was power in my small size. I could twist out of just about anything until solid muscle pinned me.

I used it all. Kicking. Screaming. I spit in his eyes and stomped down on his instep. No matter what I did, I was moved inexorably toward the cage.

It took both of Errol's hands to hold onto me, though. I wasn't going in without a fight. For some reason, he held onto the glamor that made him look like Ron Jeremy even if he was more handsome now. Maybe he enjoyed staying in the guise that had been screwed over so royally all those weeks ago.

He nodded to a man who looked like he was on the verge of transformation. He had the same look about him that Absalom had before he changed into a chupacabra. Not a vampire, I'm sure of that, but his teeth were long. Maybe wolf like. His snout began to elongate as he yanked on the cage door.

I snapped my elbow back, hoping to make contact with some vulnerable area.

Someone caught it before it could strike cheek or nose.

Someone. Not Errol. He had both arms wrapped around me to keep me from escaping.

Next I knew, I was free. One second I was caught in Errol's grip, the next, I was pulled against a different body. A warm, body. One that smelled of woodsmoke and whiskey.

"Maddox," I said, peering up at the very large man, whose arms I was gripping as though my life depended on it. It probably did.

He didn't acknowledge me as he addressed the incubus.

"I don't condone this," he said evenly.

Errol snorted. The crowds hissed. I thought I saw a woman shift into a bird and fly up over the cage.

"Doesn't matter what you *condone*, Maddox. You might own the territory, but we pay you for it. We pay well."

"She is not a slave," he said.

"She's human," Errol said. "Humans are fair play in the bazaar. You know this." He swept his arm toward the dozen servers who I now understood were indentured humans. I was willing to bet there would be no emancipation for any of them. Ever.

"She won't last one minute in there with the Witchborn."

Errol shrugged. "She entered The Kennel. It was a risk she took. No one abducted her. No one tricked her."

"I can revoke The Kennel's license," Maddox said.

"Go ahead and see how many Kindred pull their stakes out of your bazaar." He reached for me again and waggled his fingers. The crowd roared. "We come here because we trust you to leave us to our business."

"Business?" I chirped. "Surely this business isn't legal, even in your own world."

Maddox's lips were pressed tight together, and he looked like he was trying very hard not to say something. It was an expression that made Errol smirk as he stood there.

"Law can't come here," Errol said to me. "His whole bazaar is founded on operating outside the fringe of what's legal or illegal." He laughed. "It's why we pay such good money."

"Someone came in here with a human child," I said to the incubus. "What are you going to do about that?" I looked up at Maddox, but it was Errol who responded.

"Are you saying you want me to put a child in there with the Witchborn?" Errol said, pressing his fingers to his chest.

"No," I said, although some part of me perked up at the thought of escaping. I tamped it down with annoyance. "No, I am saying someone had to have abducted that kid." I stressed the word abducted because that seemed to be a point of contention.

Again, he shrugged. "We abduct all of our humans. You, on the other hand, walked right in. It's an unwritten rule that we get to play with what finds its way into our territory. It's what we pay Maddox for, isn't it Maddox?"

He laughed with delight when Maddox didn't answer. "Now, let's get this moving, shall we?"

He spun on his heel and the glamour disappeared. In its place, was the form of a stunningly beautiful man with lush black hair. Some sort of fragrance wafted off him, much stronger than it had been before. I couldn't place it. I just knew I kept inhaling, working on the smell the way I might a dream that was on the cusp of memory.

Errol made a grand flourish toward the crowds. "What say you, Kennel Kin?"

"Human, human, human," they chanted. The sound of glasses and tankards thundered against the tables.

I looked at the Witchborn. How bad could it be? I thought. She was young-looking. She might have a panther, but that panther wasn't much more than smoke. It wasn't solid. I'd taken aw-ful beatings from Scottie from time to time. I knew how to take a hit. I knew how to avoid one too.

And in the end, I'd killed Scottie. The biggest, meanest man I'd ever known. So, I had it in me. I must have. I knew I could kill. Couldn't I?

The big question was could I keep from getting killed before that.

I inhaled a bracing breath. "OK," I said to no one. "I'm no pussy. I'm not strong, but I am quick. All I have to do is find her weak spot."

I gave her a sidelong look as I said it, not quite believing my-self, but not wanting to look like a coward either. Errol jerked his head toward me as he caught the wolf's—because he was a wolf now—attention. The handler reached for me and I lifted my chin bravely.

Maddox's hand came down on my shoulder as his other held off the wolfman's grip. He shook his head with the most subtle smile, not patronizing, not condescending, just sort of... patient.

"Kitten," he said. "The Witchborn is a hundred years old. She's been indentured since her birth. She has killed every oppo-nent the Kennel has forced her to fight each week for these one hundred years."

I must have quailed at the comment because he quirked his russet eyebrow and spoke softly to me. "The Witchborn is not a violent lover who forced your hand in a moment of panic drenched adrenaline."

I scowled at the description, but I didn't argue, and he con-tinued.

"I applaud your courage, but you won't come out the Kennel alive. And you won't find a weak spot. She has none."

"So what is there for me to do?" I said, exasperated. "I can't exactly run."

I felt his hand on the top of my head. It rested there for a long moment, as though he were drawing power from it. He tugged me out of the way of the wolfman, positioning me to his right, so he could face Errol.

"I have a better option," he said to the incubus. "A battle the likes of which your Kennel has never seen. One sure to earn you top power as your clientele cash in their chips. Between the owner of the bazaar and the Witchborn."

Errol twitched his chin in our direction with a low-slung look that indicated he'd been hoping for something just like this. A victorious grin spread across his features, lighting something in his inky black eyes.

"Oh my God," I said, as I realized what that look was saying and why he was saying it.

I stole a glance at Maddox's face, and saw that he'd set his jaw in that hard line of determination. He'd made up his mind.

"That's what he was banking on all along," I said. "He wanted you to volunteer. Maddox, this is a mistake."

Maddox looked down at me, tilting my chin up with his finger. "Mistake or not, you're here, aren't you? There are unwritten understandings in the bazaar. What would you have me do? Let you die in there?"

At that, he squared his shoulders and inhaled deep enough that I could see how barrel-chested he was beneath that shirt of his.

"I'll take the human's place," he said. "I'll fight The Witchborn."

Although he hadn't shouted, the sound of his voice rose the way thunder rolls. It seemed to fill the back of the room and bounce back at us.

In the end, the cheers from the crowd nearest us were the only thing to drown out the echo of his voice. When it did, he leveled Errol with a glance.

"No matter who wins, Isabella goes free," he said. "To be clear, that's what I'm fighting for."

He said it as though he thought he could lose. He was a warrior. He'd killed demons, hadn't he? Surely, he could face off against a slip of a girl not much taller than I was. If anything, the incubus should be worried about his Witchborn, but he didn't look concerned. In fact, he looked pretty damn gleeful.

I tried to tell myself it was because he couldn't lose. The girl was a slave. If she lost, he'd find another act to fill his cage each week. And regardless, Maddox would no doubt turn a handy bit of coin.

It had to be win-win.

No doubt the battle between a human woman and his witchborn warrior would have proved dull compared to the fight about to happen.

I told myself that all of this was the reason I felt nothing over the event that was about to unfold. I might as well have been watching this all happen from the safety of a movie theater seat.

And yet.

And yet something niggled at me. That girl had swaggered to the cage. She'd paced it like she owned it. She called out for her challenger as though no one would dare oppose her.

"Break a leg," I said to Maddox as he pulled away.

He looked back at me with a mournful look.

"Don't watch, Kitten," he said. "You're free to go. I suggest you do just that."

Errol slipped in front of me, blocking Maddox from my view and I tried to push him aside. He swiveled to look down at me.

"Go, Ms. Hush," he said with a voice that sounded filled with longing and anticipation. "Or I might find a way to get around the deal your patron just made."

He didn't bother to hide his hope that I might resist. He waited for a full moment, eyes on me as I hesitated. I couldn't do anything if I stayed, but I couldn't just leave either.

"Isabella," came Maddox's voice. It was stern and sharp, and I whipped around to see him already climbing into the cage. A man with several boils on his face closed the door behind him. The wolf man was hunched over at the side of the Kennel, panting heavily and looking as though he was eagerly awaiting a meal.

I knew what Maddox's command meant. Get out of here. I pressed my lips together as I stole a look at Errol who had canted his head at me, his obvious hope I'd refuse written across his face.

Lights flashed inside the cage over the heads of the patrons. It began to rise and as it did, I saw that the bottom was see through. Electric-like shocks sizzled over the metal, and the sound of it crackled through the space, forcing silence on those who watched. It was mesmerizing.

Magic of some sort, my mind told me. Magic that sealed the fighters inside.

I heard Errol snap his fingers at someone, and I caught sight of the burly boil-faced man coming my way.

"I'm going," I said. "Fuck off."

I turned away with deliberation. It wasn't too difficult, really. I felt a sort of relief that I was free. I'd escaped something with very little effort on my part. I had the grimoire clutched in a death grip against my hip. At best, I'd been granted a bit of good fortune for once. I should use it. Not let Maddox's sacrifice go to waste.

I pushed through a puddle of vampires who looked at me with hungry looks.

"Bugger off," I said. "I have a pass."

One of them, a lean fellow with a faded green tattoo across his cheek clutched me by both elbows and yanked me off the floor. He pulled me close so suddenly, I didn't have time to fight him off. He shoved my cheek to the side with his jaw, and jammed his nose down against my throat.

Then he dropped me. Just as suddenly.

I fell backward against his companion.

"She's gone off," he said and wrinkled his nose. "Smells like brimstone."

I was still trying to find my footing after he tossed me aside, and into the back of a behemoth of a man with pointed ears, when a crack very much like the sound of a gunshot sang through the air.

The crowd whooped in unison, and I was forgotten in the rush toward the cage.

I spun in place, fighting to keep my footing amid the throng. I was carried along by them, and I bounced up on my toes and all but climbed up the back of a very large woman as I tried to see past the shoulders and heads.

Then I realized I didn't need to. I could stand perfectly still and see it. I just had to look up.

Above me, the cage had reached its zenith.
And the battle had begun.

CHAPTER SIXTEEN

The Witchborn didn't waste one second once the cage door closed. Her first shot burst from her palms in a blazing green light that was so powerful it threw her back as though she'd disengaged a high-powered shotgun. While she staggered backward from the thrust, the magic streaked toward Maddox.

It spun much like a Ninja star, slicing the air as it headed toward its target.

"Fuck," I said out loud without meaning to.

"Fucked is right, small one," said a familiar female voice, who evidently had mistaken what I'd meant. "He's met his match this time."

I was too engrossed in the fight to look at who was speaking to me. I was immobile under my own will to make Maddox storm his opponent, but he did nothing of the sort. He waited as the streak of magic sought him out. It was in the last nanosecond that he leaned, ever so casually to the left.

"He knows how she fights," said the woman at my side. "He'll let her tire herself out if he can."

"He should fuck her over," I said, surprised to hear the brutality of the words exit my mouth, but realizing I meant each one of them.

The blast of magic struck the cage behind Maddox and exploded into a thousand pinpricks of light that, in turn, traveled around the cage until they met each other and exploded again.

Now, Maddox and she were lit by magic. The electricity of the magic made her hair whip around her face and chin, as though a wind took it, his buzz cut remained stiff and in place.

"He doesn't want to hurt her, is his trouble," said my companion, and I knew who it was right in the moment I heard her voice again. I didn't need to turn to look at her. That scraping tone, that raw and unfeeling timber of it told me it was Kelly, the assassin I'd followed in.

"Emotions are a liability," she said. "His compassion will be his undoing."

I was beginning to think so, and yet some part of me wanted to argue the point.

"If he didn't want to hurt her, he shouldn't have agreed to fight her."

There was a short chuckle from beside me as the Witchborn danced backward to recover.

"Maybe he would have made a smarter choice, if his love for a human wasn't quite so strong. I smell it from here. It's a disease, the compassion. Nothing good can come from it. "

She sounded as though she was talking about someone other than Maddox, but the words dragged my gaze back to him and the Witchborn.

I cringed as I watched the panther slide around coyly to Maddox's back. He didn't even notice it.

"Two on one," I said. "How is that fair?"

"Witchborn *is* one," Kelly said, and I turned finally to steal a look at her.

She stood within a foot of me, sans child. She wore the leather jacket the child had been wearing when I'd caught sight of them. Her hair was still cropped short. She was as tall as I was, but I knew her appearance disguised a deadly, doggedly ferocious killer.

She wasn't looking my way at all, but she had to know who I was. If she did recognize me as the human she'd once tried to kill, because I'd stolen a fae rune, she didn't seem to care.

She seemed more intent on the fight. The same as every other creature in the bar. Even the human servers were enthralled. I caught sight of one of the servers with her mouth agape, her tray of drinks hovering forgotten in her fists. Humans. All of them. I remembered the child who had accompanied this assassin earlier.

I scanned the area around her legs, hoping and not hoping to see her.

"You came in here with a child," I said, when my inspection turned up empty.

Her gaze was drawn to mine by something I didn't understand at first, and then I realized the truth of what that look was saying it.

"You sold her," I said with the tiniest wince of disgust. "What's the going price for a four-year-old human in this place."

She stuffed a hand into the jacket pocket and burrowed around inside as though she were searching for something.

"Are you looking to buy an Indentured for yourself?" she said and thrust her chin toward the cage. "Strange choice for a human, but at least they're a cheaper slave than the Witchborn."

Her gaze slid from my head to my heel and back again. She was measuring me, I realized. I wasn't sure at first what it was she was considering as she looked at me, but I knew she had known all along exactly who I was. I imagined she was reliving the time when she'd last been to the bazaar with another child, hoping to flush me out by threatening the life of the young teen runaway who gathered my intel.

I lifted my chin under her gaze. I'd set that whole thing in motion by stealing a magical rune tile, but it was unintentional. That theft had cost me dearly. I considered that debt paid. She could think what she wanted.

A strange light sparked behind her gaze as it ran over me. I thought I could see a kaleidoscope in the depths. It was enough to make me dizzy. I wanted to reach out for something but didn't dare move. When she spoke again, I had the feeling she wasn't just being conversational, even if the tone suggested it.

"It's interesting how the poor Indentured that were once human are bound to this place by magic," she said. "But the kind of magic is even more interesting. The ownership needs to be transferred from Kindred to Kindred. It has a source."

She crossed her arms over her chest and turned back to the fight.

And it was a fascinating spectacle, to be honest. Like a train wreck tossing bloody body parts in all directions kind of fascinating. I could hear the sounds of fighting coming from the cage and I felt each thud and quietly dreadful sound of each bit of contact in the bowels of my stomach.

I kept trying to turn away and kept getting pulled back by my own astonishment.

"The jaguar is her familiar," Kelly said, without taking her eyes from the cage and what was going on inside. "It's part of her even if it's been severed by the magic that enslaves her. You'd be smart to leave human," she said, still staring ahead. "No matter who wins, if you're still here, someone will scoop you up and enslave you by magic, and then you too will be under Errol's thumb."

She sighed theatrically. "And then you'll make your lover's sacrifice a waste."

"He's not my..." I started to say, but I got stuck on the words she'd said.

Sacrifice. She expected Maddox to lose.

The thought dragged my gaze back to the cage. In the few seconds I'd turned away, it was evident that the fighters had both made contact with a blow or two. The Witchborn's hand taping was trailing a few inches from her wrist, and they were both bloody. Each of them had beads of sweat pooling on their foreheads that glistened in the sickening green light of the cage. Blood coated the girl's hair and there was a smear of it on Maddox's cheek. I thought he had a cut over his left eye.

Maddox, huge and towering in the space had little room to maneuver, while the girl and her jaguar paced in plenty of space. I wasn't sure who was at a disadvantage.

Just as I thought perhaps size might be the better weapon, the jaguar, spectral and blurry one moment, and solid and terrifying in the next, leapt for Maddox's back.

In one fluid motion that might have been beautiful if it had been a dance, Maddox spun on one heel. He twisted ever so gracefully to the side, whipping his hands over his shoulder to grapple the jaguar around the throat and body slam it on the glass floor. It was a huge animal, and doing so had to take more muscle than I'd given Maddox credit for.

But the beast he grabbed went to vapor beneath his grip, so that he was clutching at nothing more than air. When Maddox wrenched his whole body into the thrust, the wisp of creature floated free of his hold.

Maddox was left unbalanced, and the Witchborn used that advantage to fire another shot at him.

The blast struck him in the shoulder. He staggered.

The cage pulsed with light just as it hit him, and the crowd roared its pleasure.

I might have yelled in horror.

All I knew, was that he dropped to his knees and the Witchborn threw her hands in front of her with a gusto, that meant she was giving her next blast all of her energy.

"Sweet Jesus, he's going to get killed," I said.

CHAPTER SEVENTEEN

I had thought the leaking of my soul, as Kerri had called it, liberated me from feeling anything uncomfortable, but seeing Maddox on his knees struck terror in my throat. I realized for the first time that even though he was a man accustomed to battle, and used to being seen as invincible, all of that had been centuries ago. He was rusty. He was out of shape. He'd been battling pathetic thieves and robbers and lost his skills.

I yelled something at the cage. I hoped it was encouraging and supportive and not just terrified, but even as I did, I realized I should have kept quiet. I was supposed to be gone. He'd paid for my freedom with his body. I held my breath, waiting, praying to whatever god would listen that he get up.

As though a god was listening, Maddox straightened up slowly. I watched as he lumbered toward the Witchborn and swung awkwardly for her face with a balled fist. She, like the jaguar before her, went to smoke before the strike landed. The jaguar behind her gained corporeality in the same heartbeat.

It leapt again, this time landing on his shoulders. Its head dropped, jaws wide open, and it bit down hard into the meat of his shoulder. Maddox's mouth opened in an involuntary scream but if it sounded, I didn't hear it over the cat calls and wolf whistles around me.

The Witchborn rushed Maddox's other side at the same moment. When he grabbed to yank the cat off, it went to smoke.

The girl, however, solidified and struck him with an upper cut then blasted him again with magic.

The magic took him off his feet this time. He fell backward and landed with his shoulders smashing onto the glass floor. The wound in his shoulder splattered blood onto the floor and smeared over the glass.

The tension in my throat cut off a cry. In fact, I could barely force air down through it and into my lungs. I realized I was trembling. That my hands were balled against my mouth.

"That was a hard one," Kelly said thoughtfully. "Brava, Witchborn."

She said the last without emotion, and I couldn't help turning to watch her. She tipped an imaginary hat toward the Kennel and sent me a low-slung smile.

"You're nearly drained," she said. "But not so far that you can't feel for him. Or her. That might be useful if you wanted to do something to help."

I started to answer but the sound of glass shattering carried over the shouting and made me startle. I wouldn't look at the cage. I wouldn't.

"Goodbye, human," she said rubbing one hand over the other and stroking her thumb in a motion that drew my eye. "Try not to get killed too."

Kelly grinned at me in a way that didn't light her eyes or her expression. It was a cold movement of her mouth, as though she thought it was something she should do rather than because she felt any humor. Then she lifted both hands to her chest, running a finger over her thumb again, canting her head meaningfully to the side and holding my eye before finally turning to push her way into the crowds that surrounded us.

She didn't have to shoulder her way through any clusters, however. The groupings of Kindred parted as soon as she moved anyway near them. Every creature seemed intent on giving her the widest berth possible.

They closed back in again when she passed, pressing in on me, pushing me farther along toward the Kennel in their excitement.

When a collective groan went up, I looked again at the cage. I didn't want to. I just couldn't help it.

The glass bottom had cracked. Jagged lines crackled the surface of it in a web of silver. Maddox lay on it face down. His face looked beaten and swollen. I caught sight of Errol on the other side of the room as he raised his fist in the air. Fist pumping. Victorious. Revolting.

He eddied through the crowds toward the Kennel, shoving patrons out of the way as he went and waved his hand at the floor above him. The surface melded back together as though he'd run liquid glass into the cracks. It was as pristine as it had been when it first descended.

A pool of patrons nearby moved to pat him on the back. In response, he ran hand over his bejeweled hand proudly, as though his skin prickled and he needed to smooth it out. It was the movement of an evil villain in a Bond movie, and I imagined the magic he'd used had tingled painfully over the surface of his skin. I hoped it sucked some of his power out too.

I could see it shutting down into his skin with each pass of his hands. One particularly large stone glinted in the light and refracted toward the cage.

It sent thin rays of light toward the opponents within, and I could see clearly that Maddox still lay on his stomach. I pushed forward, so I was looking straight up at the floor of the cage. I felt suffocated by the Kindred around me, pressing against me to get the best view. Had the cage been on the floor, I'd never have been able to catch his eye, but because it was hanging from the ceiling, I had perfect view.

I caught his eye. I wanted him to see me, at least. I knew he'd expected me to run but I hadn't, and he should know that I hadn't lost all my soul. Like Kelly said, I could still show him I cared.

If I could do anything, I could root for him. He should know someone believed in him. My neck hurt for straining upward. I tried to mouth encouragement at him. Get up. Keep fighting. You've got this.

I don't know what my face must have looked like, but when he caught my eye, he winked and smiled. Though his brow was swollen and bleeding, and his mouth was leaking drool and blood onto the glass, although it must have hurt like hell, he smiled.

He was enjoying it, the bastard.

The jaguar jumped onto his back, and in a heartbeat, Maddox flipped over so quickly the cat was thrown to the side. It made the cage shudder as it struck the bars and a blast of purple shot out as the cat touched the metal. I smelled burnt hair and something else. Something like rotting flesh and swampy intestines.

I had to close my eyes to get rid of the sight of the big cat twisting and writhing against the cage as it tried to dislodge itself from the bars. Something besides magic held it there, and whatever it was, it was painful. I felt like I would vomit. I reached out for something. Someone pushed me off of them, and I hinged forward to hold onto my stomach. I couldn't throw up here. Not now.

Pink glittered sandals cut into my vision against the blackness of the floor. The delicate instep of a woman's foot swirled in place as though the owner were dancing. Her voice above me, murmured in thought to someone as her shimmer dusted feet moved once, back-stepped, and danced in again.

"He's got this one nailed down," she said in a voice tight with disapproval.

"I don't think so," said someone else, another woman, I guessed, when a pair of purple Mary Janes scuffed up next to the sandals. "My bet's on the Witchborn. She wants her freedom. She won't lose. She can't afford to."

I managed to lift my face to see them both. True fae, I thought, if I understood what the fae folk might look like. Both were incandescent and beautiful. Both had pointed ears and tiny, elegant fangs.

"You've wasted your money if you've bet on the Witchborn this time," said Pink Sandals.

"Maddox is toast." Purple Mary Janes said with finality.

"I wasn't talking about Maddox. I was talking about Errol. This was to be his fighter's last Kennel clash. He knew he had this one last chance to earn back his full power with bets on her. That's why he tricked Maddox. I'm willing to bet he's put up a godly sum of power on The Witchborn's loss."

"He'll let her die, then?" said PMJ to a nod from Pink Sandals.

I looked at the cage again. It was obvious that the bets they were discussing were based in magic and power, and that Errol had been exploiting the fights to win some of his power back.

He'd probably been doing it for years. No doubt as long as the Kennel had been open. A hundred years, did Kelly say?

The Witchborn was dancing away from Maddox, who, for all he looked battered, didn't appear to feel his pain. In fact, he appeared to be making a slow, steady progress toward her.

"Maddox will kill her," said Pink Sandals flatly. "Make no mistake. But she'll fight until she can't."

"Pity about the Witchborn. I'll miss her clashes when she's gone."

My gorge rose with my fury and indignation that one creature could, and would, exploit another. I was no stranger to it. Scottie used me. He'd treated me like a possession just like Errol was treating the Witchborn up there. Except in this case, the poor Kindred was well and truly owned. It wasn't right. I didn't care if my rage was rooted in my own memories of what Scottie had done to me or if it was true pity and empathy for the creature fighting for her life.

It didn't matter. All I knew was I felt that fury so strongly it tightened my throat.

My gaze trailed back to the cage where Maddox had gained another foot of distance. The big cat solidified and leapt at him again, but he didn't stagger backward this time. He pressed on stoically, with the cat tearing into his ribs even as he covered his face with his other arm to protect his eyes and throat.

It had to hurt. It had to be the most terrible pain and take the most dogged determination to overcome it.

I thought of the power Maddox had shown me when Scottie's goon had beaten all but the living crap out of me. He'd held me tenderly when he'd found me. Helped me wash the blood, snot, and tears from my body. And then, just as tenderly, he pulled me close so he could siphon all the pain from my body until I was healed. He bore my agony for as long as it took to track the goon down.

He'd touched the goon too, holding him aloft off his feet as he let all that pain the man had inflicted on me, and every person he'd ever harmed, funnel right back into the place it had come from.

The goon had died in agony. He'd felt everything he'd done to others. His death was a long and awful one, and it hadn't been quick. Just certain.

Maddox had done that. He'd done it to a threat to my safety. Now, faced with a threat to his own, one with a terrible power and a seemingly immortal familiar, I knew he had no choice. It was a battle to the death. It was life or death. He had to win.

In order to win, he was going to have to do that to The Witchborn.

And I knew that I couldn't let that happen.

CHAPTER EIGHTEEN

Kelly had given me the idea, actually. Whether or not it had been intentional, she'd seeded the unconscious thought as she'd stroked her thumb and casually mentioned that the magic binding the Indentured humans to the Kennel was transitory.

And that it had a source.

I knew all about sources. They were tangible. They were things that had physicality. I couldn't do anything about Maddox and the Witchborn fighting to the death. I couldn't prevent the magic that Kindred all over the bar were bidding with from going to Errol. I couldn't do anything about this being the last fight the Witchborn needed to win her freedom.

But I could do one thing.

I could steal the object that housed the magic binding the Indentured to the Kennel.

And I was pretty sure I knew where that artifact was.

Kelly had said if I failed to leave, I might end up under Errol's thumb. I'd seen a ring on his finger. It had flashed with magic. It was as good a shot as any. It was clear the little puzzle pieces she'd been tossing in my direction were to help me create a picture of indenture. And of freedom. If the slaves were all bound by the magic of that ring, and the source could be transferred, then I was going to become the de facto owner.

I tried not to pay attention to the sounds of battle above me, or the cheers and whoops and shouts of curses at the opponents within the cage. I kept my attention on Errol. Given the chance to pull the cloak of my stock and trade around me, I found it came easily. I slipped into the shadows of the Kindred jostling for better viewing, and I used their exuberance to conceal myself as I worked my way around the room.

Good pickpockets caused distraction, or they used it. There was no better distraction than the one unfolding above our heads. Like most crowds intent on that distraction, they paid no mind to someone jostling for better position. Some let me through; some forced me to weave in another direction.

All of them ignored me. I beat a sure, but slow path toward Errol. The grimoire in my grasp seemed to cling to me as I moved. I barely felt it and at times, I wondered if it found a way to disappear because it seemed weightless at the tightest throngs of contact.

Finally, I was close enough to the incubus that I could sidle up within arms' reach. I'd started out my career as a pickpocket. Picking a pocket isn't a complete cinch, but there are techniques to facilitate better success.

You can funnel the target into an area where they are crushed into others, for example. That makes any assault on them harder to detect, because they are in contact with lots of sensations. Distractions are good too. The more the better.

If this were a human club, I'd attempt to use the target's own sense of compassion to distract him. I'd drop a purse or a phone and hope they'd decide to help.

None of those things ensured a successful lift, but they upped the odds. Picking a pocket or lifting goods from the unsuspecting human is one thing. Pulling a ring off an incubus's finger was going to take some finesse.

I decided the bottleneck would be my best chance. I'd need to crush him into enough sensation that he wouldn't feel me working at the ring. Or I'd need to find a way to get him to take it off.

Or I could do a mixture of both.

I spied a brutish looking vampire nearby buying what looked like a tankard of blood. The human server passing it to him had a docile and sweet expression on her face as she leaned close to him, neck arched invitingly toward his lips.

I swallowed down my revulsion and aimed my feet in her direction. One hook of my foot around her ankle, and she stumbled sideways. The vampire caught her tray of blood drinks and flashed a look at me that spelled his irritation.

"I'm sorry," I said, trying to look like any other human server and plastered a meek look onto my face.

I reached down to help her up, guiding her ever so unhelpfully toward Errol. She gained her feet about three inches from him. Not quite enough, and not on the correct side. I had to fidget sideways, keeping my head down so as to conceal my face and eyes all while I tried to reach for the tray.

To the casual observer, I hoped I looked like I was trying to be helpful but was a terrible waste of skin. I couldn't quite reach the tray. The vampire had to step toward me. I inched backward onto the server's bare heel.

She, of course, hopscotched out of the way instinctively, moving closer to Errol's ring hand. I held out my hands for the tray. The vampire tried and missed passing it to me.

Irritated, but still assuming we'd need those drinks to serve other Kindred like him, he swore and barged forward right at the same time I pushed the female server into Errol. I grabbed the tray of drinks at the same time and 'lost control' of it.

The blood drinks sloshed out as the glasses fell. The server lost her footing and fell against Errol. Blood splattered everywhere.

With his hand drenched in viscous fluid, Errol turned to scold the server.

Of course, I was out of the way by then because I ducked and rolled around the limbs to position myself perfectly on his ring side. I couldn't be sure the vampire would lose his footing. I had no idea how graceful they were or even if they had preternatural ability to land like a cat might.

I just knew I had precious few seconds to use the slipperiness of the blood to slide that ring off Errol's finger. By the time I had hold of it, the vampire hadn't lost his footing; he'd lost his temper. The poor server took a slap to the face and Errol spun to complain about abuse of one of his things.

It took all of three heart-pounding seconds from the time I put my fingers on the ring to the time Errol swung his hand away from me, in effect removing the ring himself without noticing.

The gaudy piece of jewelry slid from his thumb so easily I almost laughed.

I didn't waste time once I knew the ring was in hand. I slipped into the crowd with the practiced ease of a dozen years' worth of spiriting myself into anonymity. The ring, clotted with blood that was cooling, was clenched in my fist and I tried not to think about why it had been warm in the first place. I weaved my way through tight-knit clusters of Kindred watching the match.

One fleeting glance over my shoulder showed Maddox had wrestled the big cat to the floor where it was panting and roaring in frustration. The Witchborn was aiming ever weaker blasts of purple at Maddox. Some of the magic missed but most struck with a force that was enough to turn his skin black where it touched. His hair caught fire when the edge of a blast caught his head and continued on to explode into the bars of the cage.

There was a moment where everything was still. Maddox almost casually patted the eruptions of flame out on his head. The cat twisted beneath his grip as the Witchborn tried her best to solidify and let the cat go spectral.

Then everything changed.

One heartbeat I was pushing my way through the crowds, trying to figure out what I was going to do with the ring now that I had it, and the next a human server standing close to me let out a shriek and then a gasp of surprise.

Then all around her other servers did the same. Then all around them, others did so too. Chaos erupted all around me in small waves that grew to a tsunami of noise. Moments later, as the Kindred watching the fight in the cage realized something was off, those same enslaved humans started to run, and the Kindred shouted in alarm.

The slaves darted in every direction at first, as though they weren't sure where they were going. They reminded me of the time Scottie had decided to purchase a hen house for his back garden. For eggs, he'd said, and then realized the chickens were past their laying prime.

He'd killed them with an axe and a makeshift block. The chickens ran much like the humans did now. They had some leftover muscle memory that told them they shouldn't be where they were, but they had no idea how to escape, or even the understanding to know they were already dead.

Like the headless chickens, they were blind, and going purely on the electrical impulses stored in their tissues.

It was terrifying to see the blind terror in their eyes as they sought to remember what they were. That they were free.

But it was the opponents in the Kennel that I cared about, and I threaded through the terror and confusion to the cage.

I heard Errol call out over the din of screaming and noise of confusion. It was a word of power, I thought, followed by one of rage when the ring in my fist did nothing in response to his words. I caught sight of him as the waves of patrons swelled and retreated and he was shaking the hand with the missing ring as though something had burned him.

I guessed something had. Metaphorically.

"Errol," I hollered, lifting my fist above my head. The ring embedded its stone into my palm.

"Errol, you bastard."

The lights of the Kennel stopped pulsing. Maddox swung his gaze toward me when he heard me call out. I noted with a flick of my gaze that The Witchborn moved to retreat to her corner. Her familiar evaporated, leaving a large pool of inky black shadow on the floor before, that too disappeared.

I expected Errol to have heard me as well, but he seemed oblivious. Maybe it was all the servers who were now caught by various Kindred and were kicking and struggling for freedom.

I pulled my hand back down and wiped the ring on my shirt. Cleared of blood, I could see it pulse with life as though it was a throbbing heart. I cleared away the last of the clots and raised it again over my head.

This time, without encouragement, Errol's head snapped in my direction. But something else happened at the same moment.

All of the servers went limp in their holder's arms.

And Errol saw it too. He looked from one human Indentured to the other and I saw in his face the truth of it.

The ring was mine.

And so too were the Indentured.

CHAPTER NINETEEN

I was a slave owner.

Me. The woman who had bucked against being treated like a possession. I owned dozens of human beings just like me.

Except they weren't like me. Not really. They'd lost some essence of themselves to the power that held them enslaved. That essence must have been in the ring, and its possession gave me power over each of Errol's Indentured.

That's what Kelly was trying to tell me when she said they were under his thumb. The magic that held their bonds was in the ring he wore on his left hand. I could have laughed at the ridiculous pun, and yet I couldn't figure out why she'd given me the information at all.

I expected it was an event that would enrage the incubus and confuse his patrons. As it turned out, I didn't have to go to Errol to demand he let Maddox and the Witchborn free.

He was coming to me.

All activity in the club halted as he strode toward me with a scowl. I caught sight of the two faery women I'd overheard earlier, and they started to eddy toward me, curious I figured, to see what all the hullabaloo was about.

"Ms. Hush," Errol said when he stood in front of me. It was polite, but tightly wound and tension filled. "It seems as though you've stolen a piece of my property."

He held his hand out, palm facing up, waggling his fingers. I had the almost irresistible urge to hand the ring over to him. There was some sort of energy coiling around my throat, making me arch toward him without my wanting to.

"You want to give it back, don't you?" he said. "Thieves are not tolerated here."

I stumbled toward him, my boots scuffing the floor as though I was walking through knee deep water. I came within inches of him when Pink Sandals stepped between us.

"You were able to steal the Solomon's Ring? " she said to me with a curious glance. "Right from the incubus's hand?"

Her face held a look of shock. She duck clapped in my direction and her friend did the same.

I met and held her eye. It seemed to ease Errol's allure and I found I could breathe again. But it wasn't without cost. I saw a flash of what she really was beneath the glamor of shimmer and long, pink hair.

She was still beautiful beneath it, but it was a terrifying beauty. She finally broke eye contact with me as she stopped applauding and turned to Errol.

"That ring gives humans the power over spirits and demons," she said. She pointed at me without looking in my direction. "She is human, is she not?"

He glared at her while I mentally choked on the information she'd just divulged. I could control demons and spirits? Holy sweet shit.

I clenched the ring tight in my fist and pulled it against my chest. It felt warm in my hand, and it grew warmer with every second.

"It's powerful, Ms. Hush," Errol said with a voice as smooth and dark as molasses. "In the right hand, it can indeed do as Elphame here says, but you are not that hand."

"Who says I'm not," I said. I scanned the room to see every human server leaning toward me like flowers in the sun.

I inched backward and bumped into someone who hissed at me from behind.

I held the ring against my chest like a shield. I couldn't even remember why I wanted it in the first place. All I could think now was that I held onto a really, really valuable relic. One that might make me richer beyond imagining.

Or get me killed. Probably killed. I swallowed nervously.

Errol inched forward as I moved back the same amount. I didn't know how many Kindred were behind me. I wasn't sure what they'd do, but if I held something that could control them, I wasn't about to give it up. Not until Maddox and I were safely out of there.

"The hand that could command demons through that ring has been entombed for centuries. Now it is a demon's ring. It has, how shall I say, *evolved* over the centuries to match what we need of it. Now all it does is control human spirits."

He spread his arm out sideways toward a cluster of servers whose faces were docile. They stared at me expectantly.

"You really want to house and feed a hundred humans who have forgotten what they are?" He snorted as though he already knew the answer. He could have been right if I did plan to keep them.

I pinched the hoop part of the ring and held it out as though it was a flashlight. I wasn't sure what I was expecting, but that did nothing.

"I can let them go," I said.

He laughed at that. "You? Your soul is leaking even as we speak. Any Kindred with a nose can smell it. You won't free them. One more day and you'll be no more than a walking zombie without emotion. You'll try to sell them, that's what you'll do. They've been used and assimilated to the special needs of The Kennel, but you might still get a small price from an unsuspecting buyer. Providing you find a buyer, and providing you can find out how to transfer the power."

"It seems I've already figured out how to transfer the power," I said, with a touch of bravado I wasn't feeling.

He reached his hand out again for the ring, ignoring my comment. I looked at it as it sat in my fist.

"I can assure you, they'll end up in my possession again anyway," he said with a note of urgency. I figured out what had him feeling so anxious when someone shouted my name.

It took me a moment to realize I knew the voice. It took me a second longer than that, to remember why I'd wanted the ring in the first place. It was when I looked up and saw Maddox leaning against the bars of the cage that the memory returned. The barbs and razors had sliced into his skin as he tried to gain that much more lift to his voice by pressing as close as he could.

I knew right away what I had to do.

Without realizing it, I'd moved almost directly under the cage, and Maddox and the Witchborn were both watching me, each from different corners in the Kennel. Evidently, it had been Maddox who had called my name. She was crouched in a defensive and terrified posture in the opposite corner. Her big cat was winding around her knees like smoke, and she was badly beaten and bloody. Her cheekbones were swollen.

Maddox looked no better. I thought his nose might be broken.

They must have halted the fight when the chaos began.

"Stop the fight," I said and thrust the hand with the ring upward toward the Kennel floor.

"Let them both live and I won't keep the ring."

He was right. I couldn't do anything about all those Indentured humans but if I could stop the fight, it would be enough. I'd have unwound the knot I'd tied into a string of events I should never have got involved in.

Errol gave me a sly cant of his head.

"All you want is the fight stopped?" he said carefully, so carefully I squinted at him. "And you'll give up the ring?"

"Isabella," Maddox shouted in warning.

I turned to Errol, waving Maddox off. He was just distracting me and I could already feel the truth of Errol's warning. I was growing less inclined to help with each passing second.

"Stop the fight, open the cage, and let Maddox leave with me unaccosted," I said, pulling the ring back against my chest. I was sure everyone saw it, and I didn't fancy leaving it out in the open like that. It was safer against my body. Close.

"Done," said Errol before I could say anymore. With a flick of his wrist, the Kennel door opened.

Maddox and the Witchborn clambered down but neither of them did so easily. I noted that he helped her when she stumbled. She leaned on him heavily at first, sagging on her feet as he held her.

"The ring, Ms. Hush," Errol said, pulling my gaze back to him. He had pressed forward another foot. Soon, he'd be close enough to snatch the ring from me or charm me into giving it over.

I stole a look at Maddox and the Witchborn, willing them to move faster, but they seemed frozen in place beneath the cage. There was no sign of the big cat.

I looked around me. The humans were all facing me. Some of them had even edged closer as though the ring was a homing beacon and they were weary pigeons.

They probably were. I felt a moment of pity for them before that too evaporated. And it was the quiet calm that told me I was losing bit by bit whatever it was that let me feel compassion for someone else.

We had to hurry if I was going to get out of there before I decided to leave them all behind and take the slaves with me.

I silently urged Maddox to step it up, but he didn't catch my gaze long enough to read my message. He was too intent on the Witchborn.

This was my payback?

"Ms. Hush?"

I shoved the ring into my pocket and hitched up the grimoire as I faced Errol.

"I keep my word," I said. "I told you I would not keep the ring and I won't."

Finally, I could feel Maddox's body heat as he drew up next to me. His smell, that of woodsmoke and whiskey curled around me, but it was saturated with something else. Sweat and what I imagined was blood.

I lifted my chin as I met Errol's eye.

"It's done," he said flatly. "The fight is stopped."

"The Witchborn?" I said.

He waved his arm toward where she stood in a pool of light with no other Kindred within a foot of her. There wasn't a single mark on her. The cat was nowhere to be seen.

"She too is out of the cage and unharmed," he said.

"Isabella," Maddox said as he tugged on my elbow. "You need to know..."

"I'm fine," I said, without turning around. "I made a bargain with the incubus. Didn't I, Errol?"

"Indeed." He smiled. "And I kept my word. Now you must keep yours."

I took a step toward what I thought was the door and Errol matched my steps like a dancing partner. His eyes remained glued to mine.

The humans came too. Proof that the ring held their spirits and freedom bound within it.

"Come on, Maddox," I said. "We're free to go."

I felt victorious. I'd won. I'd pitted myself against a Kindred and come out ahead. And I still had the ring and the grimoire. Pretty damn good for an out of practice thief.

I twisted to look at Maddox just for a second and almost didn't recognize him. If not for the russet hair and height, I wouldn't have been sure it was him. He looked way worse up close than he had in the cage from a distance.

"Sweet baby Jesus," I said. "She really put a licking to you."

Errol stepped in front of me. I wasn't sure how he'd managed to get from one place to the next without me seeing him move, but there he was. Hand extended.

"The ring, Ms. Hush."

We were close enough to the door that I knew we were good. Nothing was going to get Maddox back into the cage. Every Kindred here had seen the bargain and would accept it. They'd have to. Maddox had done his part. Now I had to do mine.

I reached into my pocket and extracted the ring. Errol's eyes fell on it greedily. He reached out for it.

"I'm not keeping it," I said and turned to pass it to Maddox, who for a second seemed to have a hard time seeing me do so. I finally stuffed it into his hand and closed his fingers down around it.

He shook his fist, as though to test the weight of the ring, but he frowned as he did so.

"What is this?" Errol said. "This isn't the bargain."

"It is," I said. "I told you I wouldn't keep it. I didn't."

For a moment, Errol looked like he would lose an eye from sheer blood pressure alone, but his face regained its careful mask.

Maddox said nothing, but he outpaced me long enough to push open the Kennel's door. It swung open with a roar that sounded like a hundred wolves about to strike.

"Well played, Ms. Hush," Errol said from behind us. "You are not as insipid a human as I'd thought."

I was about to retort that if he was going to use such big words as insipid, he should know what they meant, but Maddox grabbed my elbow and tugged me with him through the door. The Indentured followed along like puppies. When Maddox looked over his shoulder at them, a small, animal-like growl rumbled through his chest.

He waited until we were through the door into the alley before he spoke, and when he did, it was raspy.

And it wasn't to me.

The sun was coming up over the buildings. In the light of morning, I could see three large men hanging around the door—a different door than I'd followed Kelly through. This one seemed very much like the outside of a human club with velvet ropes and bouncers barring entry.

"You work for Errol?" he said, to the one with what looked like scarification designs on his cheek.

The guy unfolded from his spot holding up the stone wall.

"I work for the Shadow Sidhe," he said.

Maddox nodded as though he should have known the answer. He didn't look happy to hear it, but he didn't look upset either. He just accepted it because whoever it was the man worked for, it wasn't Errol.

He flipped the ring toward the bouncer who snatched it from the air halfway between the two of them.

"Hey," I said in protest.

Maddox turned his gaze to mine. I swallowed down sour fluid when I saw how battered his face was. The wound in his shoulder was a red mess of dried blood and tissue.

"I stole that for a reason," I said, with disappointment when I noted that the Indentured halted at the door behind the bouncer.

"I know," he said. "And I appreciate it."

He headed in the direction of his library, carrying me along with him by force of his movement. I spent each step feeling grumpy about losing the slaves to another Kindred and followed silently out of protest.

The bazaar was coming to life as we headed back to his office. Although I noticed that the life was unlike a human market. Things, what Maddox would no doubt call Kindred, sort of grew up from the cobblestones or the shadows that lay on them. Stalls that I'd not seen in the nighttime shivered into sight as though they'd always been there, patrons already in deep bargaining mode.

I wondered if they'd been there all along and I'd just not been able to see them.

He didn't speak either as we walked, and it was enough to prod me out of my own funk. I wanted the answer to two questions, but the first was the more pressing one.

It was one that had been burning in my mind since I'd seen the humans flood after me and the ring, but didn't seem to affect the Witchborn.

"What will happen to her?" I said, and didn't think I needed to say who I meant.

He looked down at me through swollen eyes and sighed.

"She is not bound to the Kennel by a ring," he said. "Her indenture is much more complicated than that."

"So all I did was stop the fight."

"Not all," he said, bumping playfully into me. "You rescued me."

"But not her."

"No," he said sadly. "Not her."

He looked down at me and wrapped his arm around my shoulder even though he winced when I touched him. He coughed and wiped his sleeve across his mouth. I didn't say anything when it came away bloody.

"You were brave to stay, Kitten," he said with an effort that made the words sound as though he had swallowed gravel. I knew the sound. I'd heard it in the men Scottie throat punched when they argued with him. His voice-box was probably injured.

"Thank you for rescuing me."

"Don't talk," I said. "It'll make things worse."

"Okey dokey," he rasped.

We walked for a few more minutes until I caught sight of the smoke-charred wood siding that meant we'd reached his office and the building it was housed in.

I couldn't help asking one more question. The other one that had been burning through my mind since we'd left the Kennel.

"You took her pain, didn't you?" I said. "Everything you did to her since entering the cage. You took it all back."

Half a smile lifted one corner of his bruised lips, but he kept his promise not to speak.

CHAPTER TWENTY

M addox had taken her pain. He didn't need to say so. A sort of ache started up in my chest as we stood in front of the door to his library slash office. When he put his hand on the iron wrought doorknob that was nailed to the very center of the door, European style, I laid my palm on the back of his wrist.

"Don't," I said, not sure I could meet his eye if he asked me to.

I felt him move, a subtle shifting of one of his feet, a swinging of his shoulders. Even to me, it seemed hesitant and pained.

I had a moment when that ache made my throat tight, and then it eased off almost as soon as I noticed it. The leaking, I supposed, because I knew what that fleeting ache was. It was longing. One so deep, that even the dissipating energy of my soul couldn't mask it. At least, not at first.

I moved into him before I could think better of it. My arms slipped around his waist cautiously, afraid I might hurt something that already ached, a broken rib, a burn from the Witchborn's magic.

When he didn't move away or wince from the gentle contact, I leaned in even closer. The toe of my boots met the spot where his arch would be in his shoes. The warmth of his breath moved over my hair. I could almost touch finger to finger along his back, but I still didn't want to squeeze too hard for fear he'd bruised his kidneys or liver. He smelled of all the atrocities he must have suffered in the cage. The blood had a distinct smell all its own, coppery and faintly of dirt. His sweat was acrid but not pungent.

For a second, I felt the hammering of his heart against my cheek as I laid my face along his chest. It echoed in my eardrums.

"I'm sorry you had to suffer all that pain for me," I said, and at first, I thought he hadn't heard me because he gave no reaction. Then he swept me from my feet, dragging me upward along his body as he hoisted me level with his gaze.

If the contact hurt him, he made no show of it.

With a practiced ease I hadn't expected from him, he cradled the back of my head in his massive hand. Those blunt, strong fingers that had balled into fists not an hour earlier and fought for his life, now splayed out in my hair. He eased me backward, putting a dip in my spine that let me see his face. There was longing in it. I could detect it in the way he set his jaw, as though an ache in his throat made the muscles clench tight.

My arms slinked around his neck of their own accord because I had to do that or fall backward.

His eyes searched mine as I tried not to look at the bruises and blood, and found the only place I could bare to look at without cringing was the blackness of his gaze. There didn't seem to be an inch of skin free of injury.

"Kitten," he said with the same rasp as before, but clogged up with something that might have been an equal amount of longing to mine. "There's no pain as unbearable as the one where I can't have you."

His kiss was soft but not hesitant. It teased a reaction from me, and I tightened my grip without meaning to. He tasted of all those same atrocities as he smelled of, but I didn't care. I wanted more. More of him. More of his taste.

It was over all too soon, but he didn't release me. Instead he held me close. His arms wrapped around me tightly enough that I knew he was clasping his forearms with his hands. His heartbeat raced against my chest and I had to burrow my face in his neck to keep from pressing him for more. He needed comfort, that much was obvious. But there was more too. I felt his desire. It wasn't fair to use this vulnerable time to tempt more from him.

And yet. I struggled not to. If it was the remnants of the after-effects of Errol's allure, or just the leaking of my soul, that made me not care about anything except my own desires, it didn't matter.

I was pulling him to me again when the door we were standing in front of swung open.

Kerri's elegant silver eyebrow lifted.

"Apparently, she's a biter," she said as she took in the battered man standing on the transom.

I scrambled out of Maddox's grip, and for a moment, I didn't think he was going to let me go. He only released me when Kerri ushered us in with an urgent hand.

"I've found something," she said, indicating with a jerk of her chin that the pile of books Maddox had flung to the floor might have yielded something useful.

She spun on her heel to face Maddox. She was barefoot, I noticed, but there was no noise to indicate her sole was even touching the floor. She looked him up and down with a thoughtful gaze.

"I'd say it can wait until we tend to those nasty wounds, but there really isn't any time. It's a good thing you found her when you did."

Maddox shrugged, as though he hadn't for one second considered taking the time to fix up his injuries.

"What did you find?"

"She's definitely being ferried," Kerri said, and she tossed Maddox a white cloth that she must have pulled out from the shadows behind her because I didn't see it until it landed on his shoulder.

"The ferryman is weak." She indicated the limp looking serpent hanging from the upended box. "Which makes me believe the connection is coming to an end."

She looked at me as she said it. "We can't argue about hiring one anymore, Maddox. If you love this mortal, you have to act now. If you don't, she'll have a body but no spirit for however long it takes till the body dies."

He pursed his lips into a white line as he gingerly rubbed at all the blood with the cloth. He pulled off the shirt that was already in tatters and tossed it onto the fire. It smelled of burning plastic.

"What?" I said, averting my eyes from his chest, because I really shouldn't be lusting after a guy who'd just taken and given a beating.

"What's the big deal? If that's the worst of it, it's not all bad." I thought of the gradual lessening of fear and guilt and decided that maybe the freedom from all that might be pretty nice actually.

"That's what you want?" he said, tossing the cloth onto the fire.

His muscles worked beneath badly bruised skin as he dug into a drawer in his bookshelf and pulled out a grey t-shirt. Evidently, he had to change clothes often if he kept shirts in his office.

I closed my eyes so I could think.

"You are the one who was worried about my state of mind," I said. "I feel great now. I'm ready to work. Get me a job. I'll steal the boxers off Satan himself if you pay me enough."

I dared look at him with bravado.

His lips pressed so close together they all but disappeared.

"Isabella," Kerri said, stooping to pick up the box the serpent had been delivered in.

She held it up for me to see.

"I don't think you realize the enormity of this. Kindred have something akin to a soul, but it's not the same thing as you ninth-worlders have. Some of us can travel the nine worlds without worry. The ferryman is one of them. Whoever rode this one rode it from hell. You stink of brimstone. So, you could very well be headed for Lucifer's boxers already when your body dies."

I stared at her. I was young yet. I had ages to go before I had to worry about that. Maybe somewhere along the way I'd find a cure. A loophole.

She shook her head as though she heard my thoughts.

"You are fragile," she said. "Like all mortals are. Except unlike them, you have been introduced to a world of Kindred. Your odds of dying young are much higher now."

I seesawed my glance from one to the other. Maddox's shoulders were tight and Kerri, while relaxed, kept a carefully guarded expression on her face that still couldn't hide the pity.

"So?" I demanded. "We go buy my soul back. What can it cost?" I remember the grimoire, and realized it had somehow managed to transport itself along with me, without me so much as feeling for it or holding onto it. I wondered if it was valuable enough to pay for an entire soul.

Then I realized what I'd just tossed back into the world of Kindred.

"Shit," I said. "Maybe I should have used the ring."

Maddox didn't answer me, and I noticed that Kerri looked away toward the fire.

"Thanks, Kerri," Maddox said to her in a tone that indicated he was good from there on in. He nodded at the woman who smiled thinly in return. "I appreciate everything."

She lifted bare arms above her silver hair and made a flourish above her head. In a heartbeat, the woman had disappeared and, in her place, there was a grey hawk. It flapped its wings and then lifted off into the shadows of the corner.

"Where in the hell is she going?" I said, thinking that I should have felt some sort of discomfort at seeing a woman transform into a bird. "And why didn't you ask her to stay?"

"She's a goddess, Kitten," he said, and the gravel was still in his throat. He cleared it unsuccessfully before finishing. "She has good intentions, but working with a god can be tricky. They are fickle at the best of times."

He strode toward the box and kicked the serpent back inside then stooped to put the cover on.

"We can't afford fickle right now," he said, and I thought his voice had gained a bit of strength. Maybe in the light of the fire he had even managed to heal up a few of those bruises.

"Let's go," he said. "If we have to see a soul merchant, then I have the last of them here in the bazaar."

The bazaar was already crowded as we rounded the street corner from his office. He shouldered a way through for us both and I tried to find some sort of fatigue in his step. I felt as though I was lagging. My feet were heavy. I couldn't imagine how he was staying on his feet after what he'd been through.

"Slow down," I said. "It's not every day a gal gets to see all this."

He looked at me over his shoulder with a scowl.

"That you're enjoying this worries me."

I kicked a pebble toward the water fountain and watched it skip over the cobblestones and land near the base.

"Don't be a killjoy, Maddox. I'm fine. I'm better than fine, even."

It was true. The last vestiges of concern or worry had left as I'd stepped over his threshold. I hadn't felt it leave, but prodding at it now like a toothache, I realized I wasn't worried. I felt truly liberated. In place of all the *humanity* that bogged me down was a wonderment at the things in his bazaar.

"The bazaar looks bigger than last time I was here," I said.

"It's not," Maddox said, absently. "It's the same size pretty much. It's your perception that's different. I can't say that's a good thing."

"How big is it, really?"

He shrugged. "Big enough. It's more like a piazza. It's enclosed by the buildings," he said. "This outer market is the public area where the cheaper stalls are and where Kindred gather. Mind you, those ones who tend to socialize are the ones who tend to come from your ninth world. The vampires who have sentience, the bogeymen, the merpeople, and mothmen. Shifters of all sorts, as you've already seen."

"You're not from my world," I said, testing.

"Some from the other worlds come too, but they don't tend to hang around the external piazza, the market as you call it."

"They're the ones in the buildings." I scanned the facade of the smokey stone that surrounded the area.

He hesitated before answering. "Rent tends to cost more," he said evasively but pointed out nine alley entrances. "As you go deeper into the streets the more the rent costs."

I was willing to bet I knew why. It didn't take a science degree to figure out that the deeper in, the older the building, the darker the magic, and the worse the trade, the more the price.

And the scarier the Kindred.

We had crossed the piazza and were aiming for a street entrance that seemed to be sparser populated than the others. The stalls were cloistered in shadow and seemed to absorb the morning sun. I hesitated to call the light sunlight. It didn't seem right, especially since I couldn't catch sight of the star at all.

"What's after the buildings?" I wondered aloud.

He hitched one shoulder up as though he needed to adjust it in the socket.

"Shadows," he said. "Shadows and nothingness. But you'll never make it that far, so don't worry."

I recognized a stall from my last visit and meandered toward it. Like a human market, the stall had open wares. Bowls of eyeballs and cauldrons of congealed viscera. It had made me nauseous last time. This time, it was mildly interesting.

Maddox hooked my elbow and tugged me away.

"Try to fight it, Isabella, won't you?"

"Fight what? Oh, the 'leaking,'" I said and put air quotes around the word. "You're putting too much energy into my soul or lack thereof. I think this is way better."

Way better. Indeed. He was looking much better too. The T-shirt did nothing to camouflage the frame I knew was beneath the fabric. He wasn't limping anymore. With each step, he seemed to move a little more freely. The great gouge that I knew was in his shoulder made just a small dimple in the grey fabric.

"I think we should go back to your office," I said. "You look...tired."

He peered down at me and I waggled my eyebrows suggestively.

"No need," he said, completely ignoring the overt flirtation. "We're already here."

Here, turned out to be a tall tower with a nondescript door, made out of a wood with a strange looking grain. It had a knocker in the middle and a long iron bar with a prying iron to bolster it shut. I'd been to Rome with Scottie once and it reminded me of the ancient locking methods those most ancient doors were equipped with. I wondered how old this door was, and exactly why the lock would be on the outside.

"Shouldn't that be on the inside?" I said.

"It might be if he was afraid of people breaking in. It's rather the other way around, I'm afraid."

He rapped twice on the door as I tried to work out what that meant.

"It's locked," came a throaty voice from the other side.

Maddox hummed to himself as he touched various spots on the iron bar. A sound like a locomotive barreling down its tracks rushed over us along with a sudden wind that took my breath.

"Hold on," Maddox said and I did exactly what he asked, clasping him instinctively by the arm as we were whipped into what felt like a twister.

"And try not to stare," were the last words I registered before my entire body felt vacuumed from the inside out.

CHAPTER TWENTY-ONE

My skin contracted painfully. Maddox's arm around me was the only thing that kept me from screaming. The liberation I'd felt from emotion, apparently was not devoid of worrying for survival. Now that I stared down the brink of my own death, I felt acutely afraid. Terrified, even.

And then it was over, and we stood on the inside of what looked like an old-fashioned watchmaker's shop had a one-night stand with a blacksmith's forge. It was a tight fit. The entirety of the shop couldn't have been more than twelve-feet sideways and ten-feet deep. Several clocks of all sorts hung on the wall behind a broad, lead glass display case. Cherry wood cuckoo clocks with ornate carvings, companioned smaller round-faced industrial ones.

The stucco walls had yellowed with age. The metronome of ticking was subtle but vibrated in my solar plexus like it was my own heartbeat.

Maddox urged me forward and I realized I'd been inching backward again toward the door. I checked to see how close I was to bolting, and realized the door had disappeared altogether.

"Oh, fuck me," I whispered, and Maddox grabbed my hand, directing me toward the rather musty smelling display case to where a thin man, with a neatly trimmed goatee and a bowler hat, stood patiently awaiting our business.

He might have been handsome but for the port wine birthmark that mottled his skin from the edge of his temple all the way beneath the collar of his shirt. He laid one palm on the case and I could see the birthmark hadn't stopped at his collarbone but stretched all the way to his fingertips. There wasn't a hint of grime in his nails.

The edges of the stain were mottled, as though he'd been dipped in scalding water and the inflammation never receded. I wondered if it went all the way to his toes.

"Is that a birthmark?" I asked, pointing at the crimson coloring that covered his skin on one half. "Or is it a tattoo?"

Maddox groaned deep in his throat, but the man only smiled.

"It's neither, and I earned it," he said. "Very painful too I might add. Sort of like the way Achilles got his invincibility, except I wasn't dipped in the river Styx but in the fires of Hell. I'll tell you about it sometime if you would be so kind as to come again without your lover for a visit. We could have...tea."

The way he said it I got the feeling tea was a euphemism. For what, I couldn't fathom. It certainly wasn't sexual. He had a most earnest look in his eyes that was anything but lecherous.

Maddox shuffled slightly sideways, edging me directly in front of the proprietor.

"He's a harlequin," he said, as if that could explain everything.

A gleam lit the man's eye as he ran his palm over the top of his display case.

"There have been very few in the history of the whole nine worlds," the man said helpfully, eager, it seemed to talk. "Only one per hundred generations. It grants me certain...abilities."

His smile at the end of his admission was enough to make me want to smile too even if I didn't particularly feel like it.

"He can harness a soul," Maddox explained. "I let him set up shop here so he can make a living without running completely amuck and getting himself killed or worse."

I couldn't imagine what this spritely man could do if he ran 'amuck', but I guessed it was bad enough that Maddox felt he needed to lock the man inside his shop. Neither was indicating any more than that, however. It might have been a simple renter and landlord relationship, but Maddox's tone indicated more. And the locks and bars on the outside made it abundantly clear that what appeared to me as a spritely gentleman, might be something completely different.

I read the understatement the way artists read an underpainting. He didn't want the soul merchant wandering around outside his bazaar.

"You're leaking," the man said to me as his rheumy-eyed gaze landed on my face. "And you smell of brimstone."

"I've been hearing that," I said.

He gave me a pensive moment of study, running his index finger along the lead glass of his display case. I thought I saw smoke trail away from his touch, but it was so subtle, I might have been imagining it. The smell of incense wafted out from the corners. It left me with the impression of a ventriloquist throwing his voice except he was doing it with fragrance. I rubbed at my nose as it had started to itch.

"I'm surprised to see you here, Maddox," he said, peering up at the man who towered over him by about a foot and a half. "After all this time. I know you're not the type to purchase soul magic for yourself."

Was that a hint of bitterness in his tone? I was trying to suss it out when he spoke again.

"You refused my services before, Maddox. What could possibly bring you here to me now? What could you possibly want in this generation that you would come to me for the same thing you refused me for an eon ago?" he said. "Is it for your lover here?"

Yup. Most definitely bitterness. These two had history.

But this was the second time I'd been called Maddox's lover, and I was getting tired of enjoying the notoriety without any of the fun.

"He's a virgin," I said, with as much undertone of bitterness as he'd used, except I stuck out my hand in greeting. Might as well get this thing moving along. "Isabella Hush."

The man looked at my outstretched hand for a moment then proffered his closed fist instead.

"I don't shake," he said. "The palms are too sensitive. But I will—what do the humans call it?—Fist bump?" He knocked his knuckles against mine. "I am called Adair in your ninth world vernacular."

He took a moment to scan me, I could swear I saw him lick his lips but it was so quick, and the room almost seemed to fragment and re-glue itself back together, as though a segment of time had been cut out of a video poorly. I had the feeling that someone had moved my hair or adjusted my shirt.

"As I was saying," Maddox said. "We are in need of your services."

Had he said it? I wasn't sure. I watched Adair for signs that he'd missed something too.

"Obviously," he said. "Or you wouldn't be here."

Nope. No indication from those two that time had just farted, but I was sure I'd seen it.

Maddox went tense beside me at the rebuke and I thought I saw him pinch the bridge of his nose. He didn't like Adair, it was obvious, but he was making a great effort to be civil.

"As you can see, Isabella is leaking her soul energy." He swept his hand over the air in front of me. "She isn't usually so..."

"Rude?" Adair finished helpfully.

"Oh she's rude," Maddox said. "But I was going to say she has lost enough of it that she doesn't think she needs it back."

"And you find that troublesome, I'm guessing," he said as he looked at me again, this time thumbing his lips thoughtfully with the hand marked in crimson stain. "Well, as you can see, I have a nice collection of soul stones. Some of them still quite fresh. She might feel a bit of deja-vu now and then for the ones that are very fresh, but nothing quite so bad as to make it insufferable."

"I don't want to buy a soul," Maddox said in a way that made it sound as though whatever the energy was in each of the stones, he believed in his marrow that it was filthy black magic. "I want hers back."

The man laughed. "Then you've come to the wrong place. I don't have it."

Even as he sighed with longing, I noted that the clocks, all pointing to one minute past twelve, transformed into small orbs that looked very much like the ethereal globes of Lucifer's menagerie. I backed up instinctively as they began to glow.

I wanted nothing to do with that sort of magic. Even without my conscience, I didn't relish the idea of housing someone else's energy stored for god only knew how long in some energy ball.

I'd seen what Lucifer did with those orbs and the souls within and even without a soul, my cell memory was so averse to them, my skin flushed with the heat of adrenaline as I fought the urge to bolt.

Maddox's hand snaked out to grab me by the elbow as I retreated toward the place where the door had been. He pulled me beside him and held me there, a comforting arm slung around my shoulder, while at the same time using me as a physical accusation against the man.

"Isabella has been bitten by a ferryman," he said, ignoring my attempts to loosen myself from his grip. "You sell them. You purchase souls. Where else would I go?"

"I barter in soul magic, yes," the man said, grooming his goatee with his fingers. "And I admit to providing a ferryman or two on occasion. I don't do that sort of magic for just anyone. I mostly deal with those ferrymen abandoned here after their task is done. There are very few available unless you know where to look. That's the problem with ferrymen. They can be very costly to acquire."

By costly, I gathered he meant something he thought was more valuable than money.

"I offer simple transference via these amulets," he went on. "Vampires buy them now and then. Mostly, to reclaim their humanity if they've lived so long, they begin to yearn for the sun. They always regret it and return here to barter that energy away again once they've worn it out. It's never worth my time by then, but I can always combine it with another if I need to."

He looked at me with interest. "Human soul magic doesn't last long even when transplanted into a body that was once human. That sort of thing takes much, much more powerful magic. Is that what you are, Isabella? A vampire who has the sun-sickness? You don't smell like a vampire. But the brimstone fragrance that clings to you is fairly overpowering, so I might be wrong."

He dug into his display case as he spoke and pulled out a small tiger eye ring that glowed as though lit from inside. He turned it over in his hand once, then laid it out on the case.

I could swear it was pulsing.

"It will cost you, a fair bit, I'm afraid," he said. "It's been used a few times, but it will let you see three sunrises before it wears out for good."

By wears out, I guessed he meant the soul was extinguished. I shivered for more than the thought of it dying in three days.

"That's not why we're here," Maddox said. "I told you. I want her soul back."

"And I told you I didn't purchase it."

He leaned across the counter and inhaled deeply of the air in my general direction. He spoke through a curled lip as though he was revolted by whatever he scented on me. "She doesn't have my carrier magic."

This time, when the video burped, I caught sight of a scaly curled tail whipping behind him and then it was gone. The residue of whatever soul I had left suffered the urge to cross itself, even though I wasn't Catholic.

Maddox didn't seem fazed.

"The box was from your shop," he said, and I snapped my attention to him. He'd said the box had come from a simple first quarter shop. He'd lied to me. I watched his face as he laid his palms down on the counter and leaned toward Adair.

"It had your handwriting on it."

"Doesn't mean the ferryman was purchased here."

"There is nowhere else to purchase one."

Adair canted his head at Maddox. "Perhaps it wasn't purchased at all."

He indicated me with a pointed finger. "She smells of brimstone more strongly than carrier magic. Perhaps the ferryman came from the other side."

The other side. Brimstone. I was feeling a bit faint at the thought of what it might mean, but Adair didn't stop talking and let me recover. I had to lean on Maddox with each new word.

"What bit her is no ordinary ferryman, of that I can assure you," he said. "It was one that can carve out a place in your soul as it leaks. I smell the void as much as the brimstone. Someone wants to take her place. But that someone was sloppy, as though they were ill-prepared. It was rushed."

"Why would they do that?"

The man shrugged. "Perhaps to make a closer fit for their own soul." He looked at me with a gleam in his eye that told me he found the whole thing fascinating.

"Do you know of anyone in hell who might want to swap places with you?"

I couldn't speak. Not at first. It was Maddox who asked the question I couldn't get out.

"Is that possible?"

"You know it's possible," Adair said and leaned across the counter, a mirror of Maddox's posture.

Maddox shook his head as though he'd been mesmerized by Adair's gaze, and perhaps he had been. I certainly felt time shift again.

He sagged backward and rocked on his heels. "Can you tell if that's what is happening to Isabella?" he said.

Adair crossed his arms as he considered it. "I'll only know if I can study her," he said, and inhaled deeply again. "I can't get anything from here. You need to come out back."

I cringed at the thought of going any deeper into the shop. Not after the glimpse of tail I'd seen. Apparently, Maddox was of the same mind.

"You can diagnose her here."

"That kind of diagnosis doesn't come cheap," he said cannily.

"I have a grimoire," I said and pulled it out from beneath my arm. I laid it on the display case with a sense of victory. I knew it would come in handy. "Can we barter that?"

Adair recoiled from it so fast, he leapt away from his display case and knocked one of the soul stones from the wall. The tiger eye clattered to the floor. It blinked once and then went out like someone had turned off a switch.

"That filthy thing." He crossed his arms over his chest. "I'd suggest you burn it."

"But it's perfectly fine," I said, looking down at the book. "It's valuable, surely."

He curled his lip. "Valuable for whom?" he said. "I know the book. I know the author. Keep it in your possession and see what payment you eventually get."

I plucked the book from the counter, uneasy about the foreboding nature of that warning, but pretty sure he wasn't going to let me just leave it there. Plus, how much worse could all this get?

"If you won't barter the book, then what will your diagnosis cost?" I said.

He thumbed his chin as he studied me. "No need for a diagnosis," he said. "Just a bit of advice."

Maddox made a thoughtful, *I knew it*, type of sound deep in his throat. I ignored it in favor of getting what we needed.

"Advice?" That was hopeful. If I didn't need a diagnosis, it couldn't be all bad. "What is it?"

Adair swept Maddox with a lingering glance.

"The carrier magic has Lucifer's scent. You have no soul. I suggest you try not to die."

CHAPTER TWENTY-TWO

For just one second, time did that fragmenting thing again, and the whole shop transformed into a bleak landscape with a rocky facade and cliffs in the distance. Just beyond him flames rose and fell. The heartbeat rhythm of the clocks became the crackling of a fire.

And I felt like I was falling off the edge of a precipice. When I looked down, my sneakers were right on the edge of a deep drop-off. I grabbed for Maddox to keep from falling and only when his hands steadied me, did I dare look up again.

His face was ashen white beneath the blood stains and bruises.

"Did you see it?" I said. "Did you see the flames?"

He didn't admit it, though I'm sure he experienced the same thing, but with his usual calm, he turned to address Adair.

"Tell us how to fix it," he said.

Adair's eye was fixed on the grimoire. He acted like he thought it would leap up and bite him.

"Find the person who has the ferryman's fare lying in wait for her space." He edged away from the display case, slowly and imperceptibly but most definitely moving away from it.

"And then what?"

Adair dragged his gaze from the grimoire to Maddox's face, avoiding me altogether.

"Then nothing. If the fare is still waiting, your human has a chance. If it isn't..." he lifted a shoulder instead of finishing his thought.

So it seemed I had gone from Isabella to Maddox's human. And why? Because I'd dared put a simple looking grimoire on his display case?

"So you're saying that the man who is in a coma is under the fare's spell, waiting for Isabella?"

Adair swept the top of the case with his elbow, rubbing out some smudge I didn't see.

"I don't know who this comatose man is, but if it's what you say, then yes. But you'd need another ferryman to trap that soul and transfer it where it belongs. But even then, you'd need a sentient ferryman. One who will work with your human and not against its nature. And even then, there's no guarantees."

"What in the hell is a sentient ferryman?" I said, turning to Maddox. This was all getting ridiculous. "Can't we just leave things as they are? I mean, I feel fine."

Adair sent me a withering look. "How you feel is immaterial. In the end, you're doomed. Now get out of my shop and take that vile spell book with you."

He picked up a cane from the corner and shoved at it with the end so that it slid noiselessly toward us.

Maddox plucked the grimoire from the case and passed it to me. I was too stunned by Adair's words to do anything but tuck the book back underneath my arm.

"We have what we need, Isabella," he said. "Let's leave Adair to his shop."

I tagged along behind Maddox as he headed to the door. His hand was on the handle when Adair called after him.

"You owe me, Maddox," he said.

I saw Maddox's jaw clench, but he didn't answer. Instead he pushed open the door and held it for me while I exited. I heard Adair's voice trailing us.

"You know what I want."

Maddox pursed his lips and nodded without turning around.

"You'll get it," he said, loud enough that there was no way Adair hadn't heard, and yet the man called out after us anyway.

"You know what I want."

I wanted to ask him what the Soul Merchant could want but by the time I oriented myself into the street, I realized the breadth of what Adair had said, and it made Maddox's debt immaterial.

"My landlord is in a coma," I said. "Whoever rode the ferryman from hell to get to me is squatting in his body." I shivered as I realized I was going to have to visit the hospital and risk hurting the man even more.

"We need Kerri," Maddox said bustling off before realizing I'd hung behind, trying to process all the information.

He swung on his heel and reached his hand out to me. "Come on, Isabella. We don't have time to waste."

"He said there were no guarantees. He said if it went wrong, I'd end up in hell now, not later." I hugged my elbows. "I can't do that again, Maddox," I said. "I can't go back there."

Lucifer kept what he called ethereal's in orbs trapped in shelves made of flesh and spidery veins of energy. When I'd been sent to Hell because of a fae general and the debt I owed him, I'd barely escaped. I'd seen what Lucifer did with those souls he kept in his menagerie. He wasn't just sadistic. He was ruthless and depraved.

I'd only escaped his torture because the Morrigan saved me. The risk of ending up back there was more than even my newly sociopathic mind could bear.

I must have looked terrified because Maddox's expression softened, and he halted to lean against the stone wall of the tower. He waved his hands at me.

"Come to me," he said, in a voice reminiscent of warmed oil and syrup. "Come here, Isabella."

When I didn't move, he snagged my elbow and tugged me ever so gently. He enveloped me, with my back to him, and his arms around my waist. Although he must have had to stoop a good deal, he rested his chin on my hair.

"I never told you about my trip to hell," he said. "Maybe it's time I did."

He found a stone bench alongside a long stretch of buildings and sat down, pulling me along with him. His arm was still around my shoulders and he rested his chin on my head again, looking up the alleyway.

I was vaguely aware that going to hell had been part of his ordeals to become whatever it was he was. I'd never wanted to press him, but I'd wondered.

I remained silent, afraid he'd change his mind, and was rewarded with a long sigh that moved my hair.

"It wasn't just immortality they offered me," he whispered, and the breeze that came from the shadows all but carried away his voice. I had to lean tighter against him to catch it all. "In my world, in my time, those who fought demons to keep our world safe were granted what we call long life. The more battles we fought, the more time we earned."

"You wanted to live forever," I said.

I felt his chin rustle my hair back and forth. "No," he said. "I didn't want to pay their price for immortality. I refused them."

"Who?"

"The Senate of wisemen who protected the Lilith Stone. The stone had cracked. They needed more warriors to guard it. I..." he halted here as though he was considering how best to put his next words. "I was good at killing."

I thought of the healing he'd done for me and for the Witchborn, and I wanted to protest that he was good at healing too, but he kept on before I could speak.

"The cost was my celibacy. I wasn't ready to be a virgin forever."

I felt his hand leave my waist and rub against his arm, and I knew he was feeling for the brand that scored his flesh.

"Your ninth world athletes understand the phenomenon," he said. "It's a stronger one in my world. Warriors are better at killing when they channel their energy. I saw strong men die beneath a demon's teeth because they'd lain with a woman—or man—not realizing they'd be called to service again."

I held very still.

"So what made you decide?"

"My brother," he said. "When I refused the offer, he acquiesced in my stead. He'd never been blooded. He'd never even gained one long life, and they let him go. They let him face Lucifer based only on the skills I showed. They presumed such a family penchant for war would be hereditary."

The bitterness in his voice was a thread I clung to. He knew the awfulness of the experience. He'd lived it too. I knew from experience that to travel to Hell and to bond with the stone created the magic that led to his immortality. I'd nearly gained it myself when we'd fought Absalom. I'd always assumed he'd wanted to pay that price. But this was the first time I'd heard he'd not gone willingly.

Or that he had a brother.

"I went to retrieve him," Maddox said. "But only after Doyle prepared to make the trip himself. I couldn't let my father go. He didn't want to let me. We'd lost too many family members to the stone. In the end, I went."

I thought of the old man who, strong though he was, would be no match for the devil, and I tried to imagine the argument between two alpha males with headstrong hearts. I thought of his comment about losing so many family members and when I wanted to ask about that, he spoke again, taking away the chance.

"I took Doyle's place," he said. "But I didn't win the argument. I stole the trip from him before he could protest. Before he could make the magic work on himself."

"You went without preparation," I whispered and my throat ached at the thought.

I'd not been prepared either. I knew how vile the devil was. I only had to think of a second's worth of my time there to feel a stone of panic in my stomach.

"I went without anything," he said. Maddox's arms tightened around me, the only real display of his angst as he described the story. "And I failed. I did everything I could to save him, but I failed and it was terrible."

He twirled me around in his arms and I could just make out the glisten of tears on his cheek. He inhaled deeply, bracing himself, I thought.

"I've never considered hiring Adair or purchasing a ferryman to pluck him or anyone else from Hell, Isabella." He held my gaze intently. "Even though I could have. Even though, as you heard, he offered it to me. He was my youngest brother. Do you want to know why?"

I didn't have to even nod. He answered his question anyway.

"Adair's magic never comes cheap. Even his information is costly."

He didn't say anything about what he'd promised Adair as we'd left the shop, but I could hear it in his words. Whatever he'd agreed to was going to pain him. The truth of it sat on his face for a long moment but then he swept it aside.

He cupped his hands around my face and lifted my chin upward. "I swear to you. I won't let you feel the bite of Hell one more time. And if by some awful magic, you ride the ferryman to Lucifer's lair, I will go back to Hell and swap my soul for yours before you can even smell the devil's sweaty armpits."

With that, he swung and pulled me to my feet then guided me toward the street again.

"But this time we have a secret weapon," he said as he crossed the piazza. "And Adair let that part slip."

I watched him pace ahead of me, a peculiar bounce in his step. I had to rush to catch up with him.

"He mentioned a sentient ferryman," I said thoughtfully, guessing that was the slip. "Is there such a thing?"

He grabbed my hand and swung it back and forth like we were schoolchildren.

"No, there isn't," he said. "But there is Kerri, and she is a shapeshifter."

CHAPTER TWENTY-THREE

Kerri's Cauldron was what I imagined an old apothecary would look like. It too, was in a tower the same as the Soul Merchant's shop, but it was a long, long walk from Adair's. I felt like I'd fallen asleep on my feet multiple times before we arrived, so when Maddox pulled on the center-affixed iron handle, I was more than ready to fling myself into the nearest chair. Let them hash out the details. I needed sleep.

But the shop itself was too interesting to ignore, and there wasn't a single chair in sight. A chandelier with four elongated gas-type hurricane lamps hung in a wood-slated ceiling. In the glow of early morning, the lights were merely a sizzle of purple, and I suspected what lit them had nothing to do with electricity.

A wrought iron spiral staircase riddled with black and red candles that had dripped onto the treads and made stalactites of the wax.

Baskets of herbs lined the top of a shop-wide medicine chest, filled with vials and clay pots and drawers with elegant penmanship denoting each container.

There was no cash register. No display cases. Just cabinets and books and baskets, and a strange fragrance that seemed to come from the floor because with each step, I got a new waft of aroma as I spun in a circle.

"Where is she?" I said to Maddox who had taken to inspecting a blue vial that appeared empty but for the label on the front that declared it as angel's breath.

"She'll be here."

"What?" I said with a laugh. "Did you entice her with a dick pic?"

"Funny, Isabella," he said. "I see with the loss of your soul, your sense of humor hasn't improved."

I trod over to the staircase and sank onto the third tread. "The problem is *you* have no sense of humor." I picked at a bit of wax and ran it between my thumb and finger. It felt oily. I sniffed at it and grimaced.

"You might not want to touch anything," Maddox said, noting me wiping the residue on my jeans.

I looked up at him. "You think I might get in trouble?"

"I think you might get hurt."

I eased more into the middle of the stairs at that. No sense taking any more chances until I got my soul back.

"So, what makes you think she'll come running when she doesn't even know we're here."

He chuckled as he set the blue vial down on the shelf.

"She knows we're here."

"But I didn't see you summon her." I thought of how he'd called to her from his office. "Is there some sort of spell in that vial?" I watched as he tinked the edge of the glass bottle with his nail. It moved an inch on the shelf toward a cluster of similarly colored bottles.

"You don't summon a goddess in her own shop, Kitten. You wait for her to decide you're worth her time."

I took that to mean she'd come out of hiding when she damn well felt like it. I sighed.

"Aren't we on a time crunch?"

Not just that, but I was exhausted. It had been, what? Twenty-four hours since I'd slept? I expected to hallucinate any moment now. Maybe I'd been hallucinating already. The things in Adair's shop had been disconcerting enough to tack it down to lack of sleep.

I leaned back against the tread behind me. Unforgiving as the metal steps were, and ill-fragrant as the candle wax smelled, I felt my eyes closing. I might have sunk down into a little ball and snored for all I knew, because the next I knew Kerri was sitting next to me.

"How long was I asleep?" I said, trying to work the words around a thick, furry tongue.

She placed her arm across my shoulder and squeezed in a comforting way.

"We've been talking your situation over for ten minutes," Maddox said.

I hadn't realized he was standing on the other side of the staircase. I had to peer through the rungs to see him.

"Not long enough then," I said with a tinge of grumpiness. "What did we decide?"

Kerri hung forward between on her legs, elbows on her knees.

"We decided that if I'm going to help you, I need a huge favor in return."

I swung my gaze to hers. Was owing a goddess as bad as owing a fae? I hesitated, and she must have known what was going through my mind. Silver eyes held mine for a long moment before she spoke.

"It's a big ask," she said. "I don't relish visiting Lucifer."

She pulled her arm away and laid it on her lap. I noticed she was holding a purple vial in her other hand, and swapped it back and forth so smoothly the glass didn't seem to leave one palm before nestling into the other.

"I don't relish it either," I said, waiting for the bottle to fall and break. "But Adair says..."

"Don't get too familiar with the Soul Merchant, Isabella," she warned.

I considered the wisdom of using the man's name and retraced my verbal steps.

"The Soul Merchant says if I don't get my soul back, I'll end up *there* if something fatal befalls me."

I tried to say it the way he had, but I doubted I'd got the words right. Didn't matter. The gist was the same.

I stretched out one leg then the other.

"I really don't want that to happen."

It was an understatement if I ever made one, but I wanted her to know I got the sentiment. That I understood what we were asking of her. I knew there were some truly evil creatures out there, but so far the worst I'd met was Lucifer.

She must have heard the regret in my voice because she rose with a sigh. The long black tunic she wore over the top of bare legs and ankle boots, started to shimmer in places as though sunlight was moving over very deep water and the surface was catching it. Her silver gaze got just the slightest of reds within the irises.

"I've never been a ferryman," she said wistfully, and her voice grew husky as she twisted toward Maddox, showing him her spine. "Maddox, would you give me a stroke along the scales and make sure I get it right?"

She winked at me as she said it and I heard Maddox huff.

"You know I hate snakes," he said.

"I don't forget anything," she intoned and then melted down in front of me to a puddle of coiled serpent at my feet.

I recoiled instantly at the sight, cell memory taking control of my muscles. I pulled my feet up onto the stairs and hugged my knees away from the snake. I worried my feet were too close even though she was several feet away.

"I'd say she nailed it, eh?" Maddox said, obviously trying to sound light-hearted but the way he edged away betrayed his own reluctance to be near it.

Kerri uncoiled and stretched toward his boot and he nudged her away. I swear I could see the serpent smile. I stood, giving her a wide berth, and picked up the vial she'd left behind. *Eye of Newt*, it said.

"I've always wondered what that was." I said, holding the vial up to show Maddox.

"Salamander," he said. "Did you know there's a species in your world so toxic it can kill a full-grown man with just enough coating from its skin to cover a pinhead?"

I shivered at his thoughtful tone.

"I'm not sure I want to know. You don't think that's what's in this bottle, do you?" I put it back down on the step and rubbed my hands on my pants as I scanned the shop for a sink and tap.

Maddox reached out his hand. "It doesn't go there," he said. "The least we can do is keep Kerri's shop neat. She doesn't like it when patrons mess with her stuff."

I wasn't sure I wanted to touch the thing again, but he wasn't taking it upon himself to retrieve the vial. I pulled my sleeves down over my hands and gripped it by the stopper, then passed it to him.

"How do you know so much about eyes of newt and what not?"

"Cleo," he said. "I don't think there's a poison in your ninth world that she hasn't studied."

"Nice," I said, but meant completely the opposite. I had forgotten that the ancient vampire had taken a dislike to me. And that she most assuredly had a major like for him. I found myself wondering how close they had been over the centuries.

"Don't worry, Kitten," he said. "I won't let her near you until you get your soul back." He tidied the shelf, skirting the serpent as it tried to wrap around his ankle.

"Blast it, Kerri," he said.

"She did manage a pretty good replica," I said without laughing. The result was uncanny and even with a leaking soul, it still scared me. "Did you two talk about how we're going to do this?"

He dragged his shoulders upward and let them drop. Not really a shrug, more a motion of resignation.

"She says she'll know what to do. All you have to do, is get her there."

"Me?" I circled around Kerri. "I'm not taking her."

He pinched the bridge of his nose. "You have to, Kitten. You're the one whose soul is leaking. And I have things to do."

He didn't say anything about Adair, but I read the message in his tone. He had to pay the Soul Merchant for the information.

Even so, I wasn't touching her, even if the ferryman was just Kerri in disguise. I jutted my chin out. "Then you have to put her in a box or a bag. I'm not touching her." I looked down at the serpent. "No offense, Kerri."

I thought the serpent smiled, but I was willing to bet it was just my exhaustion making me imagine things.

"How long do you figure a gal can go without sleep?" I said, turning to look for a bag or a box to scoop Kerri into.

Maddox watched me fiddling with drawers and didn't bother to help until I accidentally upended a drawer filled with some sort of dust. It spilled onto the floor and sprayed out across the floor in a cloud. I sneezed. Then sneezed again.

It was the impetus for him to push me gently aside.

"Up the stairs," he said, shooing me away like a nosy neighbor. "I better get this before Kerri decides to shift back and turn you into the contents for the drawer next door."

I tiptoed around the mess, keeping my eye on Kerri, who had slithered almost out of sight beneath one of the chests of drawers.

I waggled my fingers in the air in her general direction. "Butter fingers," I said apologetically, before treading cautiously out of range of the dust and up the stairs.

Kerri's second floor was filled with books and bowls of every size, shape, and make. I squinted at one big enough to boil a cow in and wondered if Kerri's shop was much like Errol's, in that he was able to make the size of it adjust magically to hold whatever it needed to.

Large porcelain bowls cradled copper ones. Copper ones held mixing bowls that looked like they were from the iron age and there were several piles of wooden ones, all in different grains and colors.

"There's a knife up there too," Maddox called up at me as though his eye was roaming the equipment along with mine. "You'll see it. Bring it down."

"How in the hell am I going to find which knife...oh."

He was right. I knew it right away. Despite a myriad of utensils and pestles with mortars, I knew right away that this knife was special. Except, *knife* couldn't be the true term for it. It reminded me of the Grim Reaper's sickle, but it was much smaller, the perfect size for a hand. The blade itself was slim and curved as though it was used for skinning hide. There was a bronze sheen across the surface, it glinted at me from the shadows as though light fell on it but there were no windows and it was out of reach of the magicked hurricane lamps below.

"Don't touch the blade," he warned. "Just grip it by the handle."

"No problem there," I said and used my sleeve again to grasp the bone handle.

I clutched it gingerly as I traversed the upstairs, still looking for a box that might hold Kerri in comfort. A wooden box, of which there were plenty, didn't seem right. Those came in as many sizes as the bowls and I pictured her up here mixing potions, then discarded the image. She was a goddess. Surely she didn't indulge in crass fairytale potion making.

The tower went up a third floor, and in a quick decision, I climbed those ten stairs to see if I could find something more fitting.

That level held chests and trunks, hinged and decorated with paint and inlay, and in some cases, burnt in symbols. I was drawn to a dark wooded one with gilt decorations that looked like gold. Several beautiful stones studded the surface in various patterns. I caught sight of something in a cobalt blue. I wasn't a foot from it before I was overrun with fragrances that I couldn't recognize, but that all felt ancient and rare.

Someone had carved hieroglyphs into it on one end. I felt the knife in my hand grow warm. A tingle ran through my palm and I itched to touch the chest, to lift the cover and investigate the things I knew instinctively were inside.

Because I knew what I had found. Whether Maddox wanted me to see it or not, I'd found that elusive treasure he'd been seeking for centuries.

Cleopatra's medicine chest.

At the sight of it, the dagger seared into my palm.

CHAPTER TWENTY-FOUR

I gasped in pain and dropped the dagger to the floor, where it landed with a sizable thud. An inspection of my burned palm showed no scorch marks or blisters. Out of a sense of self-preservation, I toed the knife aside where I could see it, but it couldn't touch me.

It had landed, I noted, with the point of the weapon facing toward the chest. I smelled a faint burning smell, like wood just catching fire. My mouth felt like ash. I croaked out a word to Maddox, not sure whether or not things were going to get nasty and if I'd need him.

But nothing came out. I coughed to clear my throat. A ball of something moved up into my mouth. Small, neat, like my own mucous but when I spit it into my palm, it burst into a bloom of red dirt.

"Oh fuck me," I said.

I wasn't sure what affinity the blade in my hand had with the chest on the shelf, but I was willing to bet that before the small trunk belonged to the doomed Queen, it had belonged to someone—something—else. And either they did not want me touching that box, or it was powerful enough that just standing near it could make a person hallucinate.

Then again, I hadn't slept in god knew how many hours except for the ten-minute kink downstairs on the stair treads. So, there was that.

I hugged my elbows and stared at the small trunk, running my gaze in a military fashion over the surface, searching for a latch that might hold it closed. I didn't think it wise to investigate with my fingers, not with the way the blade had reacted to my skin when it got close to the chest. But I did, so badly, want to know what was in it.

I leaned to the left and right, checking first one side and then the other. I noted golden hinges, so I knew it would lift open and not break into two pieces with separate cover and box. I looked down at the weapon on the floor and nudged it with my toe again to see what would happen.

It glowed red hot and smoke swirled up at me, catching me off guard as it bloomed around my face and assailed my nostrils. It smelled of old rot and semen.

I gagged hard enough to heave.

"Isabella?"

Maddox's concerned voice from below startled me enough that I leapt backwards and bumped into a chest on the other side of the small room.

"Are you alright up there?" he asked.

I waved at the smoke and realized it had already dissipated. Even the smell was gone. I could breathe again.

"Holy Hell," I said to no one.

I most definitely needed to get this day over with and get a good forty hours' sleep.

"I'm fine," I said, loud enough for him to hear as I kicked at the knife again. It sailed across the room, stopping when it fetched up pointy end first in the floor molding.

Safely away from Cleopatra's medicine chest.

I crossed the room to retrieve the knife—or dagger, or whatever it's called—stooping, and picking it up with my sleeves over my hand. It was cool again, as though it had been my imagination all along. I pocketed it in the right side of my jacket, patting it to make sure it was secure. It jutted out about an inch but it wasn't uncomfortable. Thank heaven I favored jackets with inside pockets; a habit I'd got into when I'd worked for Scottie.

Scottie. I tested the memory of the name the way you'd poke at a sore in your cheek. I guessed I should probably be concerned that I felt no guilt or lingering unease at the name. All I felt was relief that he was gone.

Maddox probably wouldn't share the relief, I knew. Best not to mention it.

Time was wasting, and I needed to package up the shapeshifting goddess downstairs, before I started to suffer worse than a few sleep-deprived hallucinations. I was already starting to feel as though something was watching me from behind. The hairs on my nape were crawling like ant antennae waving over a feast of ill-gotten sugar.

I ran my hands over the bowls and boxes, yanking open drawers and pulling on door knobs. In a cranny next to a highboy dresser, I found a black velvet pouch with a leather drawstring.

"Perfect," I said just as Maddox called to me again, this time with a note of alarm in his voice. "Coming," I said, and chuckled at the word. "Phrasing," I whispered to myself before heading for the staircase.

I descended to the second floor with the pouch clutched in my hand and the other running the surface of the spiral railing until I reached the first floor.

Kerri had Maddox cornered. She had grown to a fair size, I could see. The black shimmer of scales looked iridescent in the light of the purple magic lamps above us.

"You really are scared of snakes," I said to him amiably and he glared at me.

Kerri, in her serpent form, slithered sideways like a rattlesnake, making Maddox do a two-step in the other direction.

"I'm not afraid of them," he said. "But I've never known one to be trustworthy."

"You look scared to me," I said, and made my way toward him so he could take the bag and scoop Kerri into it.

He skirted the wall and came round me as I advanced, so that he was near the door, and several feet away from the ferryman.

"Really?" I said. "You're really going to make me do this?"

He shrugged and lifted his eyebrow.

"Coward," I said and pulled the knife from my pocket, figuring I'd use it to scoop Kerri and drop her into the bag I was flapping open against my thigh.

"Where did you get that?" he demanded.

I looked down at the bag. "In a little hollow in a dresser."

"I'm not talking about the Kibisis," he said, dismissing the bag and pointing to the knife in my hand. "I'm talking about *that*, the blade of Set."

I turned the knife out toward him, letting the light catch it. "This isn't what you wanted?" I said thoughtfully. You told me be sure to grip it by the handle."

"Because I didn't want you to cut yourself by accident," he said. "We don't want you to die prematurely, now, do we?"

I hadn't noticed another knife upstairs, but then he hadn't told me what I was looking for either. I'd just gravitated to the first thing that looked notable.

This had been it.

Maddox chewed his cheek as canted his head in the snake's direction.

"Oh, Kerri," he said coyly. "What other kinds of treasures are you hiding in this tower of yours?"

He closed the distance between us and reached for the knife, passing his thumb alongside the edge of the bone handle and as he did so, symbols lit up and disappeared again.

"You best give that to me," he said.

I gave him a long look.

"I don't think so," I said slowly, retracting the knife and putting it into my pocket. "Seems to me I might have come across a relic you might pay a girl for if she played her cards right."

He flashed me a grin that told me I had hit it spot on even if his next words were chastising.

"We don't steal from friends, Isabella."

He sent a searching look at Kerri as he said this. She, in turn splayed her snake skin out sideways at the neck the way a cobra might. Except in the ferryman's skin, Kerri looked pleased.

Maddox's jaw seesawed back and forth at her response, and I knew I'd been right. He was testing Kerri's reaction, couching his explanation of my naivete as a lesson of sorts while he gauged her response.

Oh, he was a cagey one. He wanted her to think he was completely ignorant of what was upstairs. I understood right then that this was the 'complex' issue that kept him from stealing the chest for Cleo.

The thief in me knew that the best move now, was to continue on as though there was nothing out of the ordinary. As though I'd not seen the chest, when Kerri would well know where I got the blade. She'd know I'd been to the third floor and would most likely have seen everything up there. Maddox's comment was intended to assuage any concerns she'd have about our intentions.

I knelt to spread the kibisis in front of Kerri, opening the bag to form a wide mouth. She slid into it without hesitation. I could breathe better when she was out of sight, not because I was scared of her, but because looking at the ferryman made me antsy.

I noted Maddox too, seemed more relaxed once she was out of sight.

"So," I said. "What next?"

"Next you take both snakes to the hospital to see your landlord."

"Easy enough," I said, giving the bag a little shake. "I don't even have to break in." I laughed and Maddox gave me an odd look.

"Sure, it's easy-peasy as you say in your ninth world," he said. "So long as you don't mix them up."

I shrugged. Box. Bag. What was to mix up?

"And what will you be doing?" I said.

What he was going to do was arrange for the Soul Merchant's payment, whatever that was. He wouldn't say. His plan was to usher me and the ferrymen back to his office and from there to my apartment through the Pussy Gate, which I decided in the moment to rename the man-gate because despite its warm and fuzzy feelings, it was pretty damned unsatisfying. Then he would get to whatever nefarious business Adair had sent him to.

"What did I miss while I was sleeping," I said, as he pushed me toward the portal once we'd got to my basement.

He smiled broadly. I noted his face was still healing nicely. The swelling had already gone down and the blue-green bruises were fading to yellow.

"Nothing," he said. "Kerri just wanted to know what I'd done to you to warrant such a beating."

I arrived in my basement with two ferryman serpents, a book, and a blade that apparently was rumored to be Set's own. Pretty good haul for a thief with nowhere to pawn it all.

I had the box in one hand and the bag in the other. The light through my window indicated it was nearly noon. Visiting hours at the hospital had already begun. I might have a couple of hours at best to get the deed done. I might be back to normal old soulful Isabella by the time I hit the hay that evening.

I planned to watch a few episodes of *Supernatural* as a means to do some research, and maybe spin a fantasy or two about gorgeous hunter men with no women to ease their pains. A bowl of ice cream and a bag of rippled chips too, yum.

I raced upstairs and peeled off my jacket, dropping the box and bag at the same time on the hallway floor and tossing the grimoire onto the sofa. The cat sniffed at the jacket that fell beside the box and then she sniffed the box and arched her back at it.

"Yeah, I know, right?" I said in agreement as she lifted a paw over the bag.

Then, either because she was feeling huffy or because I had no soul, the cat hissed and struck out at me.

I laid my head back along my neck to ease the tension in my muscles. I rolled it side to side, moaning at the pleasure of the fibers de-constricting from the knots they'd tied themselves into.

I bent to pluck the jacket from the floor and hung it on the coat tree. I could still smell all the Shadow Bazaar aromas on me and not all of them were so intoxicating as the whiskey and woodsmoke fragrance of the owner.

I needed a shower.

I sighed as I looked at the cat. She yowled at me.

"Hungry, I suppose," I said, pulling up one foot across my knee so I could peel off one boot and sock and then the other. "Be a good kitty and wait nicely till I shower, OK?"

I zombie walked my way to the bathroom, peeling off clothes all along the way. Naked, I entered my bathroom and left the door wide open to let the steam out that I knew was going to accumulate. I fully intended to make the shower as hot as I could stand, with the soap plentiful and foamy.

I stayed longer than I would have liked, but it felt so luxurious to just lean against the stall and let the water sluice over me in warm cascades.

I shut off the tap eventually and dried off. Just as naked as I'd entered, I stumbled to my bedroom for clean clothes. Socks. Panties. I pulled my favorite white T-shirt from the closet and yanked it down over my head. I had to sit down on the bed to pull my jeans onto my feet and up over my calves.

Everything just sort of slouched in my body as I worked to get dressed. Nothing seemed to want to work right. I couldn't remember having such a hard time pulling my jeans up to my waist. I'd have to lean back to hitch them up over my hips.

The next thing I knew, drool seeped down one corner of my cheek. I blinked. Tried to bring consciousness back. I was supposed to do something, wasn't I? Or something had woken me. That meant I'd fallen asleep. Again.

But at least then I knew something had woken me.

That was it. I'd heard a noise.

I pushed myself up and rolled over at the same time to face the doorway.

And near fainted again when I caught sight of the cat sitting next to me on the bed, a long black snake dangling from her teeth.

CHAPTER TWENTY-FIVE

I froze on the bed with my hands in the air as though I was surrendering to the feline in front of me. All I could think, was I was in one hell of a pickle. I couldn't be sure if the ferryman was dead in the cat's teeth or if she'd merely played with it to unconsciousness or paralyzation. I prayed it was the real ferryman first and then I prayed it was Kerri, the shape-shifter.

Then I realized I was out of luck no matter which one was clenched in that fishy-smelling bite, because unless they were both alive, I wasn't going to get my soul back.

"Nice cat," I said quietly, that thought top of mind. It wouldn't do to spook her.

I inched forward on my knees and got caught up in the jeans that were still around my ankles. I ended up toppling forward and scaring the cat. She flipped over herself and somehow landed on the floor feet first. She looked back at me over her shoulder, the serpent draped over her ruff and hanging along her ribs and behind her like a second, ill-placed and monstrous tail.

"Oh fuck me," I said. "You pick this time to decide to bring me a present?"

I scrambled to the edge of the bed, hitching my jeans up as I went. It was either get them on or get them off, and I had the feeling I was going to have to race to the hospital and would need every spare second.

She, of course, was off like a shot.

By the time I got both feet on the floor, the fabric was cutting into my buttocks and I had to suck in my breath to get the last bit hauled up over my backside and zippered.

"Here, cat," I said. "Good cat. I love the present. Can I see it? It's mine, right?"

I passed by the counter like I was on the prowl. I didn't dare make too sudden a move. I spied her food dish on the mat at the foot of the sink. It never moved from its place next to the water cooler.

"Pissed at me, are ya?" I said, figuring she had been scratching at it in vain and decided to investigate the smell she'd captured in the hallway.

I tried to tell myself if the snake that the cat had in her teeth was Kerri, she'd have shapeshifted back into a goddess already. I tried to reason that she'd be too quick for a mere cat to get the best of her and that she was probably somewhere in my apartment, or worse, pissed off and gone.

Thinking that didn't make me feel any better. Because if the snake that the cat was currently dragging along behind her up the stairs was the real ferryman, I was most royally screwed.

I grabbed a bag of treats from the sideboard as I passed by and shook it vigorously. It was her favorite flavor. Nothing.

I shook it again, this time calling out to Kerri to no avail.

The cat was already up the stairs. She'd dragged the snake along with her and dropped it halfway up the stairs. And there, lying in the hallway was the second snake, coiled tight, its face buried under its belly.

My mouth went dry at the sight. Whatever heartbeat managed to clock along in that second stuttered as my chest tightened like a fist.

"Oh sweet baby Jesus," I managed to get out before I recovered my wits and sprinted across the room.

I fell to my knees next to the snake on the floor, my hands running along the air above it in panic because I was afraid to get too close. How did one tell if a snake was dead anyway?

I didn't know if I should touch it, nudge it, pick it up, or what. I didn't want to even think about the fact that both of them might be out of commission. And I absolutely was not going to entertain the thought that my cat had killed a goddess.

"Bad cat," I yelled up the stairs. "Bad, bad cat."

I sank onto my heels as I studied the one in front of me. Maybe I should poke it. Or shimmy it into the bag or box. The bag. That was what. I was going to assume this one was a stunned Kerri and the ferryman that the cat had decided on as a plaything was the real one. Because I'd seen the cat take on a rat when she was nothing but a kitten.

A chewed-up ferryman where I lost my soul was preferable to taking a few bites out of a goddess.

Wasn't it? It had to be.

Don't mix them up. The last thing Maddox had warned me about. Well, I'd have to do my best.

I took a deep breath and let it go in a gust. This was a minor setback. That was all. I glanced at the clock on the wall. There was still time to gather them both up and get over to the hospital. If I was lucky, both would recover by the time I got there.

I used a spatula from the kitchen drawer to scoop both snakes up and drop them into their containers. I held the box in one hand and the bag in the other as I headed down my stairs onto the street. I caught a cab quickly, fortunately enough, and we pulled up in front of the hospital a few minutes before one.

I paid the cabbie and got out. The sun shone from behind me, casting a short shadow on the cement. I shook the bag, hoping some movement inside would alert me to Kerri's recovery. Nothing moved from inside.

I'd put the snake without the teeth-marks in the bag with the hope I was right and now I was even more worried that the snake in the box, with several chew marks wasn't the original ferryman.

But what could I do? Sticking to the plan seemed the most prudent in light of the FUBAR. If this had been a Scottie heist, he'd take nothing but death as an excuse.

I squared my shoulders and decided to press on. I headed into the building, inquired at the desk about Mr. Smith, and made my way to the elevators.

The hallway I stepped into smelled of antiseptic and in some places, sweat, as I passed harried nurses and orderlies. He was in Emerg, apparently. In a room to himself since his insurance seemed in order. I didn't consider Mr. Smith a man to have anything really in order until I'd seen inside his apartment. Having witnessed the cleanliness and perfect organization, I was willing to bet he had standing orders at the hospitals in the area.

The door to the room was open and a nurse was fiddling with his IV bag when I found his room. I presumed she was adding meds or liquids to keep him hydrated. It was obvious he was unconscious but he wasn't attached to a ventilator, so that had to be good, right?

I watched her check her watch and feel for his pulse. She noted something on a clipboard and then ran her palm down his sheets in a soothing way. She brushed his unruly hair out of his eyes.

I cleared my throat and she turned to face me with a smile. Thank god for nurses.

"He's doing well," she said. "Not out of the woods, but his readings are stable. You're family?"

I nodded. It was sort of true, and it was what I'd told the paramedics.

"I have some things for him," I said, lifting both bag and box high for her to see. "Just some essentials in case he wakes."

I smiled broadly, showing probably more teeth than I wanted. I had the feeling she could read the tension in my shoulders. I just hoped she'd imagine it was worry and concern. Maybe it was. I wanted to think so.

"I'll just leave you, then," she said. "You can talk to him if you like. I'm sure he'd like that."

"I will," I said and made a show of looking around the room. I pointed to a magazine that sported a man holding up a large fish of some sort, backgrounded by lush green trees and white water. "I'll read to him a spell."

She nodded and tucked the clipboard under her arm, then touched the IV bag again, tapping it with her index finger.

"Well, then," she said and seemed to be hesitating. "I'll close the door so you have some privacy."

She was halfway to the door before I realized what she'd been waiting for. The old Isabella wouldn't have missed it at all.

"His prognosis is good?" I asked, spinning on my heel to face her. My tennis shoes squeaked on the tiles.

This time her smile was broader. "Yes," she said. "We can't find any evidence of toxin in his blood. We pumped his stomach. The only thing that seems to be keeping him asleep is the trauma."

I tried to let my shoulders sag and was surprised to discover they relaxed considerably. "Good," I said. "He's a fighter. I'm sure he'll be up in no time."

I didn't truly breathe again till she closed the door behind her, and I didn't stop staring at the door till it clicked closed. Then I sidestepped toward the bed and yanked the curtain to conceal both of us even more so.

The blue plastic chair by his bedside was just inches from the head of his bed. The stamp of the hospital stuck out against the whiteness of the sheet. A matching blue eyelet blanket was tucked up beneath his armpits.

His arms lay outside the sheets, palms facing down. Several wires and cords disappeared under them and exited again from beneath the bed. The IV looked like it was creating a rash on the skin where it had been taped down.

"Mr. Smith?" I said as I approached the bed. "It's Isabella. I came to help you."

I didn't expect a response, but it didn't hurt to wait for one.

I set the velvet bag down on the plastic chair. I wasn't entirely sure what I should be doing, and I was beginning to have serious doubts that either ferryman was even alive anymore, but I had to do something.

The bag flopped over, with its mouth hanging forward in a frown. Not a great sign. I blew out a bracing breath and placed the box on Mr. Smith's belly, then used the Set blade to lift one corner of the lid so I could peek inside without risk of getting bit again or worse.

I didn't see any movement within.

"Rats," I said and poked inside with the handle end of the blade. "I swear if you're dead in there, I'm going to kill that cat."

I flipped the cover off with Maddox's warning ringing in my head.

"I have no idea if any of this is going to work, Mr. Smith, but there's no harm in trying."

I used the knife to scoop a coil and yanked it out of the box. The serpent lay there inert, the tiny puncture holes in its side goading me. I grumbled to myself and tried to keep my eye on it as I reached out for the bag on the chair.

The snake on the bed flicked its tongue out. Not far. Just enough for me to see it and realize it wasn't dead, or at least it had enough energy left in it to move. I whooped unintentionally and then clamped down on the sound. I didn't want the nurses thinking Mr. Smith had somehow come-to and rush in to whisk me out.

"That's it," I said to the serpent. "You're going to be alright."

I leaned in to get a better look, trying to figure out which one it was... goddess or ferryman.

In the same moment, a searing sensation shot through my wrist and up my arm. I gasped and bit down on my lip.

I suppose I should have felt panic, but all I felt was elation.

And then, both of those feelings were swept away in a tide of terror.

CHAPTER TWENTY-SIX

I wasn't sure what I was expecting, but it wasn't to get bitten a second time, and certainly not for it to hurt even more than the first. I staggered and fell against the bed as my knees went to wet bags. I grabbed for the railing with one hand and did my best not to faint.

All that ran through my mind was that one sentence. Don't mix them up.

I hauled in short breaths to keep from fighting off the serpent because this might be the last chance I had to reclaim my soul. If Kerri needed to hurt me to get my soul back, then so be it. I'd have to suck it up like a big girl.

But it hurt. It hurt like a firebrand on my skin, like acid in my veins, like a vacuum sucking out my lungs. I'd taken my share of beatings from Scottie in my day. I'd been assaulted by his henchman till I was nothing but a bruised bit of skin, but this. This felt like everything that I was and had been, was being compressed into tiny, hard stone.

I leaned against the bed, propping myself on Mr. Smith's legs with both elbows. I knew I was digging in, that I was probably bruising his skin, but I couldn't help it.

I could hear myself wheezing. The sight of that black serpent clinging to my arm with its mouth puckering my skin was almost enough to make me want to puke. It writhed as it drew on me, coiling around on itself and uncoiling again. The tip of its tail seemed to be seeking something. It wasn't finding it.

It writhed faster.

It clamped down harder.

I almost cried out, but bit down on my lip with enough pressure to keep the sobbing at bay. Tears stung my eyes and blurred everything except the inky black line crawling along my arm beneath my skin toward my chest.

It moved at a pace that worried me.

Back in my days with Scottie, he had his goons collect a fishmonger from his stall in the market who owed him money. They'd strapped the poor man to a car creeper in a deserted garage. Part of their orders were to bring along with them the knife the man used to fillet fish.

Scottie had gone to work on the man with the man's own knife, full of fish guts and blood. They let the man lie there, cut up and bleeding for two days before they let him go. I'd sneaked him in food and water and I'd witnessed how the man sweated as he lay there. I'd seen a suspicious looking line creeping beneath his skin toward his heart. I'd had to beg Scottie to let the man go or he'd never see his money.

Scottie called in a doctor to patch up the worst before sending him to the Emerg with a concerned 'son' to speak for him as the doc inspected the one cut on his arm that the man swore had been the outright result of his own stupidity.

In a way, it was. No one got away with owing Scottie money past the recollection date he graciously set.

The fishmonger ended up on I.V. antibiotics and had to return to the Emerg three days in a row with the stent embedded in his arm so they could hook him up for an hour at a time.

This creeping line looked very much like that.

Except mine was black. Coal black.

Not just that, but my skin was starting to feel as though a hundred fire ants were trying to defend a hill of sand. As if it wasn't bad enough, the snake somehow sprouted a dozen tiny clawed from its belly.

Small as they were, I had a close up enough view from my near prostrate view on Mr. Smith's bed that I could tell they looked like eagle's feet. Small. Sharp. And taloned.

Whatever was happening, I just knew it wasn't good.

"Kerri?" I said. "Please tell me that's you."

I rolled over to my side, barely able to lift my head from the bed by now. Both snakes were in view. One of them, lazily coming to, its tongue darting out to taste the air, the other drawing so hard on my wrist that it convulsed with each new inch of line that crept up my arm.

Now that I wasn't lying face first in the mattress and sheets, I could scent the fragrance I'd caught when the snake had first bit me back in Mr. Smith's hallway. It was the same smell that clung to him as he lay on the floor, the same stink that was in the box.

That thing that had hold of me was not Kerri.

It was the real ferryman, and no doubt the writhing it was doing was in a vain attempt to grapple its way back to Mr. Smith.

"Oh no," I gasped out. "Oh fuck no."

That thing was not going to finish what it started.

I knew it for sure when that writhing body sought out my landlord's arm that rested outside the sheets just a few inches away. A fuzzy sort of light started to emanate from its taloned feet.

Magic. Some sort of awful, soul-casting magic doing its best to seek out the connection it had made. I couldn't be sure, but I had a feeling the carrier magic was doing its level best to connect to the host it had mistaken for me. It didn't take a mage mind to know why.

It needed to connect to siphon off the soul it had mis-planted or to transfer what I had left.

"Hell no," I said, and mustered the energy to yank on the ferryman before it got a chance to dig its talons into Mr. Smith's arm. Just in time too.

It flung its tail sideways in frustration, seeking to fight me and reach its target.

I was blacking out now. Whatever the thing was doing to me, it was juicing more than just my remaining soul. It was immobilizing me. I was helpless as that black tail wormed its way, talons opening and closing, toward Mr. Smith's wrist.

I think I might have sobbed. Or hiccupped. Or screamed. I wasn't sure. I made a sound, I know that, and I made it the moment something whipped into view from my peripheral. It struck the ferryman with a lightning speed that reminded me of the slow-mo shots of snakes in nature. Then both of them twitched sideways, wrenching the ferryman's jaw and pinching my skin as a result.

It wasn't enough to free the bite, however, and I felt scalded where the ferryman had fought to stay impacted.

Through hazy eyesight that was already blackening at the sides, I saw Kerri subdue the ferryman. She bit down on its tail, swallowing a good inch of serpent down her throat. The macabre ouroboros bastardized itself even further when Kerri sprouted the same claw-like feet and dug them into Mr. Smith's arm.

Immediately, the ferryman attached to me spasmed. It clamped down harder, and I thought I heard Lucifer's throaty laughter, felt the raging heat of his realm. Whether the scream of pain in my head came out through my voice box or not, I knew it was more than just a response to pain. It was the primal scream of something dying. Or coming to life.

I couldn't be sure.

I just prayed, really prayed, that the snake milking Mr. Smith's arm of something I swear I could taste, was Kerri and not the other way around.

Then to my relief, my taste buds were flooded with candy apple, sweet and dopamine releasing. There was a hint of something rotten beneath it all, as though the Granny Smith coated in candy had begun to go soft and bad, but I welcomed every bit. I swallowed as though my life depended on it, and even if I had the sense that it was all metaphorical and magical, I wasn't taking a single chance.

The fog began to lift. The sense of smothering was replaced with the feel of a warm river breeze.

It was done. I felt it. I knew it was over.

The snake detached from my arm and I sagged backwards, rolling from my side to my back. My feet hung inches from the floor and I realized I was laying almost parallel to Mr. Smith. I couldn't remember writhing along the mattress but in my pain and delusion, I must have.

I hitched in a few breaths, expecting Kerri to already be standing at the side of the bed and the ferryman to be nothing but an inert coil of scales.

"That was almost too easy," I murmured to myself.

"Isabella?"

Mr. Smith's voice. He was awake. It worked.

I pushed myself to an unsteady and weak half sitting position.

"Mr. Smith," I said. "You're alright."

A look came over his face when he heard my voice. One of alarm or recognition or fear or maybe all at once. He shoved me hard enough that my back went into the railing of the bed.

He held the Set blade above his head and was just starting the arc of swing downward when I croaked out a plea for him to stop.

Because he was aiming right where Kerri and the ferryman were resting on the bed.

Too late, the blade came down on the neck of one of the snakes. Black ooze sprayed everywhere. The white sheet looked splattered by a Pollack painting frenzy. The snake's red eyes went black. Smoke curled up in a stinking plume.

"Oh my God," I said. I scrambled from the bed, still working at keeping my knees from buckling. "Stop, stop."

I grabbed his wrist to keep him from swinging again.

"Sweet baby Jesus," I said. "I hope. Oh God I hope..."

I didn't have the thought finished before the still-whole snake slithered to the edge of the bed. I might have blinked or something because in the next second, Kerri was sitting there, naked as a newborn, and looking as comfortable in her nudity as Eve must have.

I sank down on the chair without really feeling my butt hit the seat. I was aware that my breathing was ragged and I clutched my diaphragm to help stop the hyperventilating.

Kerri looked spent. Her eyes were red-rimmed. She was thinner.

But she was glowing.

And none of this had to be normal for Mr. Smith.

"Um," I started to say and he held up his hand.

"Don't bother," he said. "I know what's going on."

It took a moment to formulate a response to that, and it was pathetic.

"You do?"

He nodded as he wriggled up to a sitting position and shook the cords that strung from his arm.

"I do." He nodded silently at Kerri who grinned back.

Strange. Very strange. I jerked my chin at the snake that still lay on his bed, the head neatly dissected. The black spatter was already turning grey.

"You know what's happening," I said carefully as I eyed him. Something else was afoot and it was clear in the wary way he looked at the goddess. "Really?"

"I know *what* is going on," he said. "But I'm not sure I know *who*."

Right. The naked woman sitting on his bed. I hung over my knees, letting the last of the faint flood back down to my toes.

"Kerri," I said, taking a deep, bracing breath. "This is my landlord, Mr. Smith."

Her silver eyebrow lifted ever so slowly. "Is that what he calls himself these days?"

CHAPTER TWENTY-SEVEN

I noted she held his gaze with the steady stare of someone who is expecting an argument, but his kept flitting to the blade he'd dropped onto the bed and wouldn't roam anywhere near Kerri's face.

"You know him?" I said to her as a means to fill the awful tension that filled the air.

"Oh, that I do."

She stood and stretched very leisurely, reaching one hand toward the ceiling and slightly bent. She arched gracefully back so that her ribs rose and the muscles in her belly looked like they were rolling over small pebbles in a river.

"Do you want to enlighten your poor tenant, Djedi, or shall I?" she said to Mr. Smith.

His jaw jutted out stubbornly and Kerri, her fingers tugging some sort of silky black fabric out of thin air, canted her head at him in an obvious dare as the silk slipped down onto her fingers. It almost looked like she wanted him to refuse, but he sighed and slumped in his hospital gown.

"I'm Djedi," he said, turning his gaze to mine.

"Like in Star Wars?" I was doing my best to keep my focus but it was all so fantastic enough that the only thing I could think of was the sci-fi flick.

"Close enough," he said, smoothing his hospital gown over his legs and running his gaze over the bed.

I found myself wondering how he was able to pull his gaze from the goddess' nude body because I was mesmerized by it, and the way that silk fabric was even then wrapping itself around her in a body-hugging tunic dress that stopped mid-thigh. Her nipples stood out above the swell of her breasts, perfect globes without a bit of sag.

My hands were creeping up toward my own, almost instinctively wanting to check their perkiness in comparison, and I had to force them into my armpits as I hugged myself.

"Djedi was a magician," Kerri filled in.

"Was." I said, not posing a question, just repeating the significance of the verb. It indicated he no longer practiced.

She smoothed down the dress around her hips and stole a look at me as she did so. "Yes, was. When he was mortal, that is."

I took a step backwards. "You're kidding me," I said. There was no way this old fart, fighting with his zoning committee, was an immortal anything. I mean, why would he bother?

"Djedi was Rameses's magician in the time of the exodus," Kerri explained, as she plucked the velvet bag from the chair and passed it to Djedi. "And before that, magician to the great Khufu? Am I right?"

Mr. Smith looked miserable when he answered.

"I was never his magician. I didn't belong to anyone."

"And still he kept you." Kerri said, not unkindly. She took a moment to nudge the decapitated snake in his direction.

"You're not thinking of putting this thing back together, are you?"

He recoiled as the headless snake came in contact with his arm.

"Damned thing," he exclaimed. "Near lost myself to a damned vampire because of it." He shuddered. "I hope I got her head with that blow."

He swung his feet over the other side of the bed and caught in the cords and wires that connected him to the equipment at his bedside. His irritated glance at the IV told me if we didn't get him unhooked pretty soon, he was going to rip the thing out on his own.

"Here," I said, grasping for the IV and looping it backward over his shoulder. "Just hang on. I'll call the nurse."

He pushed my hand away. "I don't need a nurse. And you don't need the questions she's gonna ask if she comes in here and sees...you two."

He shot a look at Kerri who pointed at the snake as though he'd forgotten it entirely in his concern for what the nurse might see.

"I know, I know," he said. "Give a guy a break."

He sighed heavily, grabbed the head of the ferryman, and popped it into the drawer by his table. The body, he lifted and placed in the bag that he snatched from Kerri.

"Shame to put something so vile in a kibisis," he muttered, and then stuffed that too in the drawer. "If I hadn't been there, that thing would have taken everything you are, Isabella, and it wouldn't have cared how hard Lucifer played with you when it delivered you into his realm."

I shuddered at the words because there was a ring of truth in it that I knew from experience. Lucifer played hard with those in his menagerie and he had nothing but an eternity of time to fill. It didn't matter who had wanted to shove my soul aside and slip inside the space it had left, all of it was bad.

I edged away from both immortals and the ferryman serpent that, even if it was hidden, was far too close for comfort.

"Promise you aren't putting that thing back together," Kerri said. "I don't much care one way or the other, but I don't fancy rescuing our poor mortal Isabella again if it means me tapping into Hell's energy." She gave me a pointed look. "No offense, Isabella."

I shrugged. "None taken."

Mr. Smith struggled to his feet amid the tubes, and sheets that were now crisply white again, with no sign of the viscous black fluid that had bled from the ferryman at its decapitation.

"You have no worries about me regenerating that vile thing," he said. "What I did for Khufu was a small trick and nothing more. I don't do that sort of magic anymore."

My confusion must have been apparent because Kerri made a point of catching my eye.

"He was known for that trick back in the day," she said. "Thought it was funny to scare the kids so they'd leave his goat herd alone. It backfired. Word got out that a hundred-and-ten year-old commoner could bring a man back to life."

Djedi skirted the bed, clamping the back of his gown closed with one hand so that he could bend over to look beneath the bed.

"I was fifty," he snapped as he did so. His voice came out muffled as he peered under the mattress. "Kids think anyone over thirty is ancient."

She chuckled. "To be honest, anyone over thirty *was* ancient."

She rounded the bed next to him and sidestepped where he was busy swiping his arm back and forth along the floor beneath the shadows of the mattress. She pulled at the knob on the drawer while he checked over his shoulder, following her movements with his eye.

The drawer wasn't deep and when it was pulled open, I could make out the velvet bag and the dull black of the ferryman's head from where I stood at the foot of the bed.

Kerri plucked the serpent's head from the drawer with finger and thumb and held it aloft over her other hand for a moment, drawing a shape in the air before dropping it onto her open palm.

She gave the window a lingering glance and it squeaked open an inch, letting the curtains billow in.

When she waved her fingers over the small head in her hand, it crumbled to a grey powder.

"I told you," he said, as she blew the small pile out the open window. "I wasn't going to do anything with it. Last thing I want is to feel that vile presence again."

She pursed her lips. "And now you can't," she said and turned to me. "Never trust a necromancer. Not even this necromancer."

He didn't protest. Just crossed his arms over his chest. The flaps of his gown fell forward, caught in the breeze from the open window. He spun on his heel and headed to the small closet, uncaring of the way his backside was aimed at the door to his room and the nurses' station beyond.

It reminded me that if they saw him standing there, they'd be rushing in to check on the miraculous recovery. We really should get a move on.

Kerri must have sensed the shift and clapped her hands together.

"Now," she said to me. "I think it's time you got back home." She scanned me head to heel. "You look better. How do you feel? No strange presence crowding you from the inside out? No whiffs of brimstone when you move too fast?" She had a strange expression, like she expected me to lie.

I shrugged.

"Good enough for me," she said. "No humans harmed in the episode."

"Thanks, Kerri," I said, I wasn't sure how I was supposed to feel, all things considered, but she seemed pretty satisfied. "I owe you one."

She put a finger to her lips. "Never, and I mean this, Isabella. *Never* say you owe someone. You don't know when they'll call in those chips."

"Right," I said, recalling the sidhe lord who had sent me to hell because he thought I owed him. "Can I take that comment back?"

She laughed. "I won't ask for much," she said. "But it might be quite a few years from now before I need something from a spunky pickpocket."

She looked directly at Mr. Smith. "You give her the details. Someone has entered my shop and I'm not sure everything there is as secure as I left it." She narrowed her gaze at me but said no more.

Mr. Smith nodded and started stripping off his gown. Kerri was gone like a shadow, and I got an eye full of old man butt as he bent over to pull on his pants that he'd pulled from the closet. I turned around discreetly, mentally trying to rid myself of the image of a very large liver spot and several red pimples.

"What details was she talking about?" I said.

"You got a bond on you?" he said from behind me.

"I don't know what that is."

When his voice came again, it was muffled as though his mouth was covered with something.

"A bond. Something connecting your soul to Hell by magic."

"Oh," I said. "That. Yeah."

I didn't want to explain the connection when I barely understood it myself, but it was the reason Maddox had installed the portal in my basement. Why he gave me a job. Why he was watching over me. "There's this stone, you see..." I started to say and gave up. How did I describe what Maddox was when I didn't even understand it?

I felt his hand on my shoulder and turned around. He was free of the tubing and fully dressed in his sweater and old man slacks. His slippers were in his hand.

"I don't care," he said. "Really. It's your business. But some vampire chick wanted out real bad. She used that connection to ride the ferryman. Picked the wrong goddammed person to try to wrestle with. That much I can tell you."

I didn't have to think long or hard to figure out who he meant. "Isme," I said. "She's got..."

He held up his slippers. "Don't care about that either. She took a nice trip back across the river and she'll be paying dear by the time she gets there. All I want to know is if the bond is open. You know, if it's something she—or someone else—can use to try to connect to again."

"I don't know how it works."

"I'm thinking if I was a conduit to a world where the prince of it liked to hold a fly's wings to the fire, that I'd want to know how it works, but that's your business," he said, shaking his head.

He stooped to pull one slipper on and then the other, then made a small whooping sound as though he'd just remembered something that delighted him and surprised him at the same time.

He whirled around and leapt for the bed with an agility I didn't expect for a man his age.

I realized what had him so delighted when he burrowed beneath the sheets and pulled out the Set blade.

He chuckled with glee. "She forgot the blade," he said almost to himself. "Not quite worth the price of admission, but I can find a use for it I'm sure."

I wasn't sure I liked the sound of that, but I was happy enough to have things done and over that I was willing to ignore the crawling of my spine as he inspected it.

"It's the real deal," he murmured. "Forged by Set himself and used it cut the balls off his own brother." He looked at me over the blade and the grin he shot me was almost macabre. "See the hieroglyphs?"

I leaned toward it politely, noting that the markings reminded me of chicken scratching's, but not wanting to get too close.

"What does it say?"

"It says if I tell you, I'll have to kill you." He chuckled.

CHAPTER TWENTY-EIGHT

I knew he was joking, but I didn't find anything funny in the idea of death. "I'll pass," I told him.

"Just as well," he said. "Because then that non-man of yours would make me resurrect you, and I don't do that sort of costly magic for nobody no more. What's mine is mine, even if it's just my own damn power."

He patted down his sweater as though it had pockets, then finding none, stuffed the blade into the back waistband of his polyester slacks, gangster style.

"Now," he said. "Let's crack on."

Crack on we did. He signed himself out, dismissing the nurses' protests that they should do more tests. We hailed a cab, which he ordered to stop at his house because he was an old man and shouldn't walk so far after such an ordeal. I noted he had no trouble carting the box and blade up his sidewalk to his house. He even rearranged a few bags of dirty diapers before disappearing beneath his porch awning and reappeared in front of his front door.

I stood in the street, watching him open his door without unbalancing a single thing, and I wondered if Kerri had indeed forgotten the blade at all. It seemed a bit too coincidental for me to find an ancient Egyptian blade filled with black magic in her shop to bring to revive a man who had himself been an ancient one. And she didn't seem the sort to forget things with power the way one might forget a purse or a scarf.

I sighed and told myself it didn't matter. I was whole again. I was home. The light was on over my stoop and I didn't need to do anything at that moment but sleep.

I stumbled into my apartment without bothering to turn on the hall light. It was light enough still to see just fine without it. I didn't see the cat anywhere and it was just as well. I had a mind to throw her outside and let her face the elements for the afternoon after the stunt she'd pulled with the snakes.

Not that I could blame her, really. A snake was a snake. It had no place inside and she had probably just been defending her territory. Still. Things could have gone terribly wrong.

I tossed my cell phone on the hall table and stretched. I noted there was message bubble on the screen but I was too tired to answer it. All I wanted was a few days rest, a shower, and then gobs and gobs of ice cream.

I tripped over the cat at my bedroom door. She hissed at me, of course, the arrogant thing.

"You best find a safe place to hide for a few hours," I told her as I scooped her belly with my instep and tossed her a few feet into the kitchen. She landed neatly, facing me, her back arched high. I feigned jumping at her and she hissed louder then bolted past me for the stairs.

I fell onto my bed without pulling off a single item of clothing. I pulled the edge of the comforter over my legs and let exhaustion take me.

I dreamed of wide-open spaces. Voids, really. They were black and gaping and they called to me with a hoarse voice that sounded like frogs croaking. Something from the darkness reached out and shook me by the shoulder. I shook it off. It shook me again.

"Isabella," it said, in a gruff voice this time.

I rolled over, brushing the hand off my ribcage that I felt trying to coax me awake...

"Go away," I said.

I knew who it was. The same person who sent me a text, who seemed to think his portal in my basement gave him every right to barge into my bedroom.

"Wake up," he said.

"The hell I will," I said, without opening my eyes.

"You didn't answer my text," he said.

"Was it a dick pic?"

"You know it wasn't."

I lifted one finger before letting my whole arm drop behind me on the pillow. "Therein lies the secret to my response."

It wasn't, not really, but it was a point of honor by now for me to egg him on, knowing he would never do it. His delicate celibacy would never let him. Safe, I thought, to ride his nerves until he couldn't take it anymore. I chuckled to myself.

His palm moved over my eyes and when I thought he'd try to coax me gently awake; he peeled my eyelids open with his thumb.

It took a moment for my eyes to adjust to the bright light so I couldn't quite make out his face, but I knew it was Maddox. The smell of him was unmistakable. In fact, the woodsmoke aroma made me want to curl right back up, which I did. I rolled over to face the wall and brought my knees up.

"Doesn't the Pussy Gate come with a lock?" I said as I did so and tugged at the comforter because I felt chilly without it. "The very least it could do is scratch your eyes out when you decide to visit uninvited."

"Only a fool would do that," he said, sounding amused.

"You made the thing so it would vibrate," I countered. "So, who's a fool?"

I felt him climb onto the bed and kneel behind me.

"I didn't realize what I was doing," he said from somewhere above me.

There was something in his voice. Something I wasn't sure he wanted me to hear. I twisted so I could look up at him over my shoulder. Through my narrowed gaze, I was able to make out his russet buzz cut and stubble. He was wearing a white t-shirt that did very little to hide his size. He looked much better, healed up pretty nice if I did say so.

But that didn't excuse him, especially in light of his expression.

"Sweet baby Jesus," I said in reaction to what it said. "You did so know what you were doing."

He threw up his hands, guilty as the day is long.

I sat up, throwing the corner of the comforter still clinging to my legs aside.

"You bastard. You did that on purpose."

His face gave nothing away but I knew I was right.

"Trust a thousand-year-old virgin to make a sexually frustrated portal. Honest to Pete." I thought better of throwing the warmth of the comforter aside and pulled it over my shoulders as I faced him.

"I'm not a thousand years old," he said, but there was a glint in his eye that told me I had hit it right on the nail head.

"And what do you think you'll gain from me getting wound up every time I use the damn thing. Presuming I ever decide to use it," I said.

He chuckled and scooched down so his back was against the headboard. He tugged at the comforter, pulling me down beside him in the same motion. Before I knew it, we were cocooned together beneath the blanket. His body felt warm and solid, and it was all I could do not to snuggle in.

"They let you spoon in the priesthood?" I said.

"I'm not a priest either," he said. "I might be a virgin and celibate but there are things a man can do with that frustration if he's creative enough."

I made a sound that indicated exactly what I thought of that.

"And what I thought I would get when I made the gate," he said. "Was a little appreciation."

"It damn well stops just before it finishes anything," I said.

"I know the feeling well," he murmured. "You don't like it?"

"You really are a virgin if you think sexual frustration is pleasant," I said and tried to climb out the other side of the comforter. He might be celibate by choice but I was only so by unhappy circumstance.

"I think you did it because you can't stand being celibate and you want me to suffer for it."

"What's to be gained from your suffering?" he said. "Only a true bastard would think that way."

I didn't say that it was the kind of thing Scottie would have done. One way to demonstrate his power over me.

"I did it because I don't know the feeling of release," he said. "I can't make what I don't know."

His voice was a low whisper at that and it made me pause just long enough for him to snag me by the waist and pulled me close, maneuvering me so that I was lying on top of him, face to face. My heart was hammering so hard it felt like his was pounding into my ribcage.

"You're so cold, Isabella," he said.

"Pot. Kettle."

"No, " he said, brushing the back of his hand across my forehead. "Cold. Like, temperature wise."

"What did you come here for?" I said, because I had a feeling I was cold because he was so damn hot. I wanted to melt against him.

"The kitten," he said. "It won't eat."

There was worry in his voice and it did nothing to halt the cascade of lust that had started to sweep over me. In fact, it did the exact opposite. I wondered what he'd do if I pulled off that shirt of his and ran my mouth over his belly.

"Isabella?" he said. "Maybe it will eat for you."

"Hmm?" I said, struggling to pull my mind back to the here and now and not into the cesspool of images it was conjuring.

"It won't eat. It likes you. Maybe you can get it to swallow something."

Oh damn. Just. Damn.

"Come on," he said, somehow managing to stand up with me straddled to him for a long moment before he eased me onto the floor. The way my feet hit cold tile, was like a cold shower.

"OK," I said with a sigh. It was getting nowhere anyway. "But I'm not going by Pussy Gate. I've had enough frustration for one week."

He smiled down at me, all heart-stoppingly eager. "No need," he said. "I brought her with me. She's in the living room playing with your cat."

She was indeed playing with the cat and the sight was enough to make me stare with my mouth wide open. The cat did not play. She tore socks apart and left prizes for me all over the house, but she wasn't one to chase a string when I dangled it. If she was going to deign to swat at anything in fun it was going to be on her terms.

"Well, I'll be smoked," I said, and crossed the room to where both cats were roiling around and batting playfully at each other.

I intended to pick the small one up. My cat got in the way, though. She hissed, spine arched up, and then swiped at me. She didn't connect, but she pulled back again and I growled at her.

"You bitch," I said. "Don't you even dare."

I reached past her toward the little one because obviously, I was as bad as Maddox at learning my lesson.

Of course, the kitten did the same thing. Except she did connect. I heard Maddox suck in a breath from behind me.

I stood up, nursing the scratch that she had landed on the top of my hand.

"Ya, she's quick," I agreed.

"Isabella?" Maddox said from behind me.

I and turned to see his face had gone an ashen pallor.

"What?" I said, wondering what could have him so worried about a little scratch. "Am I bleeding out somewhere I don't see?"

"You," he said. "The kitten."

"Yeah the little beast is as bad as my cat." I shot her a nasty glare. "Both need to learn a little manners."

"That's not it," he said, approaching me with a narrowed gaze. He looked from me to the kitten and then to the cat. "You know what this means, right?"

I licked at the scratch, tasting blood. "Obviously not if you've got your drawers in a twist."

He caught my hands and held them close to his chest as he touched my forehead with his lips. They roamed across the skin as far as the temple where they rested. I couldn't help leaning in and lifting my gaze to his. Maybe he was feeling a little hot. Maybe I was too. Maybe it was time to test that damn celibacy.

I slipped my arms around his waist and arched upwards, giving him full access to my mouth if he wanted it.

His eyes held mine long enough that I started to think he was considering it.

"Go on," I murmured. "I won't tell anyone."

"Did Kerri say anything to you about the success of your visit to the hospital?"

That wasn't what I was expecting at all. I pulled away but he held me firm.

"Isabella," he said. "There's something wrong and you know it."

I yanked my arms back and swatted him with the back of one of my hands. "It's a scratch, Maddox. That's all. What's wrong is that little beast of yours should have been left to die in the alley."

I scooped up a sock from the arm of the chair and tossed it at her. "Both of you should have," I said.

The sock fell short of its target and Maddox grabbed my wrist when I picked up the cushion from the chair to do the same thing.

"You're not right, Isabella. You're cold. Your own cat hates you. But the kitten wasn't afraid of you at first. She is now. Don't you see what that means?

I stared at him, unblinking, waiting for him to enlighten me.

I watched his Adam's apple plunge in his throat as he gathered the words.

"What it means," he said. "Is you don't have your soul back at all."

CHAPTER TWENTY-NINE

"What did Kerri say when she slipped off the ferryman skin?" he said.

I was sitting in my living room on the sofa while Maddox knelt in front of me with his hands on my knees. It was a firm grip, and had been since he'd dropped me on the couch a few minutes earlier.

The cats had decided to hightail it up the stairs, the direct result of me testing Maddox's theory that I was still soulless by running at them like a banshee.

It probably didn't help that I screamed at them like a banshee either. The little beasts hissed and sprung up like rubber balls that had hit the floor with considerable force, before leaping at me and swiping with claws extended. Then they used all that spit and vinegar to flee, leaving me laughing at them from the bottom of the steps.

The laughter was probably what prompted Maddox to lift me unceremoniously by my waist and carry me like a sack of flour under his arm and on his hip to drop me down on the sofa. It was probably the spitting and fighting I did after that that prompted him to hold me there until I agreed not to move.

His question was simple enough, but I couldn't see how it made any difference. What did Kerri say? Not much.

I shrugged. "She said it was all good."

"All good," he said. "Really? That's what she said?"

"What she said," I mused out loud, because I wasn't sure I could remember her exact words, "was that it was good enough."

"Good enough?" Maddox squeezed my knees and I yelped.

"Hey, don't manhandle the goods," I complained.

"What did she say?"

"She wanted to know how I felt, is what," I told him, and held his gaze because he just wouldn't be dissuaded. "She said I looked better."

"And?"

"And then she said it was good enough. Then she left."

I couldn't see what the hubbub was all about, really. As far as I was concerned, I'd lived through the whole ordeal, got my soul back, and as a bonus, still had the grimoire tucked away for a rainy day.

Life was good.

"When she asked you how you felt, what did you say?" he pressed.

I shrugged.

He pinched the bridge of his nose but stopped just short of looking annoyed. "Well?"

"I just showed you," I told him. "I shrugged. That was my answer."

I glared at him and tried to pull my knees out from beneath his death grip. He was being stubborn and for no good reason.

"If I ask you how you feel, are you going to tell me you feel your soul? " I barked out a laugh. "I mean, really."

It had to be pretty much like your bladder or your appendix, didn't it? Unless it was hurting how would you know?

He did not take my unconcerned reaction well. In fact, he looked pretty put out over my nonchalance.

"Your landlord," he said. "How is he?"

"Djedi," I said, lifting a finger. "The pharaoh's magician turned immortal necromancer, capable of cutting off the head of a ferryman with a single blow."

I was actually pretty proud of the summation.

This time he did pinch the bridge of his nose. "Your landlord. He is well?"

"I just said so, didn't I?" I pushed him aside and headed for the kitchen. A bowl of chips was in order. Maybe some ice cream. I might still have some left over from the weekend shopping trip.

"Isabella?"

"He got up," I shot back. "Growled at us both, and is now safely ensconced in his lair next door."

I opened the cupboard and grabbed a bag of plain chips sealed with a clothes pin for freshness. "You think maybe he'll make the cats hiss too?" I spun around with the bag in my hand. "I mean, he's a necromancer after all."

I grinned at him.

"You're not helping," Maddox said and stood up to cross his arms over his chest. "I'm telling you, something isn't right, *you* aren't right." He was shaking his head. "The Isabella I know wouldn't mention killing her cat. She wouldn't pass this threat off as inconsequential. She wouldn't..."

"Wouldn't what?"

His shoulders sagged and he looked away, pinning his gaze to the floor. "She wouldn't try to seduce me."

The laugh erupted from my throat so suddenly that I choked on my own spit and ended up coughing till I was heaving.

"That's your proof that I'm *not right*?" I said when the fit ended, and pulled air quotes down around the last words aggressively enough that the clip fell off the bag of chips.

"You think my soul is still stuck in Hell somewhere because I wanted to boink you? Oh dear. You fashion me a body sized vibrator and think because it leaves me frustrated that I don't have a soul anymore. Oh, that's too rich."

I stooped to pick up the clothes pin and dumped it on the counter then brandished the bag at him. "You want proof that I'm the same old Isabella? Watch me slouch on the couch with a bag of chips and ice cream."

"I've seen the show," he drawled. "It isn't pretty."

I blinked at him. He'd just insulted me. I waited for a reaction, some sort of indignation or hurt tightening my chest.

But I felt nothing.

Absolutely nothing.

"Oh, fuck me," I said. "I really don't have my soul, do I?"

I wasn't aware I'd dropped the bag of chips until Maddox was in front of me, bending to retrieve it from the floor at my feet. Chips had flown out everywhere.

"It didn't work," I mumbled. "I don't understand. Why didn't it work." I slammed my palm on the counter, squashing several nice stray ripples into crumbs.

"I knew it was too damn easy."

"Let's not panic, Kitten," he said in a soothing voice, as he reached past me to lay the bag on the counter. "We'll work through it."

I nodded at him, a storm of thoughts colliding against each other in their haste to make me panic first.

"Right," I said. "Work through it." I started to pace. "I felt it, though, Maddox. I tasted it."

He put his arm on my shoulder. "Tasted it?"

I nodded again. "Like candy apple and rotten fruit."

His jaw seesawed back and forth while he considered what I'd said.

"I wasn't aware souls had a taste, but I'm willing to bet that if it did, it wouldn't taste like rotten fruit."

He stroked his chin, his fingers making his russet five o'clock stubble rustle. "Did anything strange happen while you were connected to Kerri and the ferryman?"

"How would I know?" I growled, angry now that the whole incident had been a waste of time and the anxiety a waste of energy. "I'm human, remember? I don't have any special powers of insight that you don't know about."

He held up his hands in surrender. "Innocent bystander here."

I stabbed him in the chest with my finger, sudden fury sweeping through me as I thought of the thing that had started all this like a house of flimsy cards on an unbalanced table.

"No, you're not." I growled. "If it wasn't for your damned Lilith stone, I'd not be in this mess. I wouldn't have some nasty bond to Hell that Isme could use to try to swap bodies with me."

He grappled for my finger and held it tight in his fist as he caught my eye. He caught my use of the vampire's name, and his eyes flashed, but he didn't speak to that. What he did was remind me ever so calmly about the true state of things.

"If not for me, you'd no doubt be dead by your lover's hand by now," he said quietly. "At worst, you'd be stuck in hell with no way to escape Lucifer's clutches."

He let go my hand and let it drop to my side. I felt my face crumble at the kindness in his tone because of course he was right. If it was anybody's fault at all, it was mine for pickpocketing Finn all those months ago, even if I'd done it out of habit and not intention. Stowing that rune tile in my pocket had laid the first shaky card that introduced the entire supernatural world into my own tumultuous one.

At best it was nobody's fault. It was awful happenstance that brought me here, and Maddox was doing his best, despite me, to help me extricate myself from it all.

It was a measure of how far gone I was that I forgot that important fact.

I sank onto the floor, my back against the counter. I drew my knees up to my chest and hugged them tight. My head fell onto them and I pressed my forehead hard into the bones so I could feel something. Anything. Even despair would be lovely. Shame would be the most appropriate, but even that eluded me, and I was exhausted at the thought that I needed all of them badly.

I heard Maddox pacing the apartment talking to himself, working it out verbally while I sat there, staring into the shadows of my legs.

His muttering did nothing but aggravate my own sense of helplessness. I sighed and pushed myself from the floor. I wanted to think of something else. What use was there in worrying over something I couldn't fix? At least not in the traditional sense. It seemed to me that the problem wasn't in not having a soul, but in dying without one.

And that particular thought seeded one more.

I had a special bond. Even Djedi had asked about it. It was one that Absalom wanted; the reason Maddox had felt it important enough to install a portal in my basement. It seemed to me that it was the one thing we were all overlooking because it was right there in front of us, hiding in plain sight.

"There is one thing that can fix it," I said. "Maybe."

He swung around mid-pace, stopping in front of the window. Sun shone in and glinted off his russet hair in a way that made my throat tight.

"Did you remember something?" he said.

"In a way." I took a tentative step toward him.

He slumped down onto the sofa, man-spreading and hanging his elbows over his knees. Everything in his posture sagged in relief and I supposed if I did have a soul, I'd be encouraged that he cared enough to be so.

But I didn't have a soul. Not anymore. And what was a human being without a soul? That was the crux of it really.

I knelt in front of him, slipping between his knees. I wasn't sure what he'd think of what I had to say.

"What if I wasn't human anymore," I said. "What if I was immortal?"

CHAPTER THIRTY

"You want to be immortal?" he said, narrowing his gaze at me. "You who gave up that chance when the stone tried to bond with you."

He didn't exactly sound opposed to the idea, but the disbelief in his voice made me want to squirm. Mostly because it was a stark reminder of the near-miss I'd had with the chupacabra shape-shifter, who wanted to use power of the Lilith Stone to increase his own.

"Think about it," I said, trying to convince him without sounding too eager. "The problem is if I die, my bond takes me straight back to Hell. If I can't die, problem solved."

He gave me a wistful smile. "While there's nothing I'd like more than to have an eternity's worth of your sassy tongue, I'm not so sure the human part of you would want that."

I canted my head at him, examining his face. There was something more to it that he wasn't admitting.

"You don't want me to be immortal, do you?"

He leaned back on the sofa. "You didn't want immortality when you had the chance, Kitten."

"But I'm not the same anymore. How can I hold myself to an impossibility? Do you want me to go to Hell, Maddox?"

There are times when you're talking to someone that their every expression rides their faces like costume. If their angry, their face grows red and tight. If they are determined, their jaw clenches. When Maddox spoke next, his voice was low. His expression gave away nothing. But the words themselves were so sincere that I was struck by the fierceness of them.

"I told you before," he said. "I would brave Lucifer's realm myself to free you from there if I had to."

"Then why not avoid it altogether? Why not just put our efforts into finding your father and the stone and re-igniting the bond?"

He held my hands. "Don't get me wrong, the thought of you dying does fill my heart with a dread I can't shake, but you don't know what you're asking. It's not just a bond you'll have with the stone. Don't you see what I am? Don't you realize the burden it is?"

I shrugged off his hands, annoyed with his reasoning because it was useless.

"Some burden celibacy is," I snorted. "I'm not getting any anyway. The only man I've wanted in years is as cold as a..."

"Not cold," he said, pinching my chin between his fingers and thumb and forcing me to look him in the eye with an aggressiveness that would have made my belly ache with longing any other time.

"You're in my veins, Isabella. It's like my own blood has been siphoned off and replaced with the spirit of you. You're all I think about. You think it's easy for me to want you and not be able to have you? You think the gate I put in your basement is just so you can portal into work?"

He pulled me toward him so that his lips were against my cheek and his voice and breath cascaded over the shell of my ear.

"No," he whispered. "It's so you can come to me. It's so I can have you near me, so I can pretend I'm a man and not just a mindless monster who executes even worse monsters or lets them barter with far worse monsters."

I was about to tell him he wasn't a monster. That even when I'd had my soul that I didn't think he was only good for killing worse things than whatever it was that he was. But he got up and brushed past me, striding across the room toward the stairs where both of our cats had reappeared and sat looking down at us.

He wouldn't look at me and I had the feeling he wasn't happy about his own admission.

"All of that is true," he said. "But you're right when you say I don't want you to become immortal." He did turn then and his hands were clenched into fists at his side. "I like you the way you are," he said. "I'm afraid of what will happen if you become immortal without that thing that makes you, well, you. What if you don't get that back? What if you become immortal without any feeling in you?"

His words took me by surprise but he wasn't finished. Not by a long shot.

"You're a conduit to the stone, Isabella," he said. "It tried to bond to you once. I don't know if it will again, and if it does try, what will happen when it reaches out to the magic in you and finds nothing."

I sucked in a breath.

"It was too easy," I murmured to myself, thinking about the ease with which Kerri was able to transfer the magic back through the ferryman. It was because there was nothing to grab onto, just carrier magic. No Isabella mojo. Just the nasty-assed vampire energy suffering beneath the coma of a necromancer.

I wanted to laugh at my naivete but I couldn't even fake the humor.

"I'd love to have an eternity with you," Maddox said, as though I hadn't spoken. "But I won't risk you harm to get it. We need another way."

Now who was being naive, I wondered as I pushed to my feet.

"What way, Maddox?" I said. "It was obvious all along that Kerri wouldn't be able to retrieve what I was losing. Everyone kept saying it. You said it."

"Said what?"

"I was leaking." I kicked at the floor. "I mean, if I was leaking where in the hell was I going anyway?"

I huffed and decided to drown my misery in a bowl of ice cream. I headed to the fridge.

"I'm so screwed."

Doubly screwed apparently, because the freezer was empty of anything but a freezer burnt pack of ground beef. I slammed the door shut and leaned with my back against it.

"So screwed."

It was overreaction, and I knew it, but somehow the thought that I was out of ice cream seemed the worst thing at that moment.

"You take things for granted," I said. "Ice cream. Chips. Souls."

I slammed my fists behind me on the fridge door. "And then they're gone and you're left staring into the abyss of chip-less-ness."

"We'll fix it." He plucked his kitten from the stairs and while it hissed at him, she let him smooth her into a ball of fluff that he tucked in the crook of his arms.

"What did Adair want from you anyway?" I demanded. "Seemed like an awful big secret."

He shrugged. "The same thing he's wanted for a thousand years. The same thing I refuse to let him have."

I raised my eyebrows to indicate I knew he was hedging and I wasn't going to let it slide.

He sighed. "He wanted something of Tamar's," he said.

"Tamar?"

"My sister."

That was news. First I find out he had a brother, now a sister? I might have felt put out if there was a spirit inside me to care.

"Well aren't you just the mystery man," I said. "You hiding a love child in your past somewhere too?"

"I'm celibate," he said because of course, the man had no sense of humor unless he was the one cracking the joke.

"Duh," I said, waving a tired hand at him. "So tell me about your sister."

He shook his head. "No."

No. No explanation, no sorry for his bluntness. The man had to have a skeleton in that closet somewhere.

"That's all I get? A no?"

The kitten reached up a paw to bat at the finger he was waving over her face. I sighed and went to the cupboard. He'd been worried about it eating. I couldn't fix my soul, but I could feed a cat. I busied myself opening a tin of flaked tuna and dumped it into a fresh bowl from the cupboard. Maddox watched me until

I plopped the bowl on the floor. He bent to shoo the kitten toward the bowl.

She resisted, of course. And I sank down onto the floor again and stared at the bowl. I caught sight of his knees when he crouched in front of me.

"If it makes you feel any better," he said. "Adair should have known better than ask. He probably wouldn't have except he saw he could take advantage of my concern for you."

"I don't know if I can feel anything," I said. "But it's nice to know you're willing to lay the blame on me."

"That's not what I was doing."

I shrugged. Tomato. Tomahto.

"Well," I said. "At least tell me what he wanted. Surely that won't crack that vault you have stuffed up your butt."

He grimaced at me, obviously not caring for the humor. It was enough to push him to his feet and he headed back to grapple the kitten and wrangle her toward the bowl.

"Nothing much," he said, finally dumping the fish onto the floor where she finally sniffed at it. "A small amulet."

The silence after this proclamation was so heavy that I thought he had disappeared into some new portal. I rolled my head on my shoulders so I could see him better, hoping it was at least one that would vibrate the shit out of his ass and leave him unsatisfied.

He was halted in the middle of the living room. Meaty calloused hands were kneading the back of his neck the way someone does when they know they've done something stupid.

Or illegal.

"Maddox?" I said. "What sort of amulet was it?"

"Sweet gods," he said and swung his gaze to mine. His brow was furrowed

"You said you were leaking," he said. "You said, and I quote, 'If I was leaking, where in the hell was I going?'"

I crossed one arm over the other. "You got an answer for that big boy? Because unless you do, I'm not impressed with your long memory."

He closed the distance between us with deliberation and so quickly I cringed against the fridge out of long-ingrained habit and cell memory. Shades of Scottie and Alvin and a lifetime of cringing.

"How do you say it?" he said. "Oh, fuck me?"

I wavered my hand in the air to indicate he was close. The inflection could use some work but the sentiment was there.

"Kitten," he murmured. "You didn't go anywhere."

He crouched in front of me again and placed his palm against my solar plexus as he said this, and the heat of him swept over me in a shiver of warmth so delicious I hadn't realized how cold I was until he'd touched me.

"You didn't go anywhere," he repeated. "You. Your soul. It didn't go anywhere."

I blinked at him, trying so hard to follow his train of thought because though he was speaking English, he was making zero sense.

He must have read the confusion in my face because he expanded on the thought.

"Your soul was clinging to you, Isabella. All that time. And he saw it."

"Who saw it?"

"That wily bastard who deals in souls for a living. Who dunked himself in hellfire so he could see them, sense them, and taste them."

He grabbed my hand and pulled me with him toward the basement.

"Where are we going?"

"Back to the bazaar to see a man who caught sight of an untethered soul ripe for the taking."

CHAPTER THIRTY-ONE

The Pussy Gate vibrated us into his office in record time. I didn't have the heart to comment on the frustration of it because Maddox wasn't speaking by the time we got to my basement. His jaw was set in a grim line that made even his collarbone tense looking. I tried multiple times to get him to talk but all he did was stride to the door of his office and pull his mace from its hook.

"Bit of overkill, or what?" I said as I rushed along behind him. He either expected me to stay put or to follow him, but he wasn't indicating one way or the other what he wanted.

So I followed him. I wasn't worried, mind you, but for the big man to shoulder his mace, it had to be bad. And I wanted ringside seats.

Besides. If it netted me a soul, then how could it be all bad?

The bazaar was in its gloaming time. The stalls were shutting down and the creatures, witches, vampires, and whatever else spent their shop time in the piazza were disappearing one by one. Some of them spilled into shadows on the cobblestones as I'd guessed from earlier.

"This is the tamer part, right?" I said to break the awful silence. "Are there humans selling things here?"

He grunted but didn't answer. His strides had picked up. I knew it was a long walk to Adair's and I didn't want to get caught falling too far behind. I had to pick up my pace and grab hold of the hem of his shirt to keep him from out-pacing me altogether.

"You're going too fast."

"It'll be midnight soon," he said. "I don't have time to wait for you. Keep up or go back home."

That stung. Enough that I shut up. Instead of walking, I jogged to keep up and I was winded by the time we got to Adair's. The moon was full as it hung over the alley. It looked drunk, sagging into the clouds that were doing their best to cover its shame.

"Bastard," he muttered to himself. "I should have known. By god, I should have known."

He fiddled with the lock and when it didn't release as quickly as he wanted, he started kicking the door with force. When that didn't do anything, he started heaving the mace at it until it splintered.

I stood back, swallowing down gobs of fear and thought how the most primal feelings—lust, fear, hunger—were baked into the cake of humanity. No need for a soul to feel those. I almost wished I couldn't as I watched him barrel through the splintered door and disappear into the tower.

I hesitated, wringing my hands.

His hand poked through the destroyed doorway.

"Don't make me carry you," he said from inside.

It took all of one second for me to decide to follow.

The shop looked nothing like it had. Gone was the counter. The walls were empty. In its place was a long corridor leading to a spiral staircase that Maddox was already climbing by double treads at a time.

I ran up behind him. I thought I could make out chanting. The air felt like I'd stepped into one of those balls that make your hair stand up.

"Maddox," I whispered. "What's going on?"

The soles of his shoes scuffed the last stair and he disappeared above me. I came out in a room lit by candles that smelled of beeswax. Another fragrance carried on the air currents to me. I wanted to call it myrrh or frankincense but I didn't know either of the aromas to name them.

I did know the other smells though.

Brimstone. Sulfur. Smoke.

And on the underbelly of those noxious fumes, I caught lavender and lemon.

Maddox's gasp was the thing that alerted me to halt, frozen, behind him. The room was open concept. Rafters spanned the ceiling. A fireplace hunkered down on one wall with a dirt floor level hearth. This place was old. Older than Renaissance buildings or Medieval castles. I had the feeling I wasn't so much in the bazaar anymore, but on a ley-line to another dimension.

Copper bowls like I'd seen in Kerri's shop were littered on their sides around the room. Quicksilver made a narrow river as it spilled from a wooden bowl and ran its way toward a glyph drawn in the dirt.

It was the symbols painted on the wall in blood that made me really start to worry for my welfare. Through all the strange markings, I could see my name at intermittent places, one letter at a time, each surrounded by ever more esoteric looking glyphs.

The room had a heavy sense of purpose despite the chaos of upended bowls and aromas. Whatever magic was afoot, I knew it had to do with me, and that kicked up my survival instinct. My fight or flight response went into overdrive. Unable to do either, I just stood there and trembled.

But it was the man who worried me the most. Just beyond Maddox, he knelt in the middle of a painted salt circle sprinkled with what had to be human blood, judging by the naked woman lying crookedly in the corner with her throat cut.

I gagged and shoved my fist into my mouth to keep from making a noise. Even as I did so, I realized I wasn't horrified, just sickened, and part of me was happy not to have to feel the compassion of a dead person on my conscience.

It shouldn't have mattered if I made a noise or not. Whatever was happening, it didn't look like anyone could stop it now. A filmy sort of barrier encased Adair and the circle. Although, if I was honest with myself, I had no idea how I knew it was Adair at all. The man I'd met earlier wasn't present at all in the circle. In his stead knelt a man who was bald and handsome. The mottling was gone from his bronze skin.

But I knew him just the same.

I reached out to touch Maddox's back. I felt as though I was going to lift off the floor, and I needed the grounding.

"What is he doing?" I whispered, not really wanting the answer.

Adair clutched a chunk of something as he chanted and as Maddox called his name, he swiveled his gaze toward us, his expression lost to whatever magic he was conjuring. He lifted the stone in his hand

"Don't do this," Maddox said.

Something crackled out of the fireplace like a bolt of lightning at his voice. It sizzled around Adair, seaming a line through the candlelit room the way a fault-line looks in rock. When I looked down, I saw the same pattern had etched itself into the floor.

"Adair."

The soul merchant swung his gaze toward us. A worried wrinkle split his brow.

"You brought her," he said. "You shouldn't have done that."

No sooner had he spoke when the magic swirling above him grabbed the stone out of his hand and lifted it high in the air. It spun in place dizzyingly, not quite level at first, then spiraling like a top as it gained momentum.

"I'm begging you, Adair," Maddox said, creeping forward now by inches. The ball of his mace hung a few inches from his fist as he held tight to both handle and chain. "Please don't do this."

Adair sent a scalding look at Maddox. "You think I wouldn't know the taint of my own magic?" he accused. "You think I wouldn't sense this girl is connected to my stone?"

"I gave you the amulet," Maddox said, ignoring the comment. "You've wanted it for hundreds of years. Let it be enough."

"You told me to find a way to bring her home," he said, and I thought there was a sob in his voice that couldn't quite break through the fury. "Well, I found a way. This is it."

"Not like this, Adair. She wouldn't want it like this."

"You said you would get her out. You promised."

"Look at yourself, Adair. Look what you've become. Do you think she would love you like this? She who spent each of her hard-earned long lives warring with creatures like you are now?"

A sob escaped Adair, one that carried a gob of spit and tears.

"So you'd save your lover, but you won't save mine," he said, pointing at me. "What makes her worth more?"

Maddox shook his head, seeming to know there was no good answer for the question, while I found myself wondering what horror Adair was planning to bring into this world.

Adair's lip curled with revulsion as he looked at me.

"The ferryman and its fare only wounded her soul. Punctured the film that keeps it host-bound. Whatever the vampire took, it was a small amount, just enough to activate the stone's magic. The rest, all that lovely potential rest swirled around her unbound."

He dropped his head back, laughter that sounded far more like sobbing burst from him. His chest shuddered. He threw his arms out sideways as he arched back so far I would have thought him a member of Cirque. At the apex of a bend I didn't think humanly possible, a word of power erupted from his throat.

The amulet froze in place, as it halted a shot of electricity flew out and snapped in the air.

Maddox jumped a step toward Adair. Then he paused. Then he pulled both arms to his chest and let go a choking sound.

Adair gagged as though he was trying to swallow and speak at the same time. His stomach undulated like a snake was moving around inside. Maddox charged, the mace held out sideways and then flung backwards as the chain left his grip. When he struck the first blow, it bounced back off the film and rounded his body to connect his ribcage. He hunched in pain at the contact.

I heard bone break.

Adair heard it too. He lifted his head and for a moment I thought he would choke on the words he was trying to form, then they came out in a rush of words that sounded like one.

"I'msorryyouhavetoseeherdie."

Maddox clutched his side.

"It's not the right magic, Adair."

"It's the perfect magic," Adair replied with a hiss. "The stone's bond on this soul makes it perfect. I can't just let the chance go."

Maddox splayed his fingers over the sac that protected Adair. "You don't know that," he reasoned. "You can't know that. What if it doesn't work?"

Adair threw his shoulders back. "Oh, but I do know. It's what I do. It's what I became so I would know when the time presented itself." He tapped his temple with a finger that had gone black, and I realized the mottling was still there, somewhere beneath the glamor and it had turned color.

"I trusted you," he said. "I let you convince me she could be free but now I see you just wanted to control me. Imprison me. Exploit me."

Those words struck me like blows.

"Maddox?" I said and crept forward inches. Adair caught sight of my movement and rolled his head on a rubberlike neck in my direction.

"Her death, her bond, her soul. All of those elements plus my alchemy will bring her back." He lifted his gaze to Maddox. "I know it will."

It was then that I saw what both men had realized was happening above us while I'd been rapt on Adair. High above us, a shape was coming into focus. A woman. Beautiful. Long black hair and full hips. Even as a mere shade, I could see she was strong. Dressed in worn looking leathers, she had the look of a primitive warrior but there was nothing primitive about the intelligence of her face.

Maddox made a choking sound.

Adair called out a word that had no English equivalent that I could imagine. It was all consonants and humming sounds.

And at the utterance of the word, I collapsed to my knees. I had no feeling in my entire body. Every muscle, sinew, and joint went limp. And yet, I was held there, in place on my knees, by some power that had no physicality.

Maddox swung around to face me at the sound of my knees striking the floor. He hefted the mace, holding it at my eyelevel.

All that flashed through my mind was that whatever was coming, it was bad enough that he was willing to kill me if he had to. He, the demon warrior, was waging war right here in this room and I was the one thing he could affect to win.

In my mind, my arms flew up over my head, wrapping around the top of my skull and protecting the vulnerable temples. But in the physical, I just knelt there, barely moving and weaving subtly like a grass in the breeze. I was held like a sacrifice by some power none of us could control.

And Maddox didn't look like Maddox. Fury and fear had stolen the intelligence of his gaze.

"Don't make me do this," he said.

"Please don't kill me," I said.

I wanted to live. With a soul, without a soul. I wanted to live.

I saw him shudder and pivot in place. His chest was heaving. His fist was clenched around the handle of his mace. Whatever he was fighting it was a battle I was afraid would win him over.

"Adair," he pleaded. "Please don't make me."

"You locked me in here for hundreds of years," Adair said. "Kept me caged like an animal, believing you could do something to free her. To fix me."

"I did it to protect you." Maddox said. "You can't be trusted anymore. Your powers make you unpredictable."

A guttural cry broke from Adair's lungs, one of pain and sorrow, and something far more primal. Lust, I thought. The air became cloaked with it.

And that was when I knew I was truly doomed.

CHAPTER THIRTY-TWO

T here are several moments in life when you know that what you do next will cause a shift in your path the size of tectonic plates rearranging. Most times, you don't know. When I'd pocketed the rune tile all those weeks ago in a dark and dirty alley, I'd had no idea that moment would bring me here. That it would put me on my knees in front of my own humanity.

Would I have done it had I known? Would I have stopped to help the man who turned out to be a dark sorcerer had I realized?

I'd been in a funk, it was true. Maddox had been right. After I'd killed Scottie, I'd wanted to feel nothing. I hadn't killed him in self-defense. Not really. The man had been taking a bath, and I'd bludgeoned him because I wanted to get away from him finally. I'd wanted his persistent hunting of me to end. I'd wanted to not have to look over my shoulder in an anxiety-filled dread one more time.

But I hadn't taken back my freedom with that blow. I'd traded it for guilt. And guilt was far worse because there was no running from yourself.

Maddox had tried to gift me Scourge as a Christmas present, so I could have that thing I wanted more than anything, hoping I'd choose happiness and peace.

But I would have chosen to feel nothing had I used the gift.

That's what he understood that I didn't. It was why he was worried about me when I didn't understand myself what was wrong.

I knew now.

I knew, and I knew I wanted to live.

I wanted to feel.

And as that realization came, a breeze seemed to move through the room. The woman becoming more and more clear in the haze of magic over the amulet sort of...shivered.

Adair's attention whipped to me and he growled. It sounded feral and unhinged. Maddox staggered. He swung around to face me again.

"Isabella?" he said.

I tried to nod because I couldn't trust my mouth to answer in anything but a sob. I needed something, some sort of movement to let him know I was still there. But I couldn't manage one. Adair let loose a litany of shrieks that sounded like a chorus of wailing women. It was high pitched enough to make me want to hold my hands over my ears.

But I couldn't.

All I could do was watch Maddox lumber nearer to me. In a flash, I saw him crouching over the kitten's crate in Fayed's back alley. I watched him cradling the crate in his arms. That man wasn't a monster. He might have killed monsters, but he wasn't a monster. I was safe with him.

I kept telling myself that, over and over, and with each image that came to me that proved me right, the movement started to come back into my body.

My hand twitched. Then my shoulder. I rolled my head on my neck to test it out. All while Maddox fought his own legs from advancing on me.

"It's ok," I said, pulling my hands up in front of me, facing him in surrender. "I'm alright."

I dragged in a breath to prove it to him.

The effect was on the woman, and not Maddox. She swung a surprised and confused gaze to me. She was almost solid now. I could see her flexing her arms as though she too were testing her movements. Both she and the amulet seemed to be lower than before.

Adair began chanting in earnest. The amulet rose. It made contact with her foot.

She gasped. Maddox threw a look over his shoulder at the sound, and I realized that I couldn't wait for someone to save me. I couldn't run. I couldn't hide.

I had to do something. But what?

If time had a way of standing still, it was doing that right then. Adair kept up his chant. Maddox slowly, deliberately, pointed his feet in Adair's direction. The amulet and the woman began to lower to the floor.

Those elements came together for me like a puzzle piece revealing a beautiful but complex picture.

Adair had recognized his magic in me. The amulet had been Tamar's. The affinity of the bond of my soul to hers was what could drive the whole damn thing. I wasn't sure how all those slots fit together, but they did. Somehow.

Whether I was right or wrong, I had to do something. I marshaled whatever energy I'd gained back and flung myself to my feet. The force of the thrust launched me, stumbling, toward the amulet. I pinwheeled toward it several steps before I caught my balance and felt the ungluing of Adair's magic from my limbs.

I heard Maddox and Adair call out at the same instant, the same one where I reached through the sizzling magic to grab the amulet from the air. The woman above me wavered.

Once, I'd been wearing a dog shock collar Scottie had bought to use on a member of his crew who looked at me a little too long. To teach us both a lesson, Scottie said, he'd tested it on me. Not a lot of shock, mind you. Not at first. Just a quick jolt to see what it felt like.

Then a larger one, to remind me who was boss.

Then the highest level to teach me never to consider looking at another man again.

I'd foolishly reminded him that it was the guy who had looked at me, not the other way around. The insubordination earned me a night's worth of sleep with the thing around my throat, getting jolted out of the blue while I slept.

This magic was much like that except far, far worse. I had the sense of dread at the same time as I felt the shocks, and it made all my hair stand up. I grit my teeth against the pain as I fought to pull the amulet free of the magic.

"God damn you," I screamed at it. "Let go."

From behind me, Maddox shouted. "Break it, Isabella."

Break it. How?

I scanned the area from dirt floor to ceiling. Rafters. Dirt. Power sizzling over me and through me, making my heart pound enough to burst. I caught sight of the fireplace directly behind Adair.

The amulet launched from my grip directly at the stones. I heard the woman sigh in my ear. Adair howled. Maddox might have sobbed.

The amulet struck the face of the fireplace and cracked on impact. Two halves fell away from each other.

The magic swept the room like a whirlwind, lifting my feet from the floor. I was thrown a yard away from where I'd stood and I landed hard on the dirt in the center line of mercury trail. My hand fell into it and it bunched into place on either side like my skin was the hand of God parting the Red Sea.

A movement caught my eye even as I was sucking air in to replace the vacuum that had drained my lungs of air on impact. Adair standing in his circle.

The film was gone.

And Maddox was already enroute.

He swung.

The mace made a whistling sound as it parted the air around it. I covered my face, my eyes, my very psyche from what I knew was about to happen.

The sound of the ball colliding with Adair's head was one I never wanted to hear again. It sickened me to my very marrow. I pitied the poor alchemist who wanted to be rejoined with his lover. My eyes blurred with tears and they wet my cheeks, running down to my chin.

I sobbed as I lay there, curled into the fetal position. Despite it all, I had liked the alchemist. I knew at one time, Maddox had too. I ached at his death because death by violence was always so damn useless.

Moments passed in which the whole room was silent. I peeked between my fingers when I managed to control my emotions.

Maddox just stood there. His shoulders had a defeated sag. The mace was on the floor, discarded.

Beyond him, Adair lay there in a crumbled heap. His head was several feet away. I don't know how Maddox had managed it in one blow, but he'd decapitated Adair so neatly, that the face still showed some semblance of the person he had been.

There was no sign of the woman.

"Maddox," I said, testing the silence.

He didn't respond. He seemed mesmerized by the sight of Adair's body. If I looked at it, I thought I could see a faint aura of what I could only describe as a tailed demon around him. Outside of that was another shell of aura, of the man with the bowler hat. And at the heart of it all, was the true Adair. He was beautiful, even in death, even with his skull completely severed from his body.

"Maddox?"

His name urged him into movement. He stooped to pick up the pieces of amulet and held them in his palm for a long moment before he closed them into a tight fist.

He swung to face me.

"Let's go," he said and strode past me to the head of the stairs.

I noted he didn't retrieve his mace. It lay there like a piece of him he didn't want to collect.

Having got my air, I pushed onto my hands and knees. Pain lanced my ribs but I didn't think anything was broken. Badly bruised, maybe, but not broken.

That had to be a good thing.

I followed him down the stairs and he led me through the bazaar, down the alleys and streets we'd come from, back to his library.

He beckoned me to the gate and bid me enter without a single word. All the while, he clutched those shards as though he'd crack himself if he let them go.

I couldn't keep his eye, and he didn't seem to want to catch mine.

I portaled home to my basement and stumbled up the stairs, feeling my way along because I couldn't see through the sting of tears that blurred my vision.

I was ugly crying by the time I flung myself onto my bed. I knew by how bereft I felt that I had my soul back.

But I might have just lost Maddox's.

CHAPTER THIRTY-THREE

I had days to mull over the events. I slept like the dead for fifteen hours, and didn't miss the irony of the term when I woke and decided I knew exactly how Jesus felt three days after he died. I'd had dreams of the bazaar while I slept, gauzy bits of images that waved away like curtains in a breeze when I tried to see through them.

Maddox's past was more complex than I'd considered before. I shouldn't have been surprised; after all, he'd lived hundreds of years in a world like my own, but nothing like my own. One lifetime of living was enough to create a kaleidoscope of memories that would alter and change a psyche. With his long life, he had to have crafted thousands, if not millions, of multiple butterfly effects and all through worlds I hadn't even known existed.

The magnitude of possibilities was astounding. If I tried to sort out how it might all have shaped him, I got too exhausted to think anymore.

One thing I did know. He wasn't an innocent. But he wasn't a monster either. His Shadow Bazaar was a pulse of things Kindred. Like the Kindred who visited, bought, sold, rented, or lived within, the space was a breathing entity, no more controllable than the wind. He could be forgiven the things that went on within its boundaries, because whatever he'd meant to create when he'd done so, it had expanded to something far more sentient.

His bazaar was his own Lilith Stone.

I didn't know if I'd ever really understand the bazaar or why Maddox had built it. Maybe it didn't matter. It had given to me as much as it had taken. I made my peace with its existence. I let it become a sort of tapestry woven into my own life, one with a hundred different story lines coded into the map.

I knew where Cleo's potion chest was, and that would be an adventure that I hoped would be remunerative but uneventful. I had my soul back. I was free, maybe not of the guilt over Scottie's death, but free to embrace the humanity of it.

I had hope for the first time in forever because of Maddox and his bazaar, and it was sad that it was so. Because things weren't right for him. Threads were still loose and ragged in the fabric. And it nagged at me that there was no easy fix that I could buy or steal.

It took me three days to decide to brave the Pussy Gate.

I did so with two things held in my hands. Both of them the best medicine I could think of for what was ailing my non-man.

I ignored the pulsing, vibrating pleasure it sent through me and when I found myself on the other side, it was to a view that was at once familiar and sad.

Maddox lay in one of the chairs by the sofa, facing a fire that wasn't lit. He knew I'd entered. I was sure he could feel it in the shift of energy, as I did.

But he didn't lift his head.

Wordlessly, I went to him. He let me push in and somehow the chair grew to accommodate us both.

I was heartened to feel that he at least put his arm around me. Maybe he wasn't too far gone.

I laid the two bowls on his belly. It was hard as a table top anyway.

"Chips," I said, pointing to the first one. "And vanilla ice cream. It won't fix what's wrong, but it'll help you work your way through it. Trust me."

His liquid gaze drew my own. "I know what you're feeling," I whispered. "It's grief. It's guilt. It's shame. And a dozen other things you can't name right now. "

I plucked a chip from the bowl and dipped it in the ice cream. Then I aimed it at his mouth. It bumped up against his closed lips and I had to jimmy it to get his mouth open.

I popped it in and he hesitated, but then chewed. Slowly at first. He opened his mouth again and I dipped another. I would feed him and I would talk and he didn't have to do anything but just be. I'd had days to think about it, and I thought I had it figured out.

"Tamar was your sister," I said, gathering all the threads of information together to stitch out some sort of understanding. "Adair was the alchemist who created the Lilith stone."

His eyes revealed I was right, but all he did was pop open his mouth again. I slipped another ice-cream laden chip inside and kept talking, remembering his comment about losing too many of his family to the stone.

"My bond to the stone, the one Absalom wanted to use, that's the thing he thought could tap into Tamar." I dipped a great gob of ice cream onto the chip. "And he was obviously right. He needed something of hers to fulfill the spell. Was she a guardian too?"

He nudged me to feed him more and I held it back.

"You have to go slow or you'll get an ice cream headache."

I waited a few moments as the frozen treat began to melt and drip. I caught it with my other hand and licked it off my palm.

"Here," I said, shoving the chip toward him. "That's enough time." I adjusted in the chair to face him better. I needed to see his eyes clearly when I asked the rest.

"The spell wasn't just to take my soul, was it?" I inhaled deeply to brace myself. "It needed my lifeforce in order to bring her out. My soul would have been swapped, trapped with Lucifer in her stead."

His gaze pinned to mine. I knew I was right.

"You knew him," I said. "You knew how real his grief was. You knew he wasn't playing around. And you let your sister stay there instead of using me to bring her back."

He swallowed.

"She's been gone a long time. She wouldn't have wanted to come back under those conditions."

My throat hurt at the longing and grief in his words.

He took a chip from me and held it over the bowl.

"I miss her," he said. "I miss them all."

His brother. His father. All the things he'd sacrificed to keep Lilith and her demons from infecting and ravishing the nine worlds.

"He broke the stone," he said, stabbing the chip into the ice cream without pulling any back out. "She had given up the warrior life. She'd bedded him. The stone cracked. She needed to fix what they had broken."

A light went off somewhere in my mind. "And because she had broken her vow of celibacy, she couldn't make it back out. She didn't have the power to fight Lucifer."

He left the chip, dug deeply into the mound of cream.

"He went insane with grief. He became a Soul Merchant and took on all that it meant, thinking it would empower him to extract her. But there was never a way. I had to lock him in to keep him from hurting anyone else."

He turned away from me and pushed the bowl aside. I had to grab at it before it dumped its contents onto my lap. "I didn't want you to know all these things. Not about me. Not about my family."

"You saw what it did to him," he said. "Over the years, he became the thing she fought so hard against. I thought keeping him in the tower would keep him safe. The worlds safe. I didn't want to..."

I put my finger against his lips. "Don't say it," I said. " You don't have to. I know."

"She would still have loved him anyway," he said musingly. "Tamar would have brought him back to himself. You saw what he looked like. She could have done it."

"Then why didn't you tell him that?" I said. "Why did you lie to him? He died thinking he was a monster."

He lifted my chin with a crooked finger.

"You have to ask that?"

I nodded and he tapped my nose almost annoyed before he answered.

"Because if he knew that, he would never stop. There was a chance I could appeal to him, make him stop the spell before it was too late." He shook his head. "But I couldn't, and I knew that when I looked at her. I knew how much he loved her. I knew the ache of it."

He sighed and leaned his head back against the chair as the kitten hopped up onto it and picked her way along the back to my side where she climbed onto my lap and curled up. He watched her with a strange expression, one that put a new thought into my head.

"Would you have let Tamar through if it had been someone else's soul he'd tapped?"

"It wasn't someone else's," he said and reached for the kitten, avoiding my eye altogether.

She batted at him once but then when he nuzzled her belly with his nose, she grabbed for it with both paws. He made a thoughtful sound when the kitten's tongue darted out and made contact with the tip.

I noted two things in that moment. One: the kitten had begun to warm up to him and that pleased him, and two: he didn't answer my question, and didn't look like he was going to either.

I decided it was about all I could expect at the moment. Maybe it was more than I could ask for under the conditions. It would take time for him to heal; I knew that better than anyone. That sort of thing couldn't be rushed.

But for now, we had ice cream and chips. And that would have to be enough.

<<<Finito>>>

There is always more going on in Isabella's world.

If this is your first time meeting her or your most recent, you can count on stories that will help you escape the chaos of your world.

HAVE YOU READ?

Rune Thief

Bone Hunter

Stone Goddess

Soul Merchant

Blood & Stone: Maddox
Slayer
Tamar
Witchborn